The Millennium Project

...toward the bright light!

Books by Cal Glover

A Grizzly Death in Yellowstone

The Millennium Project

Cal Glover

Homestead Publishing
Moose, Wyoming

ISBN 0-943972-63-9

Library of Congress Cataloging-in-Publication Data
Glover, Cal
The millennium project / Cal Glover.
p. cm.
ISBN 0-943972-63-9 (alk. paper)
I. Title.
PS3557.L6774M5 1998
813'.54—dc21 98-12659
CIP

1 3 5 7 9 10 8 6 4 2

Printed in the United States of America on recycled, acid free paper.

Grateful acknowledgment is made to the following for permission to reprint previously published material:

Shadows of Forgotten Ancestors by Carl Sagan. Copyright © 1992 by Carl Sagan. Reprinted by permission of Random House, Inc.

Savages and Civilization by Jack Weatherford © 1994 by Jack McIver Weatherford. Reprinted by permission of Crown Publishers, Inc.

Published by
HOMESTEAD PUBLISHING
BOX 193 • MOOSE, WYOMING 83012

Acknowledgments

To Gene Tyler Lee, a poet/fisherman in Sebastian, Florida. When we were all thirteen and wanted to play centerfield for the Yankees he wanted to be a writer. What? To Richard Farina, author, musician, who taught us there was more than one way to write a book or play folk music. To Tim Tomkinson and the crew at Buckboard Cab in Jackson Hole, Wyoming. Thanks for letting me drive—its the best job I've ever had. Just don't send me to the airport. To Bob Hoyle, National Park Service astronomer, thanks for the comet info, thanks for showing us Jupiter and Io from the front porch of the Science School. To Rhonda Winchell, my great agent—thanks for taking the world on from Boise. To Carl Sagan, my mentor over all these years, thanks for translating. To James Dean Day, thanks for storing 3 billion bits of trivia and keeping it handy. To Kim Carlson. Thanks for standing tall—in stature and in outlook when things looked hopeless.

It seems like total destruction,
the only solution.
Bob Marley

The Millennium Project

Book I

The Book of Geneticists

From high above, from the view of an eagle soaring on summer thermals, Yellowstone National Park is a vast area of lodgepole pine forests, punctuated with stark areas of geothermal geyser basins—steaming yellow-white scars on the earth. To the northeast and along the east of the two-million-acre park are high, jagged mountain ranges, a long barrier protecting the eastern boundary. The deep contours of the Yellowstone Plateau are filled with rushing water carving their way downhill. Drops of water trickle down the Continental Divide which accumulate into roaring mountain streams, dropping seven, eight thousand feet, to either the Pacific Ocean or the Gulf of Mexico. Lakes bejewel the landscape from the eagle's viewpoint, shimmering, reflecting the early morning sun of this late June day. From the center of the park the eagle can see the rough outline of the caldera, the crater formed following the collapse of the huge magma chamber from eruptions that occurred 600,000 years ago. Along the south is volcanic tableland, where the lava from that long ago eruption flowed southward. From its high vantage point the eagle can see movement, but it does not swoop down, for it is not prey. It is much too large. It is a man running.

Civilized society has given the man a name.

It is Doj Bolderton.

He runs along a remote trail in the southern part of this great park. There is contrast to be seen here. His high-tech shoes have cushioned air soles, flared bottoms, and rubber studs designed for running on mountain trails and slopes. He's also wearing lined nylon shorts. But the contrast, the juxtaposition, is evident in the bow over his shoulder and a leather quiver with eight arrows. Not a modern setup, with a system of pulleys and levers and a sight, but a simple hickory bow with a notch and Dacron strings. His cedar arrows have obsidian heads. And over his nylon running shorts Doj Bolderton wears a belt with a knife in a leather holster. Otherwise he is naked. He runs swiftly, smoothly, with great, graceful strides down the trail, almost noiselessly.

Then suddenly something alerts his senses. He picks up his pace and cuts off the trail through the woods. He comes to a quick stop behind a twelve-inch-diameter lodgepole pine tree. In one smooth motion he draws an arrow from the quiver and notches it into the bow, pulls back until the string creases the tip of his nose, then closes his left eye for a blink and releases the taut string so that his index and middle fingers simultaneously point in a V. There is a high whistle as the arrow flies through the air and finds its mark precisely at the front shoulder of a mule deer, a buck, and the tip pierces the ungulate's heart.

The buck, headstrong, teeming with the bravado of a dominant male, keeps running, ten, twenty, twenty-five paces. Doj springs after it noiselessly. The animal drops in front of him. Doj comes upon it when the last breaths of life are gurgling from its throat. The muscular, bare-chested man pins the animal by holding an antler to the ground, draws his knife and severs its jugular vein. A fountain of blood spurts in a strong arc, then the gushes diminish in size as the animal dies. From the *Homo sapien's* chest comes a low, guttural sound—a growl, but something more primitive. He sneers and does a 360-degree roar, as if there may be competition for his kill. He bends down and pushes his knife into the animal's back, then makes two parallel twelve-inch slices. He cleanly lifts out the steak, holds it for a moment to the sun, as if in supplication, then eats. After he finishes, he cuts six more steaks, guts the deer, and hangs the rest of the animal by its antlers between two branches.

He returns to the trail and resumes his strong pace. Thirty minutes later he is soaking in a hot spring. The temperature of the water is 103° Fahrenheit, just as he likes it. The smaller spring twenty feet away is much too hot for soaking. That's where the six steaks are boiling in a latticework of lodgepole branches.

June 21st, 1999, Jackson Hole, Wyoming, Office of Conestoga Cabs, 8:47 a.m.

Wilma Tackitt, the owner of Conestoga Cabs, and Kaela Welch, her eight-year driver, are sitting on stools at opposite sides of the counter when Wilma's day manager walks in holding the dispatch phone in one hand and the two-way radio in the other.

"Eddy, thanks for getting those numbers for me," says Wilma. "We're up eight percent over last year already."

"Let's let Kaela be your manager this summer. She's getting the computer figured out, and the paperwork's killing me. I wish I could just drive again. I was going over the figures in my head and was so unconscious I almost ran into the Budweiser truck turning into the Wort Hotel."

"You're burned out and it's only the first day of the summer," says Kaela, a lanky redhead.

"Did that new guy show up at eight?" Wilma asks, turning back to her crossword puzzle.

"No," says Eddy. "He called. He got a job bussing tables at the Alpenhof."

"More money, better hours," says Kaela, flipping through the Jackson Hole Daily. "Same old story."

"We still need four drivers so I ran the ad again." Wilma pauses. "Bumper called, asked if he could drive."

"No way," say Kaela and Eddy in unison. Eddy continues, "He ran over that drunk guy's foot the last day of ski season. We still may get sued." He tosses his cowboy hat onto the couch. "I'd rather hire Mav back."

Wilma takes a sip of coffee. "But he only spoke ten words of English and got in a fight every time he got stiffed. What's a five-letter word for a winter constellation?"

"Orion," offers Eddy.

"Someone will show up," says Kaela.

There are two raps on the wooden door before it opens, revealing a male form that immediately draws the attention of the females. He is tall, muscular, has large gray eyes, and cave-black hair, nearly shoulder-length, which frames angular facial features and a sharp profile. As he stands in the doorway his six-foot-two-inch frame blocks out most of the light before he flicks on the light switch. Kaela winces as if he were an apparition.

"Conestoga Cabs?" the man asks, his voice as clear as his gray eyes.

"Sure. Where would you like to go?" asks Wilma.

"I'm here about the ad in the paper. For a driver?"

"Where do *you* work out at?" asks Kaela.

The man smiles and then steps farther inside the room holding the classified section in his hand. "Here and there. How about you?"

"Anywhere's fine. Kaela Welch. Redhead," she says, extending her hand.

"I'm very happy to meet you." The man steps forward, reaching out.

"Kaela, please get this nine o'clock, Snow King to the airport, will ya?"

"Which airport are you referring to?" Kaela stands and faces the man, smiling, just now relinquishing his hand.

"Jackson Hole Airport? The one you've been to twenty-five thousand times in your eight years here?"

"Oh yeah, that one." Kaela reaches behind her, knocks down her radio, then fishes for it and nearly knocks it off the counter before she turns around to surround it with both hands. "What was your name again?"

"Doj Bolderton."

"Fill out this application." Eddy sets the paper and pen on the counter. "Do you have any driving experience?"

"I got in and out of Las Vegas in a '71 VW bus without getting killed."

"How long have you lived in Jackson?" Wilma asks.

"Three, maybe four hours." Doj then starts filling in the application.

The cellular phone rings. Eddy steps over to answer, "Conestoga Cabs," as Kaela waves goodbye and exits, walking backwards.

"Housing's tough here," says Wilma. "You tried to find a place to stay yet?"

"Yes, I already found a cabin for rent in town. Just the right size. Cute little place."

Eddy sets down the cellular and picks up the two-way radio, keying the transmit button. "Hey Knuckles, pick up at the dentist's office on Maple Way. Going to the middle school."

A mechanical 'got it' barks from the radio as Eddy turns back, appraising the man he guesses to be twenty-seven, twenty-eight years old, dressed in a pressed white shirt and neat jeans, far neater and sharper-looking than the average cab driver applicants who float in and out of the office.

"What brings you to Jackson?"

"The outdoors and a chance to save the world."

Eddy and Wilma stop, look at each other. Wilma scrutinizes the young man who looks as if he could get a job modeling on the runways of New York or London instead of making tips and five dollars an hour driving a cab.

"You don't look as if you're one taco short of a combination plate," says Eddy. "Why do you wanna drive a cab?"

"I enjoy taking people where they want to go. You learn a lot about people driving a cab. I don't need a lot of money. Can I listen to the radio while I'm driving?"

"I hire drivers who already know their way around town. You just got here. You don't know where anything is."

"I drove around for about three hours already. Go ahead, ask me anything."

"Where's . . . Teton Lumber?"

Doj pauses for ten seconds then says, "Gros Ventre Street," pronouncing it correctly '*gro vont.*' "You could go down Broadway and take a right on Gros Ventre, or east on Pearl—or I suppose you could even go down Kelly, if you were coming from south of town. But Carlson Lumber would probably be better if you were already on the south side of town; it's got a little bigger selection and a larger lumberyard."

Wilma cracks a smile, turns away.

Eddy studies the application. "How do you say your name again?"

"Doj. Like the Soj in Sojourner."

"Thirty-three years old . . . how's your driving record?"

"Perfect."

"*No* other previous work experience?"

"I've been a student."

"What'd you get your degree in?"

"No degree. I dabbled in . . . many studies."

"Wyoming license. How'd you get that already?"

"Got it this morning. Was hoping to work for you."

"Married?" asks Wilma.

"Nope. Single as the sun."

"Hobbies?" says Eddy, reading from the application and twisting his face as if he just pinched a nerve. "Being a messenger from God and saving the human race from degeneration?"

"That's me. I like the outdoors, too, and music, and performing an occasional miracle."

Eddy casts an inquisitive glance at Wilma, who says, "Well, he's got the prerequisite sense of humor. Hire him."

"Start tomorrow morning at eight, after we've checked your driving record."

Tuesday, June 22nd, 1999, 4:18 p.m. Offices of the *Jackson Hole News*.

Dressed in a long-sleeved white shirt, with a two-way radio in his left hand, Doj Bolderton walks to the reception desk. Tuesday is press day for the Wednesday-published weekly—hell day—and the familiar deadline panic prevails throughout the newsroom. The receptionist is on the phone jotting down information. Doj walks past her and upstairs to the newsroom where he stops between the desk of the editor, Erik Hatfield, and a staff writer, Kathy Ulrich, who click away at their computers. Erik briefly looks up over bifocals before his eyes scan back to the screen.

"Can I help you?"

"Yeah, I drive for Conestoga Cabs."

"Who called for a cab?" yells the editor without missing a keystroke.

"No, I'm also . . . well . . . the son of God, the new prophet."

Erik and Kathy both give the man a sideways glance, still typing.

"You *look* like Daniel Day Lewis," says Kathy, reaching in a folder for a sheet of paper.

"So what can we do for you?" asks Erik, his tone not changing perceptibly.

A woman leans into view from behind a partition and says, "If you're the son of God perhaps you need some ad space. I've got a four-by-two left in Lifestyle. . . ."

"We're very busy," says the editor, "so what can we do for you, Mr? . . ."

"Bolderton. Doj Bolderton. Well, I was thinking a press conference would be a good start."

Erik stops his typing, looks over his glasses. "Who the hell sent you here? Was it someone from the *Jackson Hole Guide*?"

"It was God. God himself."

Without stopping her typing Kathy asks, "What does he look like? I've always wondered."

"He's . . . a spirit. An immortal feeling of light and dark. Alpha and Omega. That sort of thing."

"Does he look anything like Peter Frampton?"

"Well yeah, sure. If that works for you it works for me."

"That's great, Mr. Bolderton," says Erik. "We need some comic relief around this place. But not on Tuesdays. We've got less than four hours to put this paper to bed. If you'll excuse us."

After a fifteen second pause Doj says, "Perhaps a couple of minor miracles. He told me you pagans may need some convincing."

"You got any real quick ones?" asks Kathy, turning over the page. "Like, could you heat up this coffee without touching it?"

"Erik, how about the time you got in a fight with Harrison Ford at the Stagecoach Bar?" There is no response from the editor, who spins around in his seat to rifle through some papers. "Or the time when you were eleven years old and you hit the home run to give Fred's Market the Little League championship in 1963?"

"Not bad. Either I know you from somewhere or you've done your homework."

"How about my coffee?"

Doj pauses, turns to her and says, "How *'bout* you, Kathy? Your grandfather met up with a grizzly bear and was thrown off his horse. Grandpa shot the bear, but not before it scratched his face severely and broke two ribs. You've got a tattoo on your butt commemorating the event. Left cheek, I believe."

Everything stops. Erik looks at Kathy. Kathy looks at the statuesque man, really looks at him for the first time.

"No one knows that," says the news writer.

"Is that true?" the editor asks her.

"How'd you know that?"

"It's my dad. God? I mentioned him before? He knows everything. How about that press conference?"

The editor swivels in his chair. "I'm impressed, but I'm not that impressed."

The radio crackles. "Doj, got a pickup at Spring Creek. You got it?"

"Got it." Doj turns to leave. "How about three o'clock Friday, on the town square?"

"No thanks," says the editor.

Doj turns back. He seems to grow, some animal seems to emerge. His voice is deeper, more stern. "Your favorite show when you were young was Zorro?"

"Yes, that's true."

Doj points to a poster on the back wall. A pencil-thin blue light emits from his hand and burns a quick Z across the poster. The middle triangles fall to the ground and the bottom section curls down, leaving a smoldering Z.

"That was my Dylan poster! That poster was signed by him! It was a collector's item!"

"Three? Town square. And Friday's OK?"

"Friday. Yeah, sure," says Kathy, rising.

Doj Bolderton turns and walks away.

Friday, June 25th, 3:08 p.m. Jackson Hole, Wyoming town square.

The imminent appearance of the son of God earned small blurbs in both local weekly newspapers, the *Jackson Hole News* and the *Jackson Hole Guide*, but both were similar in that they were tongue-in-cheek. The *News* article stated that "Through technical trickery a cab driver destroyed a valuable collector's item and directed a lewd accusation at a female reporter before demanding a personal press conference." The *Guide* was even less kind, denouncing the act of intrusion into their editor's office by stating, "we can only watch as an increasing number of freaks and attention seekers make their final mark in the most ego-driven century mankind has ever known."

But nevertheless the members of the press are there, waiting, drawn together, for in this small Wyoming community there is room for only one newspaper and two have survived. Information in a small town is spread by word of mouth; besides the press there are representatives of some of the local churches sitting on the green grass, along with the curious, a few cowboys, some youngsters, and a gaggle of tourists who leisurely shop and pass through the town square, which is bordered on four corners by elk antler arches.

A squeaky stagecoach, full of tourists, departs the Stage Stop; an Aerostar van with a western-cut 'Conestoga Cabs' logo swings in behind it, in front of the 'Taxi Parking Only' sign.

The driver speaks into the two-way radio. "Eddy, I need to take that fifteen minute break now, if I may."

"Now don't do anything stupid. We're starting to get calls requesting that God pick them up. Publicity's one thing, but this is getting out of hand."

"Clear on the square. Talk to you in a few. And you owe me five bucks from last night's game. The Dodgers won."

"You're not God!"

Doj clicks off the radio, clips it to his belt and steps over the railing.

"Oh my God!" yells a cowboy. "Yes! It's oh my God!"

"Savior . . . savior . . . savior," another group of wrangler types start ranting.

A group of women and men, several holding bibles, gaze at Doj as he passes through the crowd and in front of them.

"Can ya talk to God on that radio?" shouts a wrangler in tight jeans, black hat. "Can *I* talk to him? Can you bring back my old paint, Dapper? Been dead these eight years now. Oh, *please* bring back Dapper!"

Doj passes Erik and Kathy. The women there survey him, this handsome man, at once athletic and graceful, but also with a regal countenance, something king-like, noble. He is charismatic, but also attractive in that one is drawn toward him, attracted, like metal filings to a nearby magnet. He has the attention of everyone.

He faces them, pauses and takes a breath, then looks down at the reporters sitting in front of him.

"I'm sorry about the poster. Were you able to tape it? I really was focused on concentrating the light."

"We taped it," says Erik. "Tell us what you have to say. We've got some serious things to cover."

Doj leans down, looks squarely into his eyes. "This *is* serious."

More curious passersby meander closer. Doj straightens and looks out over the forty-some people gathered; he studies the faces, sees joy and fear, absorbs their curiosity, their doubt. A small boy asks, "Can you call up on that radio and ask 'em to bring back my dad?"

Doj smiles, touches the boy on the head, then speaks to the crowd. His voice is calm, confident. "The most dangerous place in the continental United States tonight was not the most dangerous place one-hundred-and-fifty years ago. Being here in the Tetons or Yellowstone Park one-hundred-and-fifty years ago, one feared the mighty grizzly, one feared hunger, cold, or

Blackfeet Indians. Tonight, after dark, the streets around the nation's capital, or any major city in the world, are far more treacherous, far more deadly than what we used to consider the wilderness. The wilderness now is the cities. It's not bears, wolves, lions, or wolverines, but rather the human animal that is the most dangerous. The human race has been given a chance and has failed to the degree of its dominance. Totally. We've conquered the planet, our species has, and we've come to sublimate every other life form, domesticated them, studied them, controlled them, killed them off. We've committed the most heinous atrocities in this century, the century of greatest advancement. There have been advances in human rights—the abolishment of servitude and slavery, equality. . . ."

"Wheeere's Old Dapper?" the young cowboy wails to the accompanying laughter of his cowboy buddies. "Bring back Dapper!"

"So for *these reasons,* in this, the end of the most violent of millennia, God, our father, yours and mine, has decided to end life on Earth."

Doj stops, there is a silence.

Kathy, the *News* reporter, breaks the uncertain moment. "How? Where? When?" She still has a hint of a smile on her face, eyebrows high, her tone sarcastic.

"He is sending . . . he has sent a heavenly body, a comet, toward Earth. The comet will collide with earth this year, perhaps sometime in December, before the century ends."

"Why? And why you?" comes a *Guide* reporter's voice.

"There is one reason why a human is the only animal to take its own life: It's because that person has lost hope. The God who gives and takes *our* lives no longer sees hope for humanity. Mankind has trespassed too far beyond the border of decency. His end will be more merciful than the end he sees from humankind's own volition. Why me? I did not ask. I am his son, as you are his sons and daughters. I am the messenger."

One of the bible holders asks, "If this is to be, how would we *know?* What *proof* will we see of this thing that has been portent since the time of Christ, whose time has justly come now?"

"In six days you will have your sign, your proof."

One of the larger cowboys, the young one, comes toward Doj. "You lousy little turd, why are you scaring these innocent people?" The cowboy lunges at Doj.

Doj's expression is suddenly intense as he ducks a swing, then punches the cowboy hard in the stomach, just above the heavy belt buckle, then he jerks the cowboy cleanly over his head, takes three running steps and hurls him up to the horse and Wyoming cowboy statue at the center of the town square. The cowboy instinctively latches onto the statue, sucking in breath. Doj points a finger at the aggressor just as a tomato comes whizzing from the periphery of the crowd and hits Doj in the head, splattering.

Doj wipes it off and shouts to the crowd, "Your icons and your disbelief will soon be shattered! No longer will you pay tribute to those who war and those who kill." He points to the Persian Gulf War plaques under the Bud Boller bronze. "There was no asterisk next to 'Thou shalt not kill' that said 'except in war, except in gangs, except in the twentieth century.' It's time you learned a lesson. It's time to make a change."

Doj points his finger to his assailant, but the light does not materialize. He lowers his hand, turns slowly, then walks through the silent crowd, to his cab.

Taxi drivers in any city in the world are tuned into the heartbeat of the night. It doesn't happen in the daytime. The day is full of people *having* to be somewhere—work, the store, the car repair shop—but at night people are *moving,* they're *going* somewhere. Ask a night driver. He'll tell you. You sit for awhile doing nothing, then you get one, two, three calls in a row and the night shift is happening. People are going to interact socially, especially in a resort town like Jackson Hole, Wyoming, a destination resort. Tourists dine in fine restaurants. And with the glow of great food and fine wine they climb into warm vans. Or locals and tourists go to the square, into the Rancher or Cowboy Bar, to sit not on stools but saddles. Maybe they shoot pool, or have a few drinks and kick it up with a country band. And why not drink if you want to? You don't have to worry about being pulled over by the police and 'balanced out' while standing on Broadway, in front of bright searchlights, while cars slow down and locals and neighbors gape. You don't worry about driving at all. The cabbie will do that. The hack. He's there to join in your revelry or commiserate with your suffering, for the interlude is brief and it helps the tip, then he (or she) speeds away for another pickup.

Tuesday, June 29th, 11:28 p.m.

"Doj, where are ya?"

"I'm at Taft's, having some tea."

"You're closest. Head down to the Virginian. Shelly called, says she's got a gal that's pretty drunk. Imagine that, us getting a call to pick up a drunk. I'm not sure where she's heading."

"Got it, Wolfster."

Doj pushes through the swinging doors and through the smoke to the bar. "Shelly, who am I getting?"

"Right there."

The woman is beautiful by anyone's standards. Almost as if she's been packaged. Tight black Levis, black ostrich skin cowboy boots, lavishly embroidered silk shirt with a matching turquoise cowboy hat and scarf. And she's crying.

"I'm your cab. Are you all right?"

She rises quickly, angrily, throws seven dollars on the table and scowls, "You bet," as she storms out of the room.

Doj looks at Shelly.

"Take care of Veronica," she says, stopping her wiping. "It's been rough on her lately."

Doj starts the Aerostar van, then turns down the radio. "Where to?"

"Anywhere where I can get some razor blades."

The radio crackles. "Doj, you got your fare?"

"Just got her."

"Where're ya headin'?"

Veronica starts crying again, putting her head to her knee, then stomping her feet into the floorboard.

"I'm not sure. This may take a few minutes."

"Try to hurry. I need ya."

"They can't," she cries. "They just can't! They deserve to give me some respect."

"Who?" says Doj.

"Oh, what would you care? Just get me out of here!"

Doj makes a right and cruises toward the square.

The raven-haired beauty fumbles for a cigarette, lights it, takes two puffs, then throws it out the window. "Do they care? Do any of them care if I'm gone tonight? Hell no."

She reaches in her purse and fishes out an orange prescription bottle. She has trouble with the childproof lid until it finally comes off with a jerk and she spills the contents in the front seat of the cab. She sets the bottle on the dash. As they pass under a street light Doj notices they are Tylox, a Schedule II narcotic painkiller. She picks a capsule off the floor and swallows it with a sip of blackberry brandy from a half-pint which quickly appears, then disappears back into her purse. Under a stream of cuss words she picks up the other pills, putting some in the bottle. She finds another one, which she sets on the dashboard while she reaches for the brandy.

"You don't need to do that," says Doj.

"As if you care. Just shut up, will ya?"

Doj steps on the brakes, looks straight at her, "Put those away, Veronica. Now!"

That causes a moment's hesitation, a shift in her attitude.

"How did you know my name?"

His commanding voice speaks directly to her again. "Put those away right now because I need to talk to you immediately. What's your last name?"

"Unger," she says meekly.

"Veronica Unger," Doj repeats, tucking his hair behind his ear. Ten seconds later he says in a lower tone, "Let's just drive for a few minutes, OK? Can I talk to you for just a few minutes?"

"OK. But you better tell me how you knew my name. I could have you arrested, you know."

Doj presses the button on the radio. "Wolfmeister, I've got a code blue here. I'm going to need ten, if that's all right."

"OK, Doj. I copy. We'll make it work."

"Look at me," he says to Veronica.

She looks at him now for the first time, really, and with a nervous twitch of her head she smiles a little and sniffs back tears.

He scrutinizes her for a moment then says softly, "You, Veronica, are a kind, loving and open person. You're very trusting, sometimes too much so. I think you're looking for someone to cling to. But you're afraid of something. What is it?"

She looks at him as he turns right onto Cache Street. He slows the cab and looks back at her. Her lips start quivering then she cries out, "You son of a bitch. Why are you doing this? I finish these pills and this cheap rotgut and I'm outta here and I solve everyone's problems."

In the Snow King parking lot, overlooking town, it all comes out: A father who beat her mom and ran out. Physical and sexual abuse from a stepfather. Then her mother died when she was a junior in high school. Tobacco, drug and alcohol addiction started even before high school ended. And then, last Saturday one of her closest 'friends' had taken her home and raped her; her 'friends' told her not to go to the police. There were witnesses that would testify she was making advances throughout the evening, and besides, there was her reputation, for she had slept with most of the men in their circle. She was to be at court Monday morning for her second DUI in three years. And there were the constant headaches from morning to night—that's what she wanted to get away from most.

After she finishes Veronica scoots down and puts her right boot up on the dash and her right hand to the bridge of her nose. There is silence as she looks out the right window, then automatically reaches back in her purse for the brandy.

Doj puts his hand on hers. "Your mother was a kind woman with incredible amounts of love to give. Do you remember her?"

"Yes, of course I do. We were happy. Her and I could have made it together."

"Part of your mother is within you. You're now going to start bringing that part of you to the surface. Remember that she was a strong person and could put her foot down. Remember? She knew how to say 'no'."

"Yes, she always could say no. She wasn't afraid of anyone."

"You think because you were forced to do something against your will that your will is weak now. But inside it's still there. You will start tonight, right now, with that inner foundation your mother gave you and build from there. In the past you've seen glimpses of hope, of the kind of person you want to be, but every time you near the surface you're afraid to reach that far and you give in again."

"How do you know so much about me? Have you been talking to Rachael?"

"No, but you need to. Has Rachael cleaned up her act?"

"She broke up with Todd and she's not hanging around the old gang any more. Are you that new guy she's been seeing?"

Doj laughs, "No, I'm afraid not."

"Are you seeing anybody?"

He laughs again. "No, not me."

He looks at her. Her eyes flash at him, the pupils dilate.

"No," he says.

"No what?"

"What you're thinking."

"How'd you know what I was thinking?"

"Give me the brandy and the Tylox."

"Screw you."

"Give them to me and I'll tell you a secret."

"Tell me the secret first."

"No."

After three full minutes of shifting in her seat and going back to 'what do you care' and 'no one cares' and 'you don't know me' and 'how do you know me', she throws the bottle of pills at his chest, then flings the half-pint of brandy out the window, smashing it against the one big granite boulder twenty feet away.

"Good shot," he says.

She laughs, then says, "Screw you. I can get more. What's the secret?"

"The secret is that by throwing the pills at me and smashing that bottle of brandy, you've started down the road. You're going to be all right. You just took the first step. I'm taking you home now. Where do you live?"

In the parking lot of Veronica's apartment complex Doj says, "I'm off after the bar rush, about 2:30. Will you still be up?"

"If you're coming back, I will be."

"Do you have a bathing suit?"

"I bought one in Puerto Vallarta last April. It's not much."

At 3:30 Doj is giving her a massage. Her lithe, perfect body glistens from the warm oil. He works out the knots and twists in her shoulders, her lower back, her glutes. He pushes out the toxins. Her breathing and heart rate slows. Her body goes limp. He talks to her from time to time: "And that's how it will be to be in control and off that crap. It will be as if you've lived in darkness for twenty years and the sun just came up."

"What's your name, anyway?"

"Doj. Roll over. I'm nearly finished."

"Will I see you again?"

"Can I clean out that booze closet on my way out?"

"Yes. Please."

Article in *Jackson Hole News*, June 30, 1999:

GOD SHOWS UP, KICKS SOME BUTT

A cab driver for Conestoga Cabs presented himself as the son of God in the offices of the *Jackson Hole News* on Buffalo Way on Tuesday, June 22nd, demanded a press conference, was refused, then destroyed a valuable collectors' item. At Friday's "press conference" Doj Bolderton prophesied the end of the world to a crowd estimated at fifty.

Doj Bolderton, 33, of Jackson, stated that "God, my father, yours and mine, has decided to end life on Earth." He was heckled by Frankie Holeman, 24, of Bondurant. *News* reporters observed Holeman approaching Bolderton in a threatening manner. Bolderton ducked a swing from Holeman, physically picked up the man and flung him atop the town square statue by sculptor Bud Boller.

Bolderton returned to his cab.

Police are investigating.

Article in *USA Today*, July 2nd, 1999:

COMET SIGHTED

Dr. Spencer Tennyson of the Palomar Observatory, Mount Palomar, California, has discovered a new comet which should be visible later this year. Sighted near the sun in the constellation Leo, it was confirmed by colleagues at the Special Astrophysical Observatory in Mount Pastukhov in Russia, the European Southern Observatory in Cerro Paranal, Chile, the Kiso Observatory in Kiso, Japan, and Kitt Peak Observatory in Arizona.

"Chances of it coming into our solar system appear to be extremely slim," said Tennyson. "We'll make some computations after tracking it for a few nights. On Sunday night the Hubble Telescope should be able to pick up additional data. We just hope the Hubble doesn't get confused and start snapping shots of the earth-based fireworks that night (July 4th). It's light-sensitive and likes things like that."

Further information about the new comet will be available Monday, according to Dr. Tennyson.

Owen-Bircher Park, Wilson Wyoming, Monday, July 4th. 8:32 am.

Perhaps it is because of the perfect mountain morning, with temperatures in the low sixties; perhaps it is because everything in the last year of the greatest century known to man takes on greater significance, or perhaps it is that fitness—and particularly running—has not decreased in popularity since the 'running boom' started in 1972, but there is a record crowd for the twenty-second annual Skinny Skis July Fourth 10K run. Every design of nylon, rubber and mesh is modeled, the colors as bright as the mood of the runners as they stretch, pin numbers, jog lightly, chat.

Doj Bolderton is there, striding lightly down Fish Creek Road. The newcomer. The stranger. The man who says he's the son of God. He warms up alone.

Three members of the Idaho State Cross Country Team are there. Twig Warren is also there, the former steeplechaser from Brigham Young who won the Olympic Trials in '96. Jason Lands, the longtime vice-president of the Jackson Hole Road Runners, is there. He is the course record holder. He strides up next to Doj, with a shorter runner just off his shoulder.

"Hey, you're God, aren't you?"

"No, I'm not God. I am his son, just like you. I'm simply the messenger of things to come."

"And the world's going to end, huh? Better make this a good 10K if it's the last one ever. But if you're the 'messenger of things to come', of course you know the outcome already. Can you fill me in? I might be able to make a bet. How much will I win by?"

"I will beat you. You'll probably finish sixth."

Jason laughs. "Probably? You don't know? Come on, God."

"Did the ultrasound or the massage you got this morning help that strained hamstring?" Doj asks.

Jason runs along silently for three steps. "I thought you said that was cured," the other runner says to Jason.

Jason looks at Doj. "You been talking to my wife?"

"She's not my type. Stretch marks. Ugh."

"Listen, Jesus boy, you want to make a little wager?"

"How much is a little? Not any bigger than that ego of yours, I hope."

"Fifteen dollars is the entrance fee," volunteers the smaller runner. "That's pretty standard."

"For the entrance fee, Jesus boy?"

"That's not very much. Hardly worth breaking a sweat for."

"Double the entrance fee, then—and if you lose—you'll walk on Fish Creek for us later. If you don't walk on it you'll walk in it, and it's damned cold mountain water."

"Let's round it off," says Doj. "How about thirty-two dollars and thirty-three cents since your record is 32:33?"

"Hey cool," says the smaller runner.

"You got a bet," says Jason Lands. "Excuse me if I don't shake your hand. The sweat of God might be too much. I don't want to have a religious experience while your legs are burning in hell."

With a half-mile to go, there is still a pack of six runners: the three from Idaho State University, Twig Warren, Jason Lands and Doj Bolderton. They have been averaging 5:20 a mile, and now the pace picks up. Twig Warren and one of the ISU runners open a two-yard gap. The few onlookers hear the faint sound of soft rubber soles hitting asphalt. The more noticeable sound is of deep, heavy breathing, here at 6,300 feet above sea level. Fifty yards before the final turn the pace quickens and two of the ISU runners are dropped. After the final turn they spread out and run abreast, now 300 yards from the finish banner and the waiting crowd. An electrified chorus of whoops, whistles and cheers swells as the runners swing into view. Doj pulls off his shirt, throws it aside, then forces a slight lead. Jason Lands forces his way between Doj and Twig Warren; small all-out surges produce leads of mere inches. With two hundred yards to go, the clock flashes 32:00.

In an exhalation Doj says, "Jason forgot his vitamins . . . this mornin'."

Like a horse being whipped the words galvanize Twig Warren into a wild sprint, his arms flailing, head rolling back, eyes barely open. A guttural growl emerges from the six-foot-two-inch black-haired stranger as he pushes his pursuit. Jason Lands also pursues. With fifteen yards to go, photographers snapping pictures, the crowd screaming wildly, and someone yelling out "32:28! . . . 32:29. . . ." Doj Bolderton takes three gigantic, muscular strides to step a foot in front of Twig Warren and Jason Lands. He throws back his head and thrusts out his chest as the two runners behind him get hung up in each other's arms and tumble forward.

As Doj sprints over the finish line in 32:31 he lets out a scream of primal agony followed by the two other runners splaying onto the hot asphalt in a tangle of legs and elbows.

"That was better than the demolition derby at the county fair last night!" says a young girl at the end of the finishing chute, handing Doj a popsicle stick with #1 at each end.

That evening Doj invites Taft Vandren to dinner. He is his landlord and, for Doj, he is slowly filling the role of a caring, loving uncle. Over occasional morning tea and toasted bagels in Taft's cabin, the sixty-two-year-old biologist has not once been judgmental or ridiculing. In fact he had been supportive, watching the running race that morning after Doj pleaded, for the third time, "Come, watch me win this race. I can beat these sluggish mortals!"

"Hello!" calls Taft, opening the squeaky door and stepping in. "I brought the salad."

"Thanks."

Taft takes the wooden lid off the bowl and sets it on the table and says, "I hate to leave my work, I just collected four new samples. But I know the fireworks will distract me. Might as well give in to ritualistic celebration. Speaking of which, I insist on taking my silly old plaque off the mantle and . . . here . . . replacing it with your trophy from the race today. Well done."

They eat outside. Three blocks away, at the bottom of Snow King Mountain and on surrounding neighborhood lawns, crowds slowly gather for the annual fireworks, sitting in lawn chairs and on blankets, sending their puny missiles into the sky above the ball field before the first serious boom shatters the night sky, echoing off the 1571-foot mountain, sending house pets scurrying. Doj and Taft finish their appetizers as the spectators hoot and applaud.

Tuesday, July 5th, Room 203, Teton County Sheriff's Office, 1:31 p.m.

"Mr. Bolderton, there were two men hurt at the end of that race yesterday. I want to know what happened."

"Why don't you ask them?"

"I did. What do you think they said?"

"That I blew their doors in? I out-toughed them? I beat the course record by two seconds and took Land's school money for the week?"

The sheriff tries to open the window more, but realizes he has tried it three times and it's all the way up. It's just an unusually hot summer for northwestern Wyoming, he reminds himself.

He looks at the man in the seat. Looks like a good kid, he thinks. Sharply dressed. He sighs and turns from him, toward a file sitting on top of the file cabinet, and thinks: They *had* the meeting last December. They *knew* 1999 was going to be a wilder year. Even though the year 2000 would actually be the last year of the century, the millennium, 1999 was the year everyone was celebrating The Great Countdown. What was it that criminal psychologist had said at that seminar in Denver? It was going to be like ancient Indian cave art, marking important events by scrawling on walls or blowing dye, or like the early trappers leaving their initials and the date on the trees in these parts. Or time capsules. Marking the passage of time, that's what it was. We all want to leave our mark in the—what did he say—most progressive yet agitated and aggressive century known to humankind. But hell. What a summer! For the first time in how many Fourth of July celebrations, someone got seriously injured by the fireworks in that block party over on Karns. Then there's the guy who tried to torch the Rockefeller Ranch, for no apparent reason. Drive-by shootings, crime's up in the park, and there was that backcountry rape. Now this guy's predicting the end of the world. Hell, he might be right. What's he talking about? An asteroid? Christ, we might just do it ourselves.

"They said that," the sheriff finally replies. "But they said more than that. They said you yelled or growled or something, then it was like you floated away from them. Might have been some contact; one runner said that caused him to stumble into the other guy."

"That would be Jason Lands. By the way, he still owes me two dollars and thirty-three cents. Can you do something about that? Seems Jason was just a little short, in more ways than one."

"What drugs are you taking?"

Doj peers into the sheriff's eyes. He puts his elbow on the table and rubs his nose and mouth, then points at the sheriff. "That's very good, Sheriff. That's very interesting. You don't ask *if* I've taken any drugs, but you ask what *kind*. That requires more than a one-syllable answer. Or a one-syllable lie. So it would be easier to tell if I was lying if I had to say 'I'm not taking any drugs.'"

"Well, are you?"

"Checkmate! Now I can answer in one syllable: No."

The sheriff doesn't like being sassed, but somehow he likes this guy. Hell, he had been a runner in school, for old Coach Williams at the high school. From what he's heard from witnesses he's sorry he missed seeing the race.

He looks across at the new jail and thinks: That almost sounded like the race I won in Lander back in my senior year. It's that damn Jason Lands I should throw in the clink. His daddy was an asshole, too.

"Would you mind if we cut off a couple of strands of hair? Ran a DNA test?"

"I washed it this morning. Just for you guys. Strawberry Essence all right?"

"I prefer peach."

Just then the police chief comes in and tells the sheriff, "Three other witnesses all said everything was absolutely fair."

"No elbows? No pushing?"

"Nope. One guy said it was the most exciting sporting event he'd ever witnessed in Jackson Hole. That's about it."

The police chief sits down and undoes the top button of his tight shirt. "What else did you get?"

"No record from the Internet. Nothing in California. No prior work record. Parents both died in a car accident when he was . . . eighteen?"

"Seventeen," Doj replies. "You knew that."

"He'd been a student at . . . where was that?"

"Delta University."

"Right. No degree. Worked as a research and graduate assistant. For ten years?"

"That damned Geography 101 stumped me. Took it thirty-seven straight semesters. But I'm good now with state capitols." He points his thumb behind him to the Wyoming state map. "Wyoming? Laramie!"

"Cheyenne," says the sheriff.

Doj slaps his thigh. "Damn! I studied *hard* in that class. I crammed. Dover. Now let's talk Dover. We can talk Dover."

The police chief is not so patient. "What's all this God stuff?"

"The son of God. Or something simple like my savior, or dynamic deity, or even messenger—personally, that works fine for me."

"Look," says the police chief, "some people are starting to get pretty upset about this nonsense. We have some very decent and devout citizens here. Also you've destroyed some property and three people have gotten hurt."

"The cowboy deserved it. He took a swing at me."

"That's true," says the sheriff. "But you didn't have to throw him up on the statue. He knocked off the Persian War plaque when he was getting down."

"It took one city employee one hour and three minutes to replace it, including his thirty-minute coffee break. That's fifteen dollars and eighty-three cents. I've got it here. Well, he *did* use the new glycol silicate epoxy and I don't blame him for watching it dry. That stuff should have been around in March of 1983. Remember, Chief? You ran over that bull elk while you were speeding to the Cowboy Bar for that big fight, and you pulled up with the six-point set of antlers sticking out of your radiator. Then you ran into the bar, the fight was already over, but meanwhile someone pulled the antlers out and ran off with them?"

The sheriff laughs under his breath and puts his feet up on the table. "I forgot about that."

The police chief's patience runs out. "How the hell do you know so much about some of the people in this town?"

"Dad said I'd probably have to flash a few miracles, to let them know I'm the cat's meow. It's just my special little way of letting everyone know: I'm ubiquitous. That's with three u's and one q."

"What the hell does that mean?" the chief demands.

"I've been around. I can look through your eyes, into your heart and soul. I can tell if you've been strong or weak, good or bad, naughty or nice. If you're moral. What you do alone at night. If you're quick or slow. I can read your life."

The sheriff wipes a drop of sweat from his eye. "Chief Nuxhall and I have known each other for a long time. Go on, tell me something about him that I don't know."

Doj turns slowly. "I need to face him. OK. Very good. The chief is well-trained in the art of deception, in reading it as well as employing it."

Doj closes his eyes, takes a deep breath, then peers into the eyes of the veteran police chief. The chief's stern demeanor flakes a bit under the gaze of the gray-eyed man. After twenty seconds Doj rises and paces. "At the Academy you were considered a hard-liner. You graduated, but you were practicing enforcement before you were getting paid to. Remember? That bar in Helena where that guy was roughing up his date? He deserved it though, didn't he? You're a fair person. Don't worry, you'll go upstairs when it's over. But you don't have a lot of patience. Just because that guy in Rock Springs smelled bad, was homeless and drunk and spit on you, didn't mean you had to break his jaw. But you still got a good recommendation. And now you're getting better with age. You can look into people's souls as well. You'd make a good disciple. If you'd care to fill out an application, I have one in my van. Thank you."

The sheriff turns his gaze to the chief. He can tell the young man hit the nail on the head. The air in the room is charged with potential friction, it could go either way, and it is very, very still.

After ten beats the police chief says quietly, "And Sheriff Clark?"

"Hey, great race in Lander back in '59." Doj holds out his fingertips in adolescent's newest manner of signaling approval and the sheriff finds himself automatically shaking Bolderton's hand. "Too bad about State. You were never a good runner in the wind—what was it like that day?"

"Forty. Damn gusts must've hit sixty. Damn Casper."

Sheriff Clark drifts off, reminisces, then quickly snaps back to the reality of the current situation. "I'll verify this with a phone call, so you could just tell me. Have you spent much time in the library since you got here?"

"No. I can't read. Failed that class too."

"The Newsroom? Backlogs?"

"No."

"Then how can you do that?"

"Look, guys. Can we really talk for a few moments? Can I tell you how I do it? Can I get back in my cab after that? This is a big weekend. The guys are getting slammed out there."

"There's nothing we can hold you on," says the chief. "Go ahead."

"God gave us a nice planet and we screwed it up. He's pissed. He's really pissed. He's going to end the whole thing and he just so happened to have picked me to announce it. Someone had to do it. I guess it could have been a ten-year-old girl in Mozambique. I am just the culmination of all humanity and I am his medium. So I can perform miracles. What the hell." He leans down to Sheriff Clark. "And I tell ya, 32:30 at altitude *is* a miracle, huh? The miracles are nothing. The end of the world is coming and we've all got to get ready. Time is running out."

"And how is the world going to end?" asks the chief, nine parts skepticism to one part interest.

"You know. What I told Erik Hatfield at the *News* and what he told you. He's going to do it with a heavenly body smashing into the planet. Pop goes the weasel and all that."

"I read in the papers about an asteroid way the hell out there somewhere," says the sheriff.

"A comet, actually. Yes, that's the one."

"But the article said the chances of this thing entering our solar system were almost zero."

"You should see dad's curveball. Kind of like yours, sheriff, when you played A-league fast pitch for ... Aubin Construction?"

"We had a good team."

"Listen," says the chief. "We have nothing we can hold you on, but we can probably figure out something if we try hard enough.

We already have plenty of weird stuff happening this year without any help. I'm asking you personally: Stop what you're doing."

"I can stop crime. Would that help?"

"Perfect," says the sheriff. "Then I'll be out of a job and can guide fly-fishing trips down the Snake with my brother. By the way, we are having a bit of trouble with this stopping crime thing. Just how you propose we do that?"

"What do you feel about mercenaries, murder and terrorism?"

"Not much, unless it's in the movies and the good guys win," Sheriff Clark replies.

Doj takes a breath. "On Thursday there is going to be an airplane crash in Africa, between Angola and Zambia. The correspondent from the Casper paper has informed his editor of me, my statements to the press, and this prediction, and they're going to do a story on me for Wednesday's paper where I will accurately predict this event with vivid details. I also invited the Idaho Falls *The Post-Register* correspondent. I bet you an orange soda one of them uses the word 'uncanny.' We three will know different." Doj steps to the window. "It's time to go regional. The press here is just not giving me enough ink."

The chief wipes his brow.

The sheriff folds his arms and asks, "Can you tell me who'll win the World Series this year?"

Doj turns from the window and smiles. "Texas. But only if their pitching holds up. Damn hot day, huh? How 'bout if I buy us a round of sodas? Sheriff Clark, you like orange sodas? Served very cold?"

"Mountain Dew," he says as he and the chief rise.

"Oh yeah," says Doj as they exit the room, leaving the window wide open.

Friday, July 9th, 7:41 p.m.

Doj is in his cab, cruising down Broadway toward the square. He watches shirt-sleeved tourists stroll the downtown area, posing for pictures underneath one of the four elk-antler arches.

They search and purchase, or just window shop and ponder the western clothes and artifacts. The two-way radio chatter barely pierces the music coming from Doj's cassette player. A tape from some thirty years before is playing, the Beatle's Abbey Road. He has played the second-to-the-last song three times in a row. He embraces the melodic philosophy: the love one takes is equal to the love one makes.

"Yo, Doj! Come back!"

Doj grabs the radio from his lap, fast-forwards the tape, hits the transmit button and waits until the signal bounces off the repeater on Snow King and into Wolfmeister's receiver.

"Yes cool daddy Wolf-Meister man?"

"Where are you, Doj?"

"Parked on the town square, watching the tourons shop. What's up?"

"Another request for you. Eight-twelve Mountain Oyster Drive. That's in Rafter J. You know where that's at?"

"I can figure it out. On my way west, Wolfman. You guys take some of these calls, too. Just tell them I'm spoken for."

"Hell, why should they ride with me when God personally can take them?"

"I'm not the main man, Wolfy boy, just remember that. I'm one of the afterthoughts, just like you. Did you see the papers today?"

"Yeah. Congratulations. The two local dailies, the *Billings Gazette*, Idaho's *The Post-Register*, the *Casper Tribune*, the *Denver Post* and people in every damned checkout line, barbershop, and gynecologist's waiting room are talking about you now. The details from the paper were right on. A McDonnell C-54, an army of mercenaries on a seek-and-destroy mission; you described the guns, the commanding officer, even the color of their berets. How'd you do it?"

"Wolf, I can't tell you that. There are scanners out there. Electronic ears in the evening. Someone might be listening."

"I did notice you missed the body count. There were thirty-four, not twenty-seven. My educated guess is that you are somehow affiliated with the CIA or FBI. How'm I doing?"

"Hold on a second, Wolfman." Doj puts the radio in his lap as he brakes at a pedestrian walkway and motions two elderly ladies to pass in front of him. He says, loudly enough that the two ladies hear him and turn around, "Do you know Greg Wolster? The Wolfman? Talk to me!"

The lady in the gray dress takes her friend's arm and says, "Don't go yet."

They cross and Doj drives onward, heading south. He likes this time of day, when the mountain sun takes two hours to set. The Gill meadows south of town are rich and green, the angled lighting of the early evening sun brings out the yellows, contrasts the mushroom-shaped golden haystacks against the green grass. He pops in another tape and hits the play button on Sgt. Pepper's Lonely Heart's Club Band. "With a Little Help From My Friends"—Ringo's song—fades out and "Lucy in the Sky with Diamonds" dances in in three-quarter time. Doj turns, glances at the rosy south face of the Grand Teton, then picks up his radio. "Wolfman, come back please."

"Yo."

"*You* were in Intelligence—Marines. No, Army. A Green Beret, nonetheless. Several medals in Vietnam. You are a hard man with strict values. A great sense of humor, but a realist in terms of seeing man as violent, capable of doing harm. You are a survivalist. How's that big water filter working out?"

"Jesus, Doj, I only ordered that five days ago. And it just came today. How in the hell'd you do that?"

"You were right. I'm both FBI *and* CIA. But that stands for Frivolous Bits of Information and Checking Individual Attitudes."

Three seconds later Wolfman says, "The people just called back, Doj. Are you about there?"

"Pulling in right now."

The door of the upper-class log home opens and a woman steps out and waves briefly. There are two cars in the drive, which usually means that the fare is going out to do some drinking, enough drinking so as to not be able to drive home. But the woman doesn't look to be that type. Then Doj sees a man step out and close the door behind him, carrying a boy—his son, perhaps—maybe eight years old. Something is not right with the son he is carrying in his arms; he is not well. The child's head shakes, his body quivers sporadically. He is thin and has no hair.

Doj jumps out and pulls back the sliding door of the van.

"Are you Doj Bolderton? The son of God?"

Doj sees a deep fear in the eyes of both the man and the woman. "Yes, I am."

He closes the door behind them, walks around to the driver's seat, slides in and turns off the music. "Where to?"

"Jackson Christian Center," the man replies. "But could you just drive around before we get there? If we could have a few minutes of your time. We . . . need a miracle."

The lady sobs as Doj pulls out.

Over a wailful moan of displeasure from the child, Doj speaks quietly into the radio, "Wolfman, I'm going to the Christian Center. They want to take the long way around. I'll call you when I'm clear."

"Just had another request for you, Doj, but it sounded like a bunch of drunks. I'll get 'em."

The lady cradles the child to her as the father leans between the seats and says in a trembling voice, "Our . . . child is dying. We've tried everything, every doctor, every medicine, chemotherapy . . . me . . . my . . . our life is shattered. Herbert was so full of love . . . he was the happiest kid in the world . . . a good little second baseman . . . he hit his first home run a year ago tomorrow . . . took him to Pizza Hut with the shortstop and first baseman. They almost had that double play . . . he was so happy, we were so proud. . . ."

The mother speaks through sobs. "Help us, please. We'll do whatever. Save Herbie for us."

"What are your names? What is wrong with your son?"

The dad says, "Steve and Laura. And this is Herbie."

"What is your last name?"

"Olander. We heard about you saying you were the son of God," the dad says. "We were never a very religious family, never went to church before this happened. But God can't take Herbie from us. You should have seen his smile. This doggone kid's smile could light up the world. Everyone said he was the happiest kid, real full of energy."

The mother says, "We tried for so long to have children. We finally gave up, then heaven sent us Herbie and he's just not ready to go back. The doctors say he has less than two months. . . . Why would God do this to us? To him?"

"What is the matter with Herbie?" Doj asks.

"He has cancer," says the mother, summoning reserve. "Leukemia."

"Help us," pleads the father. "God in heaven, please save our Herbie."

Doj looks skyward. "What am I able to do?"

The mother says, "Through God's healing power you can make him better."

Doj starts to form phrases, 'he'll be all right', or 'have faith' or 'God works in mysterious ways' or 'he'll be going to a better place'—but the fragments seem weak and shallow, so he says nothing.

"Could you just touch him and make him better?"

"I could touch him. I cannot make him better."

Quickly, angrily, the father scowls. "Why not? Why do you profess to be the son of God and be able to prophesy and say you can look into people's souls and you can't even help one sick child!"

Doj makes a left turn. Four kids playing catch in a front yard seem far away. The Irish setter running back and forth does not seem real. He makes another turn through the labyrinth of the South Park suburb.

"I can try to help you find the best doctor in the country, the best treatment program. What else can I do?"

"Take this left, stop in front of the building with all the cars," says the father. "We have a support group called Parents And Children Threatened, PACT. It's helped a great deal."

As they get out and head to the door the father takes Doj aside.

"Listen, I'm sorry I yelled. I've never been so confused. I don't know if you're playing a huge practical joke or what. Hell, I'm an architect; everything I do adds up, has dimensions. One beam supports another. My wife and I and the doctors have tried everything. It just doesn't feel like this should be happening. Some morning we'll wake up and our life will be back to normal, we'll be getting Herbie ready for school, rushing around . . . . Could you come in with us for a moment?"

In the brightly lit downstairs meeting room are some twenty adults, eight children, and a man who looks to be the leader, kneeling down with folded papers next to a mother with child. The mother's face reflects a sadness which pervades the room, for throughout the room are physical and, if eyes reveal inner truth, emotional defects. A girl of perhaps five is missing a leg. A woman is hooked to a respirator.

The leader glances up at the last entrants and claps his hands. "OK!" injecting the room with sudden energy and vitality. "Let's get going."

As everyone gathers themselves and their children, the leader crosses the room toward Herbie and his family and Doj. "I saw your picture in the paper today," he says, not revealing any emotion, any attitude. "You proclaim yourself to be a prophet, if the papers are accurate. Is that right?"

Doj stutters, clears his throat. "I know that I must repeat my message until everyone truly believes me when I describe what's about to happen."

"Then what's going to happen to all these people? Would you care to tell them?"

Doj looks at the man whose curled eyebrow reveals uncertainty. He looks at Steve, Laura and Herbie, then around the room. "It will all be OK. It will all. . . ."

The leader touches Doj on the shoulder. "Tell *them* that. These people need all the encouragement they can get. And not just from me."

The leader walks back to his chair and sits at the head of the circle. His energy is positive again as he says, "Tonight we have a young man who seems to have the power to see into the future and see into people's hearts. I believe he has an opening thought for us."

Doj looks like an animal poised to flee, eyes wide, skittish. As all faces turn to him he waves his radio in circles, as if trying to conjure a thought.

"You will survive . . . your spirit will survive as long as it was meant to be . . . that is all you have, I have, any of us have . . . our soul and spirit. . . ."

He leaves off, but the faces are still hungry. They are hungry for an answer, an explanation. Something solid. A miracle. Doj's hand gestures are discordant, like an unsure conductor. He starts three different sentences before he says, "I'm sorry . . . God bless you. . . ." and he is gone.

Up the stairs, out the door and back into his cab. He closes the door behind him and grabs the wheel as if it were a life preserver and he'd been tossed into the North Sea.

"Doj, come in, damn it!"

He sees that he has tossed the radio on the seat, face down. He grabs it, presses the transmit button. "Yes, Wolfman. What is it?"

"Where the hell were you just then? You were holding transmit down, wherever you were. It sounded like you were preaching in a cave somewhere. Where are you?"

"I'm . . . clear, Wolf. I'm clear at the Center."

"I just got another request for you. Sounds like Veronica."

"Veronica?"

"The girl you rescued that night."

"Those three nights."

"Eight ninety-two Alpine Way. You got it?"

"No. Repeat, no. Wolf, I'm needing a little time. Can you guys please cover?"

A five second pause, then. "Yeah, I'll get her. I'll tell her God couldn't come so she'll have to make do with Moses."

"Thanks, buddy."

Doj turns south onto Highway 89, racing the setting sun on his right. He presses the gas pedal to the floor, and the six cylinder engine roars; the vehicle rumbles, then accelerates. He turns left onto Game Creek Road, swaying through the curves and onto the gravel road. He drives fast, spewing rocks and dust behind him, only slowing briefly for two descending mountain bikers. Over the cattle guard the left wheel of the four-wheel-drive Aerostar is briefly airborne. He races up the drainage. At a creek crossing he pauses, revs the engine, then plunges through it, bounding up the other side. He reaches a cul-de-sac and can drive no farther. He stops the motor, switches off the two-way radio and steps out into his own cloud of dust.

He starts running up with a charge, a reckless anger. Up the fall line, through the sage and rocks, in running shoes, jeans and a long-sleeved white cotton shirt. He surges, sweating. Lactic acid builds in his muscles and still he bounds up in great powerful, driving strides, using his hands to pull himself above a volcanic outcrop.

He takes off his shirt and flings it to the sky, revealing the most perfect of mesomorphic human forms, rippled, smooth and glistening from perspiration. He shakes back his black mane when he reaches the summit of the mountain. He faces the western sun, just starting to fall beneath the horizon, throws his arms out in the form of a cross and screams a guttural, animal cry.

"Gooooooddd! Take me *now!*" The sounds echo off the nearest mountainsides. "Why *me?* Why did you pick *me?*" He makes a 360-degree turn, arms still held out, palms to the horizon, but hears only silence. "The pain and suffering I see here are too real. There is too much sadness on this planet! Too much hurt!" He throws his head back, and reaches toward the zenith, to the darkening blue sky. "Why is there suffering? Why cannot we all bask in the glory of the indomitable life force? Why is there so much pain, sadness and disease? Why can we not relish the gifts of this remarkable planet, this blue-green-white nest, without pain and remorse?"

He sits down, drops his head, and picks at the orange lichen growing on the rocks that are the high point of the mountain. "I can't do this thing. I can't be the harbinger of mankind's demise. There must be another way. An easier path to happiness and enlightenment for the citizens here."

He stands again, walks five steps away then again holds out his arms to the lowering sun, now a large orange orb setting behind the Snake River Range. He takes a deep breath, says calmly, "Let me bring a life of ecstasy for everyone before the tumultuous end. Let them experience the exuberance I have felt. Let me herald some kind of eternal peace, offer a chance for us all to love and care for one another before death envelopes the people of this third stone from the Alpha star."

A grasshopper rattles and lands closeby. There is no breeze, it is silent around him.

He walks in a circle, his hands raised, not in supplication, but reaching. "There are children who will fear the end. I can't bring fear. Can we not make this quicker? Why must they know so soon?"

With a long sigh he drops his hands. "Yes, I see," he says submissively. "I see that for the sake of eternity this must be done. They must see the end. A chance to exterminate the evil. Yes, it is harsh. But in the end the hearts and souls of these beings will be better. You will make their hearts pure and in one thousand years Earth will be the heaven you have described to me." He lowers his head. "I will not waver again."

He starts down the steep slope, retrieving and putting on his shirt. "But what about Herbie? Am I powerless there? Can I offer only compassion to those who suffer? That's not enough for me. I want more."

Chess, the Game of Kings, was invented in India fourteen hundred years ago. There have been few adaptations or improvements to the game since that time, and it has challenged the most gifted minds in the world. In this twentieth century where technology has exploded into every facet of life, where computers have enabled man-made devices to venture out of the solar system, where computers not only do a great deal of work but even control the lives of humans, it is only now, in this last few years of the century of technology, that computers have been designed which can regularly beat the great chess minds. And still not every time. Chess has been the subject of written volumes, examining the myriad possibilities from a relatively few logical openings. It is a game of *If* and *Then* played to an infinite degree. It is a game which stimulates imagination to the point of self-willed hallucinations, a state of hypnosis; a great player can actually imagine the pieces in different positions. It is the only game ever invented where luck is never a factor. Good players are called prodigies. Or geniuses. In 1858, Paul Morphy, at the age of twenty-one, played an exhibition against eight accomplished players at the same time and won all eight . . . *blind-folded.* Such is the power of imagination of a grand master.

Two men sit opposite one another in the Snow King Resort Grand Room, about to vie for the Region VI Open Championships. The table is in the center of the large hall; the contestants are surrounded by a hundred spectators. Four feet above the crowd are large monitors which show a computer generation of the board and pieces—arsenals preparing for war.

Among the crowd are the tournament losers. Big-bellied and unshaven is Hank Kaiser, the top-ranked player in Idaho with 1385 masters points. Across from him is Kansek Reshevsky, a late loser in the lower bracket, whose father was a Russian champ. Kansek, while never rising to the ability of his father, makes a living travelling in his famous van painted with chessboard and pieces, winning smaller and regional tournaments. They stay to watch the finals because of the two finalists. They are unknown to the other players. Neither of them has a record of accumulating a single master point; the tournament director has searched their names on his laptop, in the latest quarterly of Chess Monthly.

Besides being unknown, one of the men is black. Not only is he black, but he has the clothes, jewelry and persona of a reggae musician. He wears a paisley kaftan and bracelets adorn both wrists. Over the weekend his opponents had come to associate the rattle of those wrists to the warning of a rattlesnake before it strikes with killing venom, underscored by the ring on the middle finger of his right hand, a huge black snake coiled upon a large plate of gold. Two of the earlier players had complained that when it was the black man's turn, he gestured in sinuous motions, as if conjuring the pieces into moving. But the tournament umpire stated the rules they both knew, that when it was his turn, it was not considered a distraction. Nor was it considered a distraction when the man made his move, a radiant white smile broke across that very dark face, a face as smooth as glass, and he would shake his head, making his long dreadlocks click with the strange collection of beads and adornments.

His name is Toby Tiler.

The other finalist is Doj Bolderton.

At the press conference two days before, on July 29th, one of the last questions from the group of news media was, "Well, we really haven't seen any miracles, you know." The reporter from the Boise television station was speaking tongue-in-cheek. "I'm here for the weekend, could you make a river go upstream or something?"

"I will win the Teton County Open Chess Tournament," Doj had replied.

"Are you a chess player?"

"My master just taught me the moves. And I can see into the future."

"I'm here also to cover Kaiser's victory. There are only a handful of men in the country who can beat him. I don't believe you are one of them. Would a hundred-dollar bet be in order?"

"How about ninety-nine dollars and ninety-nine cents, since it's nineteen ninety-nine?" said Doj. "Then there would be a penny for your thoughts."

"You've got a bet," said the reporter.

The black man smiles and extends a braceleted hand.

Doj winks at Taft, shakes the proffered hand, and smiles. "Good luck. Toady, is it?"

"Ahhh. Good first move. Demean your opponent; goad him into responding emotionally. The name's Toby. But I am not offended. In fact, if it soothes you, I will take the black pieces."

It is a gesture that has astounded the officials throughout the tournament. Before each match Tiler has offered to take the back pieces, the second to move, a disadvantage at the start. The one time that Reshevsky demanded a pick Toby Tiler stared at his hands for a full twenty seconds before choosing the right hand and the black pieces. Toby Tiler won that game (playing a Sicilian Defense) in forty-seven moves.

"These pieces blend in so well with the color of my skin, don't you think, Mr. Bodwellton?" says Toby with a heavy Jamaican accent.

"I will accept white. But don't you think my pieces should be a little tanner, Mr. Tiler?"

Toby Tiler smiles broadly, gestures with his hands as if receiving vibrations and says, "Your aura is red today, Mr. Bolderton; you came to play. Your pieces should be red. I believe it's your move."

After seven moves Kaiser mutters to himself, "They're playing the Capablanca/Marshall match of the Ruy Lopez defense of 1909." It is a classic match. The preferred eighth move for Black is now pawn to king's knight three, or G7 to G6.

Doj follows with pawn to queen three, hits the clock.

It is Tiler's move. "You are the one who calls himself the new prophet, are you not, Mr. Bolderton?"

Bishop to king two.

"I am just one of the pawns for the white king, Mr. Tiler."

"Oh no, Mr. Bolderton. I see you have the power of the bishop and the knight together. A very unusual, but a strong combination. You can slide along the diagonal of either color, or you can hop one and over two, like the knight."

"Then there must not be any rook in me and your queen is still stronger, Mr. Tiler. Your queen moves very well. Are you the black queen, Mr. Tiler?"

"Oh, but you do have some rook in you, Mr. Bolderton. I can see your aura. But it only goes so far. My weak pawns block its advance, then you retreat into your world. What world would that be, Mr. Bolderton?"

Queen's knight to queen two.

"The world of possibilities, Mr. Tiler. Possibilities of things which can happen to you. To your fortress. Possibilities of things that may happen to my world and your world. And what world would yours be, Mr. Tiler?"

"The world of the spirit, Mr. Bolderton. Life and beyond. I play with the spirit of the pieces, of games gone by, for I have seen into the afterlife and now I can see the lives of so many games with pieces, games of people."

Bishop to knight four.

"Then of what spirit are my pieces, Mr. Tiler?"

"The color of your pieces reflects your aura, Mr. Bolderton. Your spirit is deep green now, with some blue, like the colors of the vast ocean near my home. There is not much salt in *your* spirit, though—it is very pure."

"I believe your clock is running, Mr. Tiler."

He smiles and plays knight at bishop two to rook three.

At move twenty-seven Kaiser reacts to Black's move with a slap of his palm on his trousers, for he sees it: Black's breakthrough move, four moves result in an equal exchange of material; from there, Black should promote his queen's rook pawn; three moves from there, it should be a passed pawn and he would easily promote it to a queen at the eighth rank.

Two seconds later Reshevsky sees it as well and his audible grunt affirms Kaiser's gesture; the two masters have communicated, they both see the line of victory for Black. They nod in appreciation. Very well done. Beautifully played.

Doj's eyes shift back and forth as he sees it as well, and looks up. He moves king to king two, for he must, or he will lose his bishop with no restitution. He captures and hits the clock.

"Oh, Mr. Bolderton, your aura has changed a little, the sea is somewhat paler. Could the tide be ebbing in your emerald ocean?"

Toby's hands gesture as if he were forming a pound of clay into a ball; He offers the imaginary ball across the table. "Would you care to call it a draw? We would be even. Then perhaps you and I could walk into the mountains and get to know one another without playing such a game."

The offer of a draw shocks and an audible murmur of disappointment escapes those informed onlookers. Doj moves the hair behind his left ear and lets it fall back. He looks at the beaming man who smiles and offers the ball. Doj rises, puts one hand on the tall leather chair, closes his eyes and stretches, bringing his right leg behind his buttocks. With his eyes closed he calls aloud the positions of the ten remaining pieces on the board. He switches legs, twists his torso a few times, then stretches his tall frame toward the sky, fingers reaching.

"Orion!" Doj says, as if in a trance.

"Aaahhh," says Toby Tiler. "The warrior star-god of the sky." He presses his hands together, as if making the clay ball disappear, then flicks it into space. "The warrior who fights and never gives up. I thought that might be your decision, noble Doj Bolderton. Even after you go down to defeat, I hope that we might go to the mountains when the match is over and speak with no remorse. Is this possible? There we may share the same time, yes?"

"I have a better idea, Mr. Tiler. Why don't we both bring our guitars and see if we may forsake our castles and knights and play a tune or two."

"Ooohhh, yes, Mr. Bolderton! Very well played. You do see much. How did you know that I play?"

Rook takes knight.

Move thirty-one causes a stir in those gathered. It breaks the spell. For as even a game as it has been, neither player has made a salient error until 31: rook takes knight. Doj holds the gaze of Toby Tiler and smiles. "Ahhh, Mr. Bolderton, your aura is blue-green again. You are back. The red is gone. Are you giving up? Slipping back out to sea?"

It is the third move from that point—king to queen two—when what was an apparent bad move is revealed as a brilliant sacrifice of Doj's rook, successfully drawing attention away from queen to rook seven, (check!), which will lead to a fork and checkmate in two moves. The observing players gasp in astonishment—white has pulled off a victory against a deficiency in material and what appeared to be a lost position.

"It's a miracle!" says Reshevsky, standing next to the Boise reporter whose reaction reveals shocked confusion—he does not see the line, but realizes he just lost all but one penny of the hundred dollars that was his expense money back to Boise.

"Let's see the wonderfully sculptured finale," says Toby Tiler, quickly playing out the final three moves.

He offers his hand with a broad smile. The crowd erupts into reverent applause, the loudest of which are Kaiser's and Reshevsky's, appreciating an ending that even those seasoned strategists did not foresee.

Outside Toby and Doj walk together, each carrying a trophy and a case of chess piece glass mugs. Doj commands a four-inch advantage, but the black man's walk is livelier, bouncier despite just having played a highly charged two-hour chess match.

"You had me beat, Mr. Tiler," says Doj.

"You can call me Rastjahmon now. The war is over," he smiles, his Jamaican accent now more relaxed, thicker.

"Doj."

The two shake hands in the style of brothers—hands between thumbs, then fingers clasping fingers, then just touching fingertips—a gesture which takes more time and establishes a longer bond.

"Doj Bolderton. I will now call you Bolderdoj, the messenger from God. A pretty heavy chore, mon, but I, too, have seen life from the other side. I have come from very far to see you, for like you I am of the spiritual world. Around you are many hues, some beautiful shades, but I do not see the light of the one who has come to herald the Armageddon."

"What color do you see?"

"That of the man whose prism can be divided into most every color of the spectrum, but not all at once. Why did your aura turn so pale when you realized the winning combination?"

Doj surveys the man intently. "For some reason I have the desire to tell you everything I know. Why is that? Why is it that your skin is so black, yet so much light comes from your face? Everything about you—your chess game, your gestures, your beads and bracelets—is rhythm and cadence."

"Ahhh, Doj mon, it is simply the outward pulse of my heart that is happy at this time."

Rastjahmon points three vehicles down. "My chariot is here, she beats with a happy heart too."

"A sixty-nine VW van!" says Doj.

Its basic color is black, but all around it are rainbow stripes in different thicknesses and detailed acrylic paintings of various spiritual symbols: the yin and yang, a peering eye, the sun, wizards and mystics, a hand with a shining ring, and on the passenger's side door, a chess piece: the bishop with Tiler's smiling head on top.

"Nice ride, Rastjahmon."

"Aaahhh, this is Rainbow Annie the Rasta Vannie."

"Seen some places, has she?"

"Aahh yes, she believes in anthropomorphism. Her spirit and her motor are strong."

"Original engine?"

"I rebuilt her myself. I rubbed a little good juju on every little camshaft and rod. She is my warm mistress on cold nights. Where would you like to go and play?"

Doj glances west. "It's too dark to go into the mountains. How about the town square? We could sit and play on the benches. Do you like reggae music, Rastjahmon?"

"Oohh no, Bolderdoj, can't you tell? I'm from North Dakota. I like elevator music. Grain elevator." He laughs loudly as he slides his guitar case out. "I bring a flute too. It is only seven blocks. Let us walk and talk a little."

They walk down Willow Street toward the square. Rastjahmon says, "I was in the great city of Denver with some good people. I was reading the aura of this one troubled girl—oooh, so much trouble!—and she told me about you happening here. I hear about these miracles. But then I hear it's maybe not so much miracles but that you have the gift like I have the gift. What makes you think that you are this messiah, this messenger from God, Bolderdoj?"

"Let's just say, Rastjahmon, that I was sent here to make the world a better place before the end, which is destined to be very soon. I was sent here to let the unholy ones get their houses in order before king to king three, so they may go down the path of righteousness, or the yellow brick road, whichever comes first."

"Aahhh, your answers are as clear as my Caribbean when the hurricane approaches. What is your sign, Bolderdoj? What is your ascendancy?"

"I'm an asparagus, Rastjahmon, broccoli ascendancy. My rebirth started here, on the first day of summer."

"Aahh, the cusp of Gemini the twin then. And what, my good new friend, is your religion?"

"Why Rastjahmon, can you not see? I am a practicing pedestrian!"

"Aaahhh, yes. Very good. I see I will have to play some with you before the harmony comes."

On the town square they start slow but soon their notes mesh, intertwine. Rastjahmon is a heavy strummer in the reggae style. Bolderdoj works out melodious riffs with bends, twists, and slow hand crescendos in the style of Eric Clapton. They play new stuff, old stuff. Doj's arpeggios blends sweetly with Rastjahmon's flute. Soon there is an impromptu jam session going on as people join the celebration with tambourines, drums, and harmonicas. The police show up, but do nothing. No one is charging money. It is simply a happening.

"It is like a miniature Rainbow Gathering, Bolderdoj. Look at all the beautiful people here in the Hole! Jah love! All is Irie!"

If there is any place in the United States, perhaps the world, which so accurately and vividly illustrates the far-reaching changes in the twentieth century, not only technically, but socially and culturally—it is Jackson Hole, Wyoming. At the beginning of the 19th century no one but Native Americans had yet to see this beautiful valley bordered by a fault-block mountain range with no foothills, the Tetons. Then in 1806 John Colter left the Lewis and Clark Expedition, went on a 500-mile winter journey to establish Indian trade, and beheld the majestic peaks before turning north into what is now Yellowstone. Colter heralded the arrival of the mountain men who named the mountains *les Trois Tetons*, the Three Breasts. The mountain men trapped, plundered, and nearly exterminated the furry water-rodent, the beaver, before "the shinin' times" ended abruptly in 1840. It wasn't until 1884 that anyone came to this valley to settle—it was the Mormons then—and by 1900 there were only 638 residents. In a hundred short years what had been small log cabins with mud and grass roofs and dirt floors became multimillion dollar homes with high-tech security, Jacuzzis, in-floor radiant heat, and window quilts. Jackson Hole became a playground for the wealthy who had made their fortunes, then demanded their personal mountain sanctuary.

The technological onslaught eventually arrived: cable or satellite TV, computers, digital sound, fax machines, and virtual-reality visual disc-players. Mountain climbing guides for Exum, the oldest alpine climbing school in the country, report accidents and initiate high-altitude rescues via cellular telephones. Backpackers use hand-held Global Positioning Systems to pinpoint backcountry location via satellite. Now, in 1999, Jackson Hole is truly a technological melting pot. The past, present and future is in evidence; there are still ranching families whose style of life hasn't changed in nearly a century, but it is also a favorite nesting site for the 'hatch', the annual invasion of kids just graduating or taking a break from college, taking a year off to sow wild oats before resuming the course of life plotted out by them or their parents. In the seventies Jackson Hole was a refuge for many baby boomers as their ideals from the sixties were washed away and diluted. And now those baby boomers have houses, kids, and their escapes. Garages are stocked with mountain bikes, assorted skis, kayaks or canoes, climbing gear, windsurfers, and so forth. There is at least a dozen different kinds of footwear per person, appropriate for the many different ways to *re-create* in this great playground. It is the birthplace of the slogan "he who dies with the most toys wins."

Communication and entertainment has changed as well. Now, from what started as news and mail being carried on horseback or skis over Teton Pass from Idaho, it has come to this—its own TV show—*The Whole JaHo Show*, from Whole *Ja*ckson *Ho*le Show. The show's young creator, Bill Francis, is also the station manager and the cameraman in this small media market.

It is now 9:47 p.m., thirteen minutes until the live broadcast of the August 14th edition, the eighteenth week of *The Whole JaHo Show*, purposely slotted to compete with the Idaho, Salt Lake City and Denver newscasts.

Its ratings have skyrocketed.

Regina Ivonson, from a longtime Wyoming family, is the host. Her critics cite her as rather dry, but they cannot deny her proponents in that she is well versed in Wyoming history and politics, and she chooses her guests and themes with great aplomb. And Jackson Hole provides a seemingly endless supply of controversial characters and stories to choose from.

The cameraman/stage manager/creator helps Toby Tiler pass around condensating mugs of ice water; for it is warm under the lights, and the studio is small. The glass and pewter mugs which give the set a sparkle are in the shape of chess pieces, rooks, and are gifts from Doj Bolderton and Toby Tiler.

As the guests take their chairs against the backdrop mural of the Tetons, Regina adjusts her notes on the wooden table and announces over the din of pre-show conversation, "OK, everyone, remember, *we are* live. This subject matter, particularly with *this* combination of guests, can lead to some volatile verbal exchanges, so let's try to be polite and in control, shall we? Let's have one person speaking at a time."

Bill Francis steps behind camera two and says, "Nine fifty-nine and fifty-five and five . . . four . . . three . . . two . . . one . . . Go!"

"Hello and welcome to the Saturday, August fourteenth edition of *The Whole JaHo Show*. Tonight my guests are the Honorable Reverend Marvin Throop of the Our Lady of the Mountains Catholic Church, in Jackson; Mormon Elder Caleb Jukins of the Church of Latter Day Saints, Third Ward; Dannette Cather, an avowed atheist and president of Atheists Perpetuating Evolution or, as they like to call it, APE; Doj Bolderton, a fascinating young man, recently moved here from California, who professes to be the messenger of God; and Toby Tiler, who likes to be called Rastjahmon, and who says he has been in touch with the spiritual world since a near-death experience at the age of five. Tonight's topic is The Place of God and Religion in the Year 2000. Mr. Tiler, I'd like to start with you, if I may, and get right into it: Tell us about your near-death experience."

"Aahhh, Regina. It was when I was five. It was a day in July and what a hot day it was. So hot, Regina, that the blue-green sea did not provide relief. Young Rastja did not like it so hot. He knew it was much cooler in Uncle Jenolee's freezer, where he stored the tasty dolphin and snapper, and young Rastja opened the freezer, crawled inside, and shut the big metal door above him and laid down on those cool fish. Then Rastjah heard someone come into the shed and knew he was in big trouble, so Rastjah stayed very quiet and didn't move. He heard steps on the wooden floor and someone making a big noise, then a noisy thud right above his head, then more steps, then a second and third thud above Rastjah, and then the footsteps leave. Rastjah Toby wanted to get out; it was dark and cold and getting hard to breathe. I pushed the door, but nothing happened; the door would not rise up for me. I pushed harder and tried to use my legs; I pushed so hard a lobster claw broke through the wrapping paper and into Rastjah's back. Oh, Regina-woman, so cold and so dark in there and quickly I was so very scared. Rastjah yelled and yelled, but only the frozen fish could hear. Rastjah screamed and yelled and pushed and I will tell you the young Rastjah-Toby panicked, he did. Rastjah pushed with all his might and screamed and kicked and yelled until I went into the other world, Regina.

"It was dark and I was floating—then no longer was it dark. There was bright light and I was in another place. There was a long corridor with light at the end and I was walking toward it, over the Caribbean night sea. Then I saw my father, dead some three months before, drowned on the big squall, and there he was, luminous in the ocean, under the blue surface; I asked him to come up to walk with me. We walked and talked and it felt so good to see my loving dad, young Rastjah loved him so. And Rastjah saw his grandfather, Grandy Zeke, and he walked with us, too, over the sea, and some of the fish that swam below us were luminous. Then Grandy Zeke said, 'Toby-boy, you better think. Look around you. Look back. You have so much more of life. Are you sure you don't want to go back?'

"I turned back, looked at the shore and saw my short life, Regina: the time I won the swimming race against my cousins, and the night of the bad hurricane, and the big marlin that Grandy and father caught that time. I remember feeling very serene with Grandy and my father, so I turned back around to the light and could not decide. I looked ahead and the horizon was brighter and the feeling walking that way was very good, so we walked on and Rastjahmon was happy, but there was still something back there, something I kept looking back to. For so long, Regina, we walked ahead and I kept looking back. Then I looked back again and I saw Uncle Jenolee come into the shed and put the three fifty-pound bags of fertilizer on the freezer then walk out—and I could hear young Rastjahmon, shouting so loudly for help. Then I saw my own mother walk into the shed; and my father told me to go back to her because she would need Rastjah-Toby, so I ran back quickly, skimming over the water, before mother could open the freezer door. I remember, Regina, because I sat on a shelf and watched from above as my mother found me; she yelled for Uncle Jenolee and they put me into the sand and covered me and she breathed for me but no, they could not bring Rastjah-child back yet." Rastjahmon smiles. "I wanted to watch for a little longer."

The cameraman pivots camera one for a different angle.

"Soon the doctor come running and give Rastjahmon a shot with a needle. I knew it was time to go back in and live the life that I knew then would be forever special, because I had seen the spiritual world and felt content in returning to the present life."

"Were you going to Heaven, Mr. Tiler?"

"Ooohhh, I did not name it, nor did my father or grandfather. We just knew we were going to a place where we felt good to be together and were happy to go."

"Dannette?" says the hostess.

The cameraman closes in on Dannette Cather tightly enough to where her pin comes into focus: APE, against a background of a huge mountain gorilla, a male silverback.

"What Mr. Tiler had is a near-death experience, or NDE. When someone is dying, certain biochemical reactions take place in the brain which can produce hallucinations. It is common in many victims of sudden accidents, or any near-fatal occurrences, especially in cases where the victim suffers from hypothermia. Ask any EMT. You never give up on someone who has fallen in very cold water and exhibits all the signs of death, especially in the young."

"Aaahhh, no, my dear APE woman. I was there. I saw it with my eyes."

"So," interjects Regina. "What you're saying, Dannette, is that this phenomena has a natural explanation. But how can you explain the fact that so many of these NDE survivors have similar experience: walking toward a brilliant light of some kind, often meeting others, particularly deceased family members; feelings of serenity; then making a decision to go back, often because of some unfulfilled obligation?"

"They are common. Hemingway had one—he wrote about it in Farewell to Arms—so did Rickenbacker. The images of near-death experiences are similar just as our dreams are similar. Haven't we all had similar dreams? Dreams of those closest to us whom we depend on for survival? Dreams of falling, dreams of snakes, dreams of being chased, our legs getting heavy? It all goes back to our earliest fears about survival, back to our primate beginnings when we had to live in trees. Dreams and hallucinations are sensations associated with the pineal gland, one of the oldest and deepest glands within the brain. Spiritualism is said to be centered there, as are dreams and hallucinations. Threats from the known and fear of the unknown, i.e. death, are the bases of spiritualism. For millions of years in our evolution, simply surviving from day to day was a spiritual fulfillment."

Dannette takes a sip of ice water and camera one moves back.

"Reverend Throop, what would the Catholic church say about this event?"

"The church would be happy for Mr. Tiler and his father and grandfather, for they had lead good lives and followed the word of God and were awarded the Kingdom of Heaven."

The Mormon Elder asks Toby, "How has this great event altered your life, my son?"

"I can see into the spirits of things and people. Everything has the spirit, everything has an aura visible to me."

"Really, Mr. Tiler? What color is my aura?" asks Regina.

"Ahhh, so black and white, my lady, you can see both sides of any issue; things are good or they are bad. You are very skilled at what you do. But there is so much tension in the other colors, I think from all the electricity in the TV. Too much TV is not good for you."

"TV is my life, Mr. Tiler. Now how about Ms. Cather's aura."

"So much red, so much of the anger. Did you eat meat tonight, Ms. Dannette?"

"She had pepperoni pizza at Pizza Hut, and a large iced tea," says Doj Bolderton.

"Which brings us to our Mr. Bolderton, a man who has caused quite a stir in Jackson Hole since his arrival on the first day of summer. For those of you not already aware of all of Mr. Bolderton's exploits: there was the strange beam of light which reportedly emanated from his mind and destroyed an editor's collector's quality poster. There was his prediction of a comet that he said would end civilization, only to have a comet show up in an astronomer's telescope heading *somewhere* in our neighborhood in space. There was what some athletic observers said was a miraculous finish when he won a six-mile running race against some extremely tough competition. There were his revelations, in explicit detail, of the lives of our police chief and town sheriff. There was his accurate prediction of an air crash involving Angolan guerillas headed into combat, and his victory in the Region VI Chess Championship, which one expert observer called 'a miraculous comeback against a defeated position.' How did you do it?"

"Well I started with pawn to king four."

Rastjahmon laughs, gives five fingertips to Doj.

Regina asks "Reverend, could something like that chess match—or any of these other events—be considered a miracle by the Church?"

Reverend Throop, laughing: "No, I'm afraid not. The coming of Christ will be much heralded. There will be the trumpeting of angels so all will know of the return of His Glory."

Doj leans forward, "Hey, my brother Rastjahmon and I play strings, flutes, a little blues harp, some vocals, tell a few jokes. Maybe we can warm up the crowd before the big guy shows up."

Toby smiles, "We play for you good people if you like. Our axes are in the green room."

Elder Jukins: "Chess . . . is a game of the mind. His running is of the physical body. The arrival of Christ will bring the spirit in the form of the father, the son, and the holy ghost."

Regina: "Then, Elder Jukins, how can you explain these two men, who are totally unknown in the chess world, winning over some of the best players in the region, if not the country?"

Dannette Cather answers quickly. "For the first twenty-one moves they were playing a Ruy Lopez defense. It was a replay of a classic game played in 1909 between Capablanca and Marshall; we entered the moves in a Dlr 385 Chess Computer and found a match. The endgames deviated, and did reveal a mastery, but then again, four-year-old child prodigies have mastered the game in no time. Bobby Fischer, for example, won the United States Championship at the age of fourteen. Capablanca was a master in three years."

Doj says, "You mean the Copa Cabana had a chess team? A bar?"

Toby Tiler: "Ahhh yes, Dannette, my Uncle Jenolee, when I was recovering from my awakening into the spiritual world, taught me the moves. I saw the aura of the pieces. He told me 'Relax and the pieces will tell you where to move them' and to let the calm mind see them go there. I beat Uncle Jenolee the third time we played. My horsey ate his rook, forked his king and queen. So angry was my horsey that day! So angry was good Uncle Jenolee!"

Regina: "Dannette, you seem to have a logical explanation for these supposed supernatural activities. How can you explain Mr. Bolderton's predictions of the comet and the airplane disaster?"

"The airplane crash appears to have been the result of espionage. They are still piecing the plane back together. The comet . . . well, perhaps somehow Mr. Bolderton knew at the same time an astronomer did, but the astronomer held on to the facts for six days. Who knows what reason." Danette shrugs. "There could be many logical scenarios. He could be involved in some kind of intelligence."

Regina: "That has been proposed. But Mr. Bolderton is a simple cab driver, and before that he attended the same college for fifteen years."

Doj Bolderton: "Hey! Intelligence! Check this out, everyone. The capitol of Wyoming is . . . um . . . hold on . . . it's coming . . . Casper!"

Regina: "Cheyenne."

Doj: "Damn! Cheyenne. I've *got* to remember that. Like a shy woman named Ann. Shy-shy-shy."

Regina: "OK. Back to the subject. Reverend Throop, now, in 1999, religion is losing more and more followers as more and more of the mysteries of the universe, from the infinite to the infinitesimal, are being revealed by science. How do you react to this?"

Dannette: "Religion *is* losing followers; church participation dropped twenty-eight point nine percent from where it was in nineteen sixty-nine, a mere thirty years ago. Scientists can manipulate life at the genetic level and create. . . ."

Reverend Throop: "I believe she asked *me*, Ms. Cather. No, our church is stronger than ever and our followers more devoted as people see the biblical prophesies of the Second Coming realized."

Dannette raises her voice another notch, "Yes, that prophesy is coming true. Our earth *is* burning and the April Wrightwood quake killed over eight hundred people, but the Wrightwood was from a compression bend beneath the earth's surface and not because of some mythical fable written by storytellers and power-brokers some two thousand years ago—and, in case anyone is confused about this, some forty years *after* the death of Christ. No, these so-called prophesies coming to light are the result of greed, overpopulation, and defiance of nature, which both the Catholic church and the Mormon church propagate in an attempt to rule the earth by sheer numbers of converts."

Elder Jukins: "Regina, I believe Ms. Cather is letting facts get in the way of the truth. The church has known about these prophesies for many years; we call them the Signs of the Times. We have long known of the Second Coming. All of recorded history can be traced back to the four thousand years before the birth of Christ, yet the prophesy is of *seven* thousand years. One thousand years of man equals one day of God, so we know that right now the prophesied first six thousand years are coming to a close. The chaos, disasters and turmoil which are occurring precede the coming of Christ. We know that there will be one thousand years of peace—this may be here on Earth, maybe not.

Married couples and families that are sealed will be sealed for eternity—perhaps here on Earth, or perhaps in Heaven."

Dannette Cather: "Yes, they will be sealed. There are so many of you people now, and so much overcrowding, that you're stuck together. No big surprise there. You people breed like white-tailed deer."

Reverend Throop: "But you see, Dannette—or may I just call you Danny?—you *are* a female of your race, are you not? God's mercy somehow encompasses pagans like you as well. The Second Coming will be announced—lower your hand Mr. Bolderdash, it's not you, and you're not God, but even people like you may be allowed to repent. That will be up to God."

Dannette Cather: "Second Coming, hell. Wake up to the truth, Reverend. The Second Coming will be the first going before your carpenter friend ever shows up."

Regina: "Now please let's try to be germane to the. . . ."

Reverend: "Stop clapping your beak, woman. If you. . . ."

As the war of words builds Doj and Toby look at each other, then nod. Off-camera, they point to one corner, catching Regina's attention. They hold up their sweating mugs of ice water to her and sip, and Regina drinks after an unsure toast. Doj and Toby shake their heads and point again; Regina forces an unsure smile and nods. They retrieve their guitars, regain their seats, tune briefly and start plucking softly in the background. Camera one switches briefly to them before cutting back to the verbal thrust-and-parry.

Reverend: ". . . and further more, Danny old boy, you may *be* a lesbian, in which case you are purposely slandering the name and design of God, so you must work harder to repent."

Dannette: "At least I'm not a pedophile. Reverend, please reiterate for the television viewers the events of June twenty-eighth, nineteen eighty-three, at that summer camp in Montana."

A silence follows. Finally the Reverend says, "That matter was settled. The allegations were incorrect."

"Not according to Doyle Thomas, the young boy you made pose naked in the canoe for you. He's one of our members now. While you were wearing a pink bikini? Now come on, Reverend Marv."

Elder Jukins turns to Reverend Throop. "That's where I know you from! There was something about flatulence bubbles in the lake and this poor child having to pop them with his nose."

"These things happened many years ago. God has forgiven me and enlightened me again to the correct path to righteousness. My work is to spread The Word."

Dannette: "Also to hear the word too, if I'm not mistaken—is that what all those 900-calls on the church's phone are for? The words of Busty Bleu and Little Oral Annie, the punishment—reward specialists? And how about that porno video that got stuck in your VCR so you had to take it in to get repaired? I believe the correct path you refer to, Rev Marvy, leads to the post office where you pick up those brown packages."

Reverend: "Ms. Ivonson!"

Regina: "The ratings will skyrocket!"

Elder Jukins: "OK, if you want to play dirty, Danny, let's talk about your addiction to Demerol. Does that lessen the pain of being a card-carrying dyke in a God-fearing country, where women shop for bargains, bake a pie, and volunteer at the ward in the same afternoon, all the while raising four kids to be respectful human beings?"

Dannette fires back, "And you, Elder Jukins—drank that water pretty quick, didn't you? Is that because the alcohol dehydrated you a little? APE is glad you have such a good time on those junkets to Jackpot, Nevada. You're a pretty good hold 'em player, a good bluffer, we hear. But you better be careful next time you fill a straight flush. You knocked your fake moustache loose—and you never know who's sitting there at the table, trying to read your eyes."

Reverend: "Ha!"

Elder: "I've done no such thing!"

Dannette, a notch louder: "No? Would you like to see some pictures of you in the Jacuzzi after the steam and the hooker caused your moustache to fall into the hot water?"

Elder: "That flash! I mean . . . that flash . . . from God! Yes! When I was a missionary in Cambodia. That flash from God showed me the way of Mormon. I would never, could never, care to do—I mean want to do—anything like that."

Regina: "Wow, you guys are savage. I was afraid twenty-three questions wouldn't be enough, and I've barely asked two. Did you check out these guys playing guitars over here? They're too *good*."

Reverend, to Danette: "In these lesbian deals, how does that work? I mean how much can you do with nothing dangling out, no protrusion? And how do you decide who gets on top—you play Spin the Dildo or something?"

Dannette: "You're disgusting. How can you even give yourself a title like Reverend? Shouldn't it be more like Pinky Fartface?"

Reverend: "Maybe APE stands for aggravated penis envy. Your group says that we came from apes. Do you come from apes or do you come *with* apes? Is that how you chicks get off? With apes? Oooh oooh oooohhhh!" He mimics scratching his underarms.

After a progression of fifths on the guitars, Doj and Toby slip into an old Bob Marley song, Coming in From the Cold.

Elder Jukins looks up, hands in supplication. "Welcome each rebuff that turns earth rough . . . each sting that bids not sit or stand, but go. . . ."

Regina: "Robert Browning! Let's just focus on *my* religion here for a moment, all right? I mean, my parents tried to raise me as a Catholic, but then I got to my freshman year of college and Spoody Alexander read that Robert Browning poem to me under the black light. The next thing I knew, we were naked and—whoa! Did I see God or what! He was that tight end from Laramie. Hell, we did it in a haystack, in his dorm room, on the fifty-yard-line with his cleats on, you name it. We even did it in the same room with the black running back and his cheerleader girlfriend who was a white girl from Tensleep. Which brings me to the next question: Elder Jukins, what the hell are you laughing about?"

"Pinky Fartface!"

Regina: "OK, Momo. I've got one for you: Why do all the Mormons come to Jackson Hole to party?"

Reverend: "Why?"

Regina: "Because God can't see over the Tetons!"

Dannette: "Touche'!"

Regina: "Oh hell, let's just skip all these questions and get to the last one, which is really the balls of it all. Please quit laughing, Elder Jukins." She tosses away four pages. "God, who comes up with these questions? OK, here we go. In this age, where total self-annihilation seems probable in the most advanced but also most violent century in history, when brother turns against brother and the prophesies of early Christianity appear to be coming true, what proof is there that God exists?"

Elder Jukin's is the first then the loudest voice. "It is a faith one has. One knows and can feel the spirit of the Lord inside themselves."

Dannette: "The spirit of Jack Daniels is more likely."

Reverend: "Devils can be driven out of the heart by the touch of a hand on a hand. . . ."

Dannette gestures to the Reverend. "More likely with you, it's the touch of a young boy's hand on your unit."

Regina: "Hey Reverend, you just quoted Tennessee Williams, didn't you?" She whispers intently, "Did you know he was gay?"

Dannette: "Hello! The light goes on. Somebody's home! No, there is no proof of God because an omnipotent being does not exist. Welcome to the world of atoms and molecules and quarks and sub-quarks and empty space. The fact that we haven't accepted this, but have pinned our hopes on a cosmic being returning to save us, and whoever tithes ten percent, so that when we die we walk around with empty smiles and say 'damn glad to see ya', has gotten us into a helluva lot of trouble. We've nearly exhausted the planet with our greed and avarice."

Regina: "OK! Good point, Dannette. If this was Jeopardy you would have just swept the category. You've convinced me! By the way, I forgot to compliment you on your blouse, *very* nice. If you'd let me buy you a glass of wine at the Cadillac Grille after the show, perhaps we could discuss it, where you got it, how it feels without a bra. . . ."

Doj hits a loud chord on his guitar. From out of the body comes a thin blue line of light which quickly burns a treble clef on the world map, then one flat. "Key of F—for shut your freakin' traps! Billy, camera one tight on me, camera two at these people with their jaws down around their knees. Rastjahmon, a little background music, if you please."

Regina: "Mr. Bolderton, if you and Rastjahmon would like to join the two of us at the Caddy, perhaps you'd tell us how you just did that."

Doj: "Shut up before I hit a diminished seventh chord and blow the roof off this place. OK, keep that camera rolling, Bill, 'cause we want everyone to be able to see this. This is the way it is and is going to be. There might be life on other planets and probably is, somewhere out there in the universe. Can any one here argue with that?"

"Could be," Regina says.

"Probably most certainly is," Danette agrees.

Reverend Throop: "The Catholic Church would not deny that possibility. Can I see that guitar?"

Doj hands it to him.

Elder: "We do not pretend to know the whole mind of God, but yes, son, there could be life on other planets."

Doj asks, "How about your dog, Elder Jukins—does he exist?"

Jukins nods. "I love my little spaniel."

Doj: "How about time? Does anyone doubt that twenty-four of the show's thirty-eight minutes have passed? Does anyone doubt the passage of time?"

All shake their heads or mutter no.

"Then how about matter, does anyone doubt that the Tetons exist?"

All shake their heads no.

"Then who can describe what was here before there was time or matter, a time when there was no time and the cosmic clock was plugged in, a time when matter just appeared? Or a time when there was no life and suddenly there was life—in one second time just *started*. Can someone please describe that?"

No one motions. The Reverend stops looking inside the guitar and hands it back to Doj.

Doj continues, "So then, if there must have always been time and always matter and always life and always eternity, was there not always a life spirit? A life force striving to exist, just as every plant and animal on the face of the earth is striving?

"Oohhh, nice chord change, Rastjah.

"And if there is a life force, an intangible will, is that not the same as a spirit? And if there is a will and a life force, and there is a spirit is that not how we describe God? I'm not talking about some guy who looks like Peter Frampton or George Burns, but about a spirit, a soul. And now this spirit, this God if you like, is pissed off. He's really pissed off. The last time he was this mad was 64,389,221 years ago, when he smacked the earth with a comet. OK, granted, he was aiming at the equator and it hit off the coast of Mexico; the Big Guy's not perfect. But the dinosaurs had gotten greedy, they were right on the verge of taking over, not giving the little furry guys a fair chance. And God wasn't all that pleased with Tyrannosaurus Rex. Now he's again throwing a hard breaking slider down and in. I told you this once before and you didn't believe me: the heavenly body, this comet, is coming closer. In three days God will let us glimpse it again, because he wants us to prepare. Perhaps then you will believe. So everyone had better start treating everyone else a little damn more kindly or he might land this thing right on top of *you*."

He points at the camera.

"Time to clean up your act because the boss is walking down the hall and you've been in the break room for too long. Following the Ten Commandments would probably be a good place to start. Does everyone out there get the picture? Now, if the studio guests would be so kind as to permit us to do the song *without whining or bickering*, we would like to play "Coming in From the Cold" by Bob Marley. Billy, hand out the tambourines to Elder Jukins and the Reverend, the drums to the ladies. Play or I'll bring back the light and carve a little treble clef right between your scrunched up little eyebrows. One time with feeling, key of F, Rastjahmon. Three and four. . . ."

As the strange little sextet starts to fade out the cameraman gestures 'fifteen seconds to go'. Regina cuts in, "Thanks for tuning into *The Whole JaHo Show*. Join us next week when our topic will be 'What to do with the last two grizzlies in Yellowstone: Capture and captivity or can natural copulation be forced?' Please join us."

She turns to Dannette and whispers audibly, "Now, about that glass of wine and that blouse. . . ."

Monday, August 16th, 9:18 p.m.

"Hey Wolfmeister, man-king of the cab world, this is cab nine. Come in."

"Yeah, go ahead, Doj, holy exalted one, he who foresees all things, runner dude, guitar-playing chess champ, talk show guest, cab driver of great ubiquity."

"I'm clear on the town square. Where do you need me?"

"If you foresee all things, you should know that I need you at the Acadian House, heading out to the Mangy Moose at Teton Village."

"Got it. Well, at least my tips have been better since Saturday night's show."

"Yeah, you're about to single-handedly put Caribou Cabs out of business; everyone wants to ride with the son of God. I have to tell fares I'm one of your disciples. And what the hell happened to those people on the show Saturday night? Not even on Geraldo or Sally—or even Jerry Springer—have I ever seen civilized people so hostile."

"I think the mood music of Bolderdoj and Rastjahmon must have broke down their psychological barriers and permitted them to say what they really felt. My last fare said he was glad as hell the world was going to end and he tipped me twenty bucks. I can pay off my Scrabble debt to you from last night. Although I don't think X-ray should count; it's hyphenated."

"Who are you working for?"

"You, Wolfman, you just sent me to the Acadian House. Here's my party. Look at this fat hippo, dribbling chantilly cream sauce down his chin."

"Don't let that comet hit him in the gut and get it all over the cab. Call coming in. Hey, before I forget, Wilma called. She wants to talk to you. Come in a half-hour early on Wednesday."

"Got it, Wolfmeister. Good evening sir! To the Mangy Moose?"

Article in *USA Today*, Wednesday, August 18th, 1999. Section A, above the headline:

COMET BOUND FOR SOLAR SYSTEM

Tennyson's Comet, discovered on July 1st, and expected to pass far from our solar system, is now being predicted to come as close as the orbit of Uranus and quite possibly visible to the naked eye, according to Dr. Spencer Tennyson of the Palomar Observatory. The astronomer's original calculation gave it a 'slim to none' chance of coming into our solar system, but recent calculations have it arcing much closer than previously thought.

"This is not a short-period comet," said Tennyson. "It appears to be a long-period comet on a long ellipse, with origins in the Oort Cloud. We have seven other observatories around the world which have collected some data in regards to its trajectory. Our annual meeting is here this year, so in a couple of days we will compare all the data, run it through both the math coprocesser and the multiple depression statistical analysis programs and see what pops out. This is one of the topics we'll discuss, maybe the most exciting topic."

A comet, referred to in lay terms as a 'dirty snowball,' is material left over from the origin of the solar system. The Oort Cloud is matter a great distance from the sun, but bound to it by gravitation. A possible reason that Tennyson's comet has escaped from the Oort Cloud, according to its discoverer, is that something has 'perturbed it', something of interstellar origin.

Dr. Tennyson now gives the comet a 'very good chance' of being visible to the naked eye later this year.

Other items on the agenda at the annual meeting of the International Astronomical Union (IAU) at the Palomar include the observance of the one-year anniversary of the death of its former president, Garland Stein, who was killed when his South American observatory was destroyed by rival factions August 21st of last year, and the final testing of a space-based radio telescope to be launched by NASA later this year.

Doj sits on the one chair in his cabin, lacing up his trail shoes, buzzing with the promise of yet another perfect summer day, and psyching for his morning run, 12.5 miles up Granite Canyon to the top of the Jackson Hole Ski Area's Aerial Tram, gaining 4000 vertical feet to the summit, 10,450 feet above sea level. Last week he improved his time to 2:05, and the unofficial record was two hours.

There's a knock on the door.

"Come in."

Taft opens the door. "Good morning, Doj. There's something in the paper this morning that may be of interest to you."

"Dr. Vandren, every morning I come over for orange juice, tea, and toast. It's always good. And we watch the news. It's always the same. Life isn't that bad, Doc, just take a look outside. Come running with me. Or ride the tram and bring me dry clothes so I don't stink out the tourists riding the tram back down."

"The orange juice is fresh-squeezed, the tea, my own blend, and when I drop the bread in the toaster the wheat berries shoot out like crunchy little comets."

He shows Doj the front page. Doj reads the headline first and he gazes wildly at Taft before he grabs the paper and reads the article aloud. He stands up and says calmly, "It's happening."

Ninety minutes later he is nine miles into the run, entering "Dread Meadows," the steep, wildflower-laden slope that strangely appears flat, and Doj is charging uphill. His mind and body are in the present tense, the Buddhist state of *samadhi;* he feels all of life peaking around him, the high, alpine mountains in their most resplendent summer glory. He absorbs the message of the flowers, grasses, trees, elk and moose—everything living is *thriving*—there is no better time to peak than on these most perfect of days.

Doj wipes the sweat off his brow and thinks: Then the grasses and flowers will die and I will die as I should but it is fine now because I see heaven on earth and whether I live forever or stop existing before the millennium's end doesn't matter because I see God's wife Mother Nature and behold her most splendid wardrobe.

Doj exhales, then breathes deeply, and whispers between breaths, "A request . . . please . . . "Stairway to Heaven" . . . by Led Zeppelin?"

August 18th, 4:32 p.m. Office of Conestoga Cabs.

The powwow consists of Wilma, the owner; Eddy, the manager; Wolfman, the night manager; and Doj.

"Now don't get me wrong," Wilma continues to Doj, "Our business is up eighteen percent over last year, partially in thanks to you. I mean we're right on the verge of driving Caribou Cabs out of business. But now it's getting to the point where half our calls are for the son of God, or the messenger, or the prophet of the visualization of whirled peas. . . ."

"That's world peace," interjects Eddy.

"Or *whatever* you've been calling yourself. These range from crank calls to some really stressed-out people looking for a miracle."

"One guy last night was willing to double the going rate of forty-two dollars an hour," Wolfman says, "just to have you drive him around so he could talk to you. I just couldn't do it; I don't have the cabs. Some of our old drunken regulars aren't able to even get through on the phone. Hughie Dukes ended up driving himself last night. I pulled him over and made these rich people double-up with old Hughie and his wife. Then the rich guy's wife wouldn't take a sip of old Hughie's homemade, so Hughie started cussing at her. Not a pretty sight."

"Now we're having people ask that the Christmobile show up at their homes," says Eddy. "When are you going to stop this stuff?"

"I guess when everyone believes me. You believe me, don't you? I mean, folks, we ain't got far to go, to coin the old blues phrase."

"Well, you've given Eddy and me some good conversation

topics," Wolfman says. "I was still thinking FBI, or CIA when . . . well, Wilma, you better tell him."

Wilma lights a cigarette.

"Wilma, those things aren't good for you," admonishes Doj.

She raises her voice. "Well, it doesn't matter a damn if the world's going to end like you say, does it!" She pauses. "Sorry, Doj, didn't mean to yell at you." She takes a breath, looks at Eddy then the Wolf, then at Doj. "Doj, we had a couple of guys from the FBI show up in the office yesterday, asking about you."

"It's about time the FIB boys showed up; I've been waiting. What'd you tell them?"

"Nothing that's not common knowledge. They asked to see your application."

Eddy adds, "They seemed to think that was a joke as well. They were somewhat light-humored about it—at least for those thick-skinned varmints."

Wilma continues, "The point is, we don't want those guys around here at all. We keep good records, but you know they can always find something if they look hard enough. We don't need that pressure."

"You're not going to fire me, are you? This is the best job I've ever had. Well, now, come to think of it, it's the only job I've ever had."

Wilma puts down her cigarette, brightens her tone. "Well, you know we offer guided sight-seeing tours of Yellowstone Park. Sharon, our current tour guide, is eight months pregnant and wants to take her leave. We were wondering if you might like to take her place, do some Yellowstone tours for awhile."

"No more cab shifts?"

Wolf says, "We can let you drive some night shifts, but hell, everyone in town knows your schedule. The damn *Guide* even printed it. So we just won't have you on a regular schedule. We'll say you're filling in here and there."

"The people on the tours are mostly from out of town," says Wilma. "They won't know you're the son of God."

"By the way," Eddy says, "can I get your autograph in my bible?" The others turn to him. "Well, just in case!"

"The Indians used to think Yellowstone was an evil place

because of all the thermal features," says Doj. "Some said it was the place of the devil. It is one of the most geologically primitive places on earth. I've been learning about it. I've spent a little time in the back country up there. In fact, my landlord has told me some interesting things. He was a part-time naturalist for three years after he retired."

"Who's your landlord?" Eddy asks.

"Taft Vandren."

"Old Daffy Taffy!" exclaims Wilma. "He *is* one of the characters in this valley."

"Can I take him for the first few days? He could fill me in."

"Sharon has tours tomorrow and Saturday. Ride shotgun with her, see what she says, then take Daffy on your first few tours if you'd like. Old Daffy, I'll be damned. I used to go to some of his lectures around here. He was a botanist too, now that I think about it, always messing with the plants. I took a nature walk with him on edible indigenous plants. Smart man. Wrote some books. Taught at Montana State, I believe."

"He makes a pretty good venison stew, too. I've had dinner with him on occasion."

The Palomar Observatory on Mount Palomar in southern California is a state-of-the-art observatory. The 200-inch reflecting telescope with five-meter reflector gathers light older than any living thing on earth. The intricately balanced 200-inch mirror weighs $14^{1}/_{2}$ tons. Its Brucato Planetarium is popular with visitors of all ages; field trips with school-age children are booked well in advance. There is also a walk-through museum, viewing area, and learning center.

But on this day, Monday, August 23rd, there is no one in the observatory, there are no children in the planetarium's reclining seats, no one strolls through the museum or learning center. It is quiet everywhere but the lecture hall. There, bright lights are being focused on the long table displaying name cards for eight of the most prominent astronomers from around the world; the placard of Dr. Spencer Tennyson is at the center. There is a microphone behind each name card and a cluster of four mikes at the center.

Twenty-two members of the news media are mingling, chatting animatedly, rehashing recent assignments, anticipating what the astronomers might have to divulge. The pecking order of the cameramen has been settled. A boom man murmurs 'test' into each of the microphones.

Precisely at three o'clock Langdon Stofford, the 1997 Nobel Prize winner in physics, opens the door and stands aside as the astronomers file in. As they take their assigned seats Earl Roth, of the *Los Angles Times*, says to the *Chronicle's* reporter, simply, "This looks serious."

Spencer Tennyson clears his throat then starts, "We'd like to thank all of you for coming. We have called this press conference to announce our data relative to the trajectory of the comet now known as Tennyson's Comet."

It becomes very still in the room; The hushed whirl of the video cameras seems to harmonize with the lower drone of the air-conditioning.

"For three days we have fed the data from the eight major observatories, located around the world. These eight observatories, using the most powerful telescopes in the world, including the newest Chilean additions, the sixteen-meter VLT and the Gemini four-meter telescopes, are represented here by the heads of those observatories. We have fed this information into the most advanced computers we have for this type data: the Schreier Math Co-processor and the Quammen Multiple Depression Statistical Analysis Program. We have performed calculations both independently and as a group. We performed the calculations with each of the eight different sets of data, coming from eight different sets of coordinates independently, and finally once each with data only from Mount Palomar's coordinates. It appears the Tennyson Comet is coming."

"Coming where?" a reporter calls out.

"Here?" asks another.

"To Earth?"

"Where, Dr. Tennyson?"

"It is still too far away to say exactly where, but closer than we previously thought. Closer than the orbit of Uranus. We think at least within the orbit of Jupiter."

"Could it hit us?" ask three reporters nearly in unison.

"Dr. Cooper?" says Tennyson to his left.

"Very unlikely at this time," says Cooper, British accent. "But as the comet moves closer, it is actually going to be in opposition from us, on the other side of the sun. For thirty-two days we will not be in position to monitor the Tennyson or collect data. There is some chance solar flares could influence its orbit."

"So you're saying there is a chance this comet could hit Earth?"

There is a splattering of flashes throughout the room, then another barrage as the astronomers look around at one another.

"This comet will come close enough to Jupiter where that planet's gravitational force will have some bearing on the comet's trajectory," says Dr. Cooper. "We have seven days to gather more data on both the comet and Jupiter and we hope to have a more precise idea at that time."

"Where would it hit?"

"How big is the comet?"

"What would happen if it did hit earth?"

Tennyson looks to his left, holds up a palm to the continuing barrage of questions. "Dr. Hoyle?"

"The nucleus—the head of the comet—appears to be quite large after some rudimentary computations. It's strange, but there's really not much of a coma at all."

"What's a coma?"

"The outgassing, the burning-off of gasses and water vaporizing. The coma burns and the debris fans out in the solar wind. That's what we can usually see, the coma and the tail. But that's not the case with the Tennyson. There's very little coma," Hoyle explains.

"Compare it to the Shoemaker-Levy which hit Jupiter in '94."

"The Tennyson is perhaps much bigger, but these statements are all speculative at this time. As it approaches we will acquire more reliable data to work with."

"When?"

"When would it hit?"

Dr. Hoyle nods. "If—now this is a huge if, the chances are still quite small, and we do not want to create a panic here—if it hit, it would be late in the year: November, December, perhaps January. We are a long way from making such a statement, though."

"If this comet hit what could it do?"

"How much damage?"

"Could it end life on earth?"

Tennyson says, "Dr. Singer?"

The only woman at the table leans forward. "Let me reiterate that this is a small chance, one in thousands. Thousands. And a comet of this size impacting earth would not end life. At least not right away."

Twenty, thirty questions come at once, each louder than the others. As the cacophony of human voices crescendo Dr. Tennyson raises his hand. The din subsides.

"Ladies and gentlemen, we have approximately seven days to get to our stations and gather more data before the Tennyson goes into opposition. We have a lot of work to do. We will meet back here in eight days and reevaluate the data. We should know more at that time. We trust and hope your reporting will not over-sensationalize what we have said—we are predicting nothing for certain. As soon as *we* know more, we will let *you* know. Thank you."

The astronomers file out of the room ignoring questions and camera flashes. After Stofford closes the door behind him, the tidal wave roar that comes with a big news event follows.

In the middle of the tumult is Hank Boorstin, the *Denver Times* correspondent, who looks shell-shocked. He stares ahead, oblivious of Phil Hayden, the *Sacramento Bee's* reporter, talking directly to him.

"Hank, did you hear what I said? Let's get out of here!"

"My God!"

"What? What is it, Hank?"

Five seconds pass before the Denver reporter turns to face the *Bee* reporter. "There's a cab driver in Jackson Hole, Wyoming who has been predicting the end of the world. He said by comet. He said life on Earth will perish before the millennium ends. Phil, he predicted this!"

The *Bee* reporter grabs the Denver reporter; before they are out even of the room he has autodialed the Bee's editor.

". . . and a charter to Jackson Hole, Wyoming right away! Commence vocal-type, edit and run, priority twenty-nine to A-1. Palomar Observatory. The Tennyson comet may be on a collision course with the planet Earth. . . ."

In fairness, most of the major wire services and dailies accurately reported what the astronomers had said, but the papers given to sensationalism exaggerated mightily. That next day, in every newspaper in the world, headlines read something more or less accurate than the *Los Angeles Times* headline: KILLER COMET HEADING EARTHWARD. Over the next days more articles start appearing about the cab driver in Jackson Hole, Wyoming, who had predicted the event on June 25th, six days before Tennyson's discovery and again, on August 14th, before a live TV audience of thousands, nine days before some of the sharpest minds in the world would verify its path.

The reaction in the United States is indicative of the reaction throughout the world, a curious reaction unprecedented in the annals of time: It is at once a degree of gratification, something to talk about the next day, almost like the home team winning the big game, a topic which unites everyone around the boss' desk, or at the town post office, or over the phone lines, and the overall mood is strangely positive, on the verge of being cheerful, for after all. . . .

"The chances of it actually hitting Earth are small."

"It gives some kind of meaning to my whole life."

"Even if it hit here, we'd know where it would hit long beforehand."

"They said it had one chance in thousands of hitting here, but that's a lot bigger chance than winning the lottery, and someone always wins that. I'm going to start preparing, just in case."

There is excitement at the supermarket and at the hardware stores, like being along the Gulf Coast or south Atlantic seaboard as a hurricane approaches, and people look at one another in a new light. "What's the latest you've heard?" is echoed from neighbor to neighbor, store clerk to customer. People start buying large quantities of water and canned goods.

But if they talk about the other element of the comet story in public, more hushed tones are used. "What do you think about this cab driver in Wyoming who predicted this and said he was the messenger from God?" is asked between close friends, between parishioners and clergy, between rabbis and their congregations, between husbands and wives at night before the lights are turned out, between lovers. This adds a different element to the comet. Around the neighborhood, around the world, in every language, belief is expressed:

"I've been a good person and I have nothing to fear from the coming of the Almighty, but I know some others who I will worry about."

"And just maybe this could be real, because there were always prophesies about this happening."

"Just like the Bible always said."

"Nostradamus predicted all this stuff, man, years ago. He predicted the extermination of the Jews and Poles, World War Two, Kennedy's assassination, AIDS, earthquakes, the shuttle disaster and even the comet, man:

Sang, main, soif
faim, quand
courra la comette."

"What's that mean in English?"

"It's the last verse of a prophesy that goes like this:

Mabus shall come, and
soon after will die
Of people and beasts
shall be a horrible destruction,
Then, on a sudden, the vengeance
shall be seen:
Blood, hand, thirst,
famine, when
the comet shall turn."

"Oh, that's heavy, dude."

In Jackson Hole, Wyoming, reaction is stronger, the range of emotions wider, for over two months residents have discussed, made jokes about, and threats toward this upstart stranger who says he's a messenger from God. Sure, he's done some pretty amazing things—and, oh yes, the woman, and even the men, describe him as handsome, charismatic, and appealing, in that something-about-him kind of way. But now this is serious.

"He's focusing all this national media attention on our town. Why did he have to pick *our* town? I feel as if I have to be extra pure or something."

"He *predicted* this all along; it's been in the paper."

"Where does he get those strange powers, like that light source coming from him?"

"I met him and it felt like he could look right through me."

And more than one reporter has found his or her way to Jackson Hole. They want to photograph Doj, they want to interview him.

"The interview of the year," said Idaho's *The Post-Register* reporter.

"Of the millennium," said the Casper *Star-Tribune*.

But the only thing Conestoga Cabs company can tell callers is the truth: "It's his day off; we don't know where he is."

Nor is Doj at his small cabin at 185 East Hansen. A reporter from the AP news service even walked in and looked around. "The door was open. I thought it might be his cathedral, open to the public. . . . Well it could be."

They call the cab company, they call the Chamber of Commerce, the sheriff's office, the police department, the *Jackson Hole News*, the *Jackson Hole Guide*. No one can explain the disappearance of this much-sought-after young man.

"Hey, Rastjahmon, hand me that joint, will ya?"

"Aaahhh yes, Bolderdoj, and pass it to the young ladies, my irie brother," Rastjahmon laughs.

There are ten thousand thermal features in Yellowstone, and Doj has led Rastjahmon and his two lady-friends to two of the secret ones, two of the hot springs that meet the temperature and outflow prerequisites for soaking, for 'hot potting'.

As Rastjahmon hands the rolled *cannabis sativa* 'joint' down to Doj, his arm touches the naked breasts of Aisha, a strikingly beautiful black English woman; firm of breast, young and birdlike, and with her right forearm she holds his strong arm to her warm, wet breasts and turns the bracelets on his wrist. She runs her left arm lightly down the center of Rastjahmon's back and up again to spread out his dreadlocks. She slowly caresses Toby's shoulders; he sighs and lets his head drop.

Lisen leans back to reach for her glass of chardonnay, can't quite reach it, then stands. Her thin patch of pure-blond pubic hairs contrasts with the darker-skinned woman next to her. Lisen's breasts, her buttocks, are not as full nor round as Aisha's, but she is of regal carriage and portrays a splendid and fearless grace in her movements as she pours more wine.

Lisen takes a sip of the Ferrari Carano and a small toke from the hemp cigarette, then backs up three steps. With a Finnish accent, she commands "Hold still, Doj." She exhales the smoke, then runs toward Doj's back. Using the broad shoulders of Doj as a springboard Lisen launches herself high in the air, into a jackknife dive; she enters the 103° Fahrenheit water with hardly a ripple. She surfaces quickly to a round of applause and a chorus of cheers from the shoreline audience.

"A ten! Lisen, that was most definitely a ten that time. You really did dive in competition, didn't you?" says Aisha appreciatively.

"Three meter and one meter," says Lisen in slow, clear diction. "That was my escape from piano. And piano was my escape from springboard."

Lisen cups her hands and squirts Doj in the face. She laughs then sits on the submerged log which allows her shoulders and head to stay above the water.

"Now let me get this straight," says Doj. "I thought you played keyboard, Aisha."

"I do," says the coquettish alto. "You gig with Jake you'd better be versatile."

"I've loved Jake K. Solstice for years, never thought I'd party with his band," says the tall Caucasian man, now tanned to a deep bronze.

"Toby was his rhythm man and his main man for three years before he decided to branch out on his own," states Aisha.

"Ahhh, the Rastjahmon likes it on his own sometimes. I can let my light shine and choose my own chords to blend with others. Jake's light shined so bright it washed out every other light. I still love my brother Solstice though."

Lisen dog paddles back to the edge of the pool then stands unashamedly in front of the other three, flipping her hair back. Aisha says, "He still loves you too, Toby, and wishes you'd come back to the band. We have three weeks off before the east coast tour. No Paramount, Toby. This Halloween we're at the Garden. Think about it for him. For me and all who hear you and bask in the music coming from your good soul."

"Ahhh, my lovely Aisha. So beautiful by the warm water springing from the Earth. You are like a gorgeous angel from that other world."

Toby lifts Aisha and sets her on his lap as Lisen lowers herself into the steel-blue spring.

"Your desire is tempting, but good brother Bolderdoj needs me. He says the world will end and all the brothers and sisters in the world need a black disciple to believe. Praise Jah."

"Well," says Aisha, "he certainly has the body of a God."

"Aisha!" scolds Lisen, "You noticed?"

"Yes I have. I think we have the pick of the litter here. They're brilliant. They both possess hard-bods and God-rods."

"Aisha! You are, do I say it right, a scoundrel," says Lisen. "You make me laugh too much. Maybe you would like to trade? Mine is defective. I swam up and hugged him and he sprang an air leak. Worse than even the sulphur."

They all laugh. Doj nods and smirks, then slides into the hot spring. His hand comes up and he splashes the entwined bodies of Aisha and Toby. Lisen starts to hoist herself onto Doj's shoulders in an effort to push him under water. Doj back paddles, says sharply. "Don't push me under! I can't swim."

Lisen raises her eyebrows. "That cannot be true."

"Ahhh, young Aisha," says Toby, shifting position, "you'd better get off my lap at this time 'cause the Rastjahmon is growing right in front of your eyes. Oh yes. . . . Ooohhh, you haven't touched me there in a long time, lovely one."

With an embarrassed smile Toby lowers himself into the water. Aisha follows and says to Doj with a soft English accent, "So you're the one who beat Toby in chess. In three years no one on the bus could beat him—band members, managers, producers, agents, even a record executive. No one. Solstice even bought a computer, but Toby beat that. How'd *you* do it?"

Toby and Aisha embrace in each other's arms like eagles plummeting through the air, immersed, floating, then settling on the underwater log.

Doj moves his hair back. "He had me beat. I sacrificed my soul to the white devil for the answer."

"I love this place, Doj," says Lisen. "How did you find it?"

"My landlord and neighbor Taft Vandren. He drew that map. He's spent quite a bit of time up here. Remind me—he wants me to bring him water samples from these pools."

"Doj, brother man, now that the whole world is aware of your ability of prescience, you may be a marked man. Are you ready for some notoriety?"

"Is the world really going to end?" asks Lisen.

"Not the world. Not the earth. Just all—or at least most of—the life on Earth. We have treated each other and the planet too badly for too long."

Toby says, "Then Aisha and I will start right now by treating each other better. We will slip over to that other spring by ourselves. We must discover if we can still harmonize together."

The two perfectly-formed bronze and ebony bodies rise, dripping, out of the hot mineral water and Lisen and Doj watch as they stroll arm in arm over the rise and out of sight.

"But there have been good people who have not caused harm," says Lisen. "My mother is one."

"Yes, some. Perhaps it is just time to start over. There has been too much hate between too many people lately, too much take-grab-me-mine. It's really annoying."

"But beauty and sharing, too—yes? And many examples of unselfishness and generosity."

"Yes. That's why it is hard. But God, or nature, made humankind to be survivalists. After we obtain love and safety and warmth, we have a drive, an implacable urge, to obtain more, to go faster, to climb higher. It is a fault that must be corrected after the big crescendo."

"Then I shall be one of the ones who will not make it, for I've been good and I've been bad. Right now I feel like being really bad."

Lisen rises out of the water. She takes Doj's hand and guides him to sit on the shore. She stands between his legs, lifts his head in her hands and kisses him lightly, softly on his closed eyelids, on his steam-moistened cheeks, then on his soft, yielding lips.

His heart rate quickens, his senses sharpen, and moans of pleasure accentuate his peaking arousal. He slides his hands along her warm, muscular legs, the length of her exquisite form, up to her lips. His blood surges. His trembling fingers skim her perfect face, then fall down to delicately circle her breasts. She arches her back and thrusts her chest toward him. He surrounds both of her firm breasts with his large hands, barely touching her full nipples until his fingers make a V, then he slides his palms over them and continues his feathery caresses to her slender neck, then up, with eyes half-opened his fingers slowly explore her radiant, vulnerable face.

She moans, touching him with only her fingernails, then lowers her hand down his chest slowly, tracing his sculpted physique, her fingertips making light, concentric circles at various spots, occasionally pinching him at the center of the circle. She moves from the sensitive area just under his armpits to circle his nipples, then spreads her fingertips out and draws tiny swirls down his hard, flat stomach. She moans softly, then lets her head fall back. Doj glances over the glistening form of the Scandinavian; there is not a dark hair on her body; light hairs of silk protrude from skin of satin.

Lisen spaces her fingernails around his chest, puts her thumbs on his nipples with a firm but steady pressure, and forces him to lie back on the grassy shore.

She kneels between his legs. Her toes tickle the bottom of his feet as she runs her fingernails up his legs and lightly caresses both sides of his scrotum.

She scoops a palm full of hot water, rises high on her knees above him, and wets him once before she slowly, very slowly takes him into her, just a tiny bit at a time. With each little motion Lisen moans and her head falls back; she immerses herself in feeling.

Doj tries to remember the last time he had a lover, but consciousness gives in to sensation. They move together for awhile, half-opened eyes watch the other's increasing pleasure; caressing fingers discover ways to arouse and titillate.

A rising crescendo starts with long, slow movements, then smoothly builds under the blue sky; synchronous cries of pleasure are uttered. There, awash in the rays of the sun, next to the warm spring, when they've abandoned every civilized pretense, when there is no way to hold back, they climb together, moving faster, caressing, kissing, pinching, gasping. The climax is mad and vocal and almost violent, the lovers clutch and intertwine as if to literally bring their physical bodies into one another's, as if attempting to physically merge into one being, muscles tense and taut. After the squeals and moans of a long, shared, physical ecstasy, they giggle together like adolescents. Then their bodies relax, spent, before slipping like amphibians back into the warm spring, embracing, carressing, floating.

She holds him there, in the water and kisses him and they dance in a slow circle. Lisen whispers, "So is this my baptism, good Lord Bolderdoj?"

They rise early on the morning of August 25th. Radiant floor heat, courtesy of the earth's core, kept the tents warm and moist and one by one they slide naked out of nylon tents and slither through chilled mountain air and steamy gray fog into the hot spring. They dress in the rising sunlight then share a long breakfast next to a rekindled campfire. By noon Lisen and Aisha are airborne for Denver. Twenty minutes later Toby steers Rainbow Annie onto East Hansen.

At the same moment Toby and Doj lean forward to see over seventy people scattered in their front yard; some are camped out, some sit in front of tents, some just have sleeping bags; they are lounging, reading, waiting. As soon as the doors to Toby's VW van are opened they are accosted.

"It's him!"

"It's Doj Bolderton!"

"It's God!"

The throng quickly gathers around Doj, cameras start flashing, and a television camera is thrust in his face. The sheriff approaches with two men in nearly matching suits, and the din of all the voices talking at once becomes unintelligible.

"I don't think they're camping on our front lawn to hear us play "Natural Mystic", says Rastjahmon. "Be careful, Bolderdoj. Rastjahmon sees a green and yellow aura about this place."

Doj gets out of the van's passenger side. His neighbor/landlord Taft Vandren smooths back his gray hair, smiles, gestures broadly, and says in perfect East-Indian imitation: "Dese are your *people!*" He laughs loudly. "I didn't know if you'd want your followers waiting here or not."

Doj hands Taft his day pack with its uneaten food, one empty wine bottle and five full specimen bottles, before he turns to the crowd and says, "I have told you what you need to know. Yes, it is going to happen; the world is going to end. Prepare ye the way of the lord and all that."

"When! When is it going to end?"

"When do you think?"

"We don't know. We've come a long way to hear your words."

"You knew all along. On New Year's Eve of 1999. He's aiming for midnight, but he gets this great rotation on the nucleus so he could be off a few seconds. Gotta keep those heavy-hitters guessing."

"And will we be saved?"

"Remember when we all believed in Santa Claus? We were all good as saints in the week leading up to Christmas, weren't we? Think of this as God's cosmic Christmas. We're gonna find out who's naughty and who's nice. I mean, come on, haven't we all heard this our whole lives? The prophesy of the Second Coming?

He did not make us deaf! And wait till you get a load of Frosty the Snowman. Now please, out of my yard before I bring down that dragon from the sky!" Doj points and looks up, as do those gathered. "Oh hell, it's only the twelve-ten Delta. Our cabs are in the holding area. I can feel it. Now, sheriff, if you and the two FBI guys could again request that these people step off my yard, they've already trampled my raspberries."

Doj sits and watches as the sheriff moves the crowds, tents, sleeping bags, and bibles off the lawn, back into waiting rental cars, beat-up Subarus, television vans. After ten minutes the sheriff comes to him.

"Doj, these two guys are. . . ."

"Russ Hayes and Al Morgan of the Federal Bureau of Investigation," finishes Doj. He stands to face them. "Let's see if I got this right. Our government is very much concerned about public reaction to this astronomical event, which may be nothing more than a passing comet in space. The concern is panic, and our government is very curious as to how I found this out and came to predict potential world-altering events." Doj pauses. "I'm the messenger; that's all I'll tell you now, but you want some proof for yourselves, because you don't believe the good sheriff here about some of my abilities.

"You, Russ, I want to thank personally for finding—and yes, killing—that child molester in Albuquerque two years ago. The guy was a real sicko. In the last three years you've broken a major cocaine ring between the US and Mexico. Good job again, Russ—that cocaine is bad juju. And you were also on that team which tracked that serial killer in Arizona. My bet is that you played an integral role. Your pleasure is not only in breaking these cases, but getting recognition from your peers, and you enjoy being a field agent.

"And you, Al—how does it feel to get out from behind the desk after three years? Good, huh? But you should have just shot that drug pusher in Denver in 1995, rather than make him bungee-jump from the tenth story of that crack house. That building was too short, wasn't it, Al? He hit and bounced, dangled there for the other pushers to see until morning, and by then he bloated up and all. But God likes stuff like that—the devil takes it personally—and yes, you're going up there where Hoover never quite made it. Is there anything else?"

A full ten seconds lapse. Sheriff Clark smiles and looks away.

"Since we're being so damned candid, yes," says agent Hayes. "We want to know your activities and your whereabouts in the future, while we further our investigation. There's lots of dead ends. Why don't you tell us a little more about how your parents died?"

"Car accident. And as to my future whereabouts: the Jackson Hole Open Tennis Tournament starts Friday. If you could possibly do a little real investigation and find out the time of my first round match and my first opponent's style, I'd appreciate it. Good day, gentlemen, Sheriff. Toby, we're missing *Days of Our Lives*."

Three percent of Teton County, Wyoming, where Jackson Hole lies, is available for private ownership; the other ninety-seven percent is federally owned: the National Wildlife Elk Refuge, Bridger-Teton National Forest, Grand Teton and Yellowstone national parks. Many large landowners have easements on their land, precluding development in return for lessened property taxes. That leaves relatively little space in which people may reside. In the last ten years land prices and housing costs have skyrocketed, which drives up property taxes. Unless residents of low-to-average housing are innovative, only the wealthy can afford a home in Jackson Hole. 'The playground of the rich' describes resort towns of the west in the late 1900s—Telluride, Vail, Aspen, Lake Tahoe, Jackson Hole. In these places the wealthy seek activities, escape from the travails of maintaining lofty positions: golf, dressage, polo, boating, and tennis.

At Teton Pines Tennis Center, nestled under the Teton Mountain Range, there is a reverent hush as first-round matches are being played on the blue asphalt hard courts. Spouses in tennis warm-up suits sip on sparkling spring water under umbrellas, watching their peers battle it out. The setting is a favorite, and good regional players use the annual Jackson Hole

Open to incorporate a vacation with a tournament. World-class players have come to train at this high altitude club: Richey Reneberg, Yannick Noah, Gabriela Sabatini.

But now the club pro, Ray Lucas—the number one-ranked singles player in the state, a 6.0-rated player, and the winner of this tournament five years running—is having little trouble with a newcomer, registered locally, an unknown: D. Bolderton. Lucas' booming overhead emphatically decides the first set, 6-1 Lucas.

The lawn chairs are turned the other direction to face court four, where an interesting mixed doubles match between former champions is just getting underway. While Ray Lucas leans over the fence to talk to someone Doj ties his black hair in a rubber band before putting his tennis hat back on and changing sides for set two. Reaching in his tennis bag he selects another racket, a Wilson Pro Staff, and checks the tension by hitting the strings with the edge of his first racket.

Toby strolls up and hands Doj a water bottle. "Try my sports drink." He turns Doj around and rubs his shoulders with both hands. "Your aura is pale today, your energy is so low."

"I keep hitting the ball long," says Doj, leaning back against the fence, toweling his face. "I think it's the altitude."

"Aahhh, Bolderdoj, there's the problem: It's not the altitude, it's the attitude."

"My mental state?"

"It travels down through your heart and down your arms to the racket, where it reflects the attitude."

Doj gazes at him, not understanding.

"Ready?" Lucas says.

"Yeah. Let's go."

Bolderton's service is broken, then Lucas holds to go up 2-0.

Doj glances at Toby, who makes the same peculiar wavy motion with his hands he used in their chess match. He makes a motion starting with his right palm upward, then gracefully traces a semicircle, curving his palm downward.

"I get it!" says Doj. "Why didn't you say that before?"

"I did, brother Bolderdoj. Check your attitude!"

In game three Bolderton holds serve. His ground strokes become crisper; instead of hitting a foot out, the balls land a foot in. The rallies last more than two strokes, his footwork improves, and after a long baseline rally, the momentum swings, the pressure is coming from Bolderton's side of the court instead of into. The applause, cheers, and jangling of bracelets from the black man annoys, distracts, then draws the attention of those facing the mixed doubles match.

"What's the score over there?" asks an older man, turning in his chair.

"Twenty-one goals to fifteen." says Toby.

"There's no such score," scowls the man, just as Bolderton runs up to put away a mis-hit to take the second set, 6-3.

"Ray, what's the score?" asks a spectator.

"One set apiece."

A quiet murmur goes down the line, then chairs turn back to court five.

As Doj towels off he notices the two FBI guys standing to the side, in polo shirts, under the spruce trees. Doj waves, pantomimes a backhand and bows.

By 3-3 in the third set, everyone not playing is gathered outside of court five, watching what has become a close match with long rallies and deuce games.

"I'll be damned," says one of the old-timers who watched the early part of the match. "The kid switched to a western grip in the middle of the match!"

Toby looks over and smiles. "That, my good white sir, is called the Caribbean clasp. It's new."

The man nods, "No kidding! Who's your friend?"

"He is blue and red now. A good combination for this sport, would you not say, sir? Look at that aura!"

"He's wearing all green."

"Take off those expensive glasses and look."

At 5-5 in the third set the level of play of both men picks up. The rallies are long, precise and there is seldom an unforced error. Applause punctuates the good rallies, for it has been a long time that Ray Lucas has held court and proven himself king in these parts, and many who have fallen victim to the confident pro are secretly glad to see a challenger to the throne. A hundred of Jackson's *creme de la creme* have gathered around this suddenly surprising and tight first-round match, and comments can be heard between points:

"I don't think Ray's playing badly. I think this other guy's playing well."

"Who is he?"

"I recognize him from somewhere. Someone go find out his name."

"Who's that black guy? His coach?"

"Looks like one of those Rasta Aryans, something like that."

"I think it's Yannick Noah."

"Now there's a mixed doubles team!"

"I've seen this guy. He's got such good control of his top spin. I wonder if he's single."

They go to a third set tie-breaker. First one to seven points, win by two.

Ray Lucas is a steady player. His composure is his strong suit—he plays every point the same, regardless of the score—'Controlled aggression' as he preaches to his students. Just the slightest pursing of his lips reveals that, for all of his determination, he can't put away this guy who he handled easily for an entire set.

A stab volley from Lucas, then it is 7-6 in the tiebreaker, Lucas with a match point—a point away from victory. But Bolderton hits a drive down the right sideline, runs in behind it, and stabs at Lucas' plummeting return—a clean, crisp volley to save set and match point.

Doj's serve starts a long ground-stroke rally of cross-court forehands, each a little harder than the shot before. Lucas comes over a forehand early and hits the sharp angle. Bolderton scrambles to his right, starting to stretch as he reaches out. He hits a ball with little pace on it, a low chip shot with heavy backspin, but it lands a foot inside the baseline and a foot inside the backhand corner. Lucas has to lunge at the ball; he flicks at it with a loose wrist and open face, a defensive lob. Amazingly, the ball is headed over the net. Doj surrounds it, but the ball bounces in the doubles lane, a foot out.

Match point, Bolderton. Lucas's serve, 7-8.

"Come on, Ray!"

"Ray-*Ray*!"

"Let's go Luc!"

"Aaahhh, come on, Bolderdoj. Do it for these people before they snap."

Lucas' serve crowds Bolderton, he must back away and hit a weak return, bouncing short. Lucas comes up, runs around the backhand to hit the short forehand with heavy topspin, with so much spin the ball takes on an oblong shape to Bolderton's backhand. Doj can only hit a defensive lob and pray. It is high, appearing to sail out, but an early evening Wyoming gust picks up the high lob, takes the spin out, and the ball lands lazily in, forcing Lucas back to the baseline. Lucas hits topspin to Bolderton's forehand.

"Now, Bolderdoj! Pure red!"

Bolderton loops his backstroke and brushes the strings up and over the ball, imparting a huge topspin; he is aiming for the short angle. For the first time in the match he grunts loudly with the shot. Lucas charges cross court to the point farthest from him. The fuzzy yellow orb hits the back and top of the net, but it has so much rising topspin on it the ball crawls up and dances along the net cord for four inches before it drops weakly onto Lucas' side of the court. Lucas scurries to the ball but can only flick it cross-court. It hits the underside of the net cord, bounces twice on top of the cord then falls back onto Lucas' side of the court like a gun shot duck.

Game, set, match—Bolderton!

The crowd erupts in shouts and robust applause, and Lucas can only stand there gasping, hands on hips, glaring at the net before the young man he's never seen before runs up, his hat and his racket in his left hand, and his right hand extended to him. Lucas shakes Doj's hand, says, "Well played," and walks off the court.

"That's they guy who says he's God! The guy in the papers! That's where I've seen him!"

"The guy who's predicting the end of the world?"

"I'm just his messenger, ma'am. I'm just his little backhand drop shot. If you think that was smooth, you should see the big guy's game. Power, finesse, and grace all in one."

"Is God just? Is God good?"

"He's more than just good, sir. He's great. His court's the size of Nebraska, and he uses balls the size of King Kong's."

On Sunday night Doj accepts the trophy for winning the championships, having advanced easily in straight sets through the final. The final was played on court one, there was standing room only. People who had never held a tennis racket came to watch. Newspapers and television covered the final.

On the way out Doj overhears a man telling his daughter, "No, Judith, that wasn't God and that wasn't a miracle. That was just very good tennis. Icons just don't appear out of nowhere like that."

The young girl glances behind her and Doj hands her his trophy, mouths "Shhh," and leaves quickly through the men's locker room.

In the week that follows the International Astronomical Union's press conference, after the initial reaction—one nearly of optimism—if there is one word that can describe the reaction of adults from around the world, it is *reverence*.

The next meeting of the International Astronomical Union is scheduled for Wednesday, September first, and though everyone awaits further word from Mount Palomar, the astronomers have resolutely sequestered themselves in their lofty aeries. It is almost as if these astronomers have become gods, or at least heralding saints, as the masses await their word: what will the future hold?

Much is printed and spoken about the Chicxulub, the 150-kilometer-wide underwater crater off the Yucatan Peninsula. The crater was caused by a meteoric impact which occurred around 65 million years ago. Scientists believe this event caused the demise of the dinosaurs, they were the dominant species on Earth for 200 million years.

Television, the Internet, magazines, and daily major newspapers give a barrage of information about comets, their origins, their effects:

". . . subsequent dust clouds blocked out the sunlight and chilled Earth for several years before spawning a global heat wave, a heat wave lasting a thousand years, a millennium."

". . . a three-hundred-kilometer-wide crater could result from a nucleus only ten kilometers wide."

"If the comet hits in winter, it would probably hit the southern hemisphere because of the tilt of Earth's axis."

"This will be Jesus' return, prophesied two thousand years after his birth. Jesus will be here for one thousand years, a millennium."

"Just look through a pair of binoculars at the moon's craters to see the power of comets and meteors."

Validity is diffused in an inverse correlation from the proximity of the large population and media centers of the world, so that by the time the story trickles down to remote parts of civilization, carried by mouth to mouth, facts and scientific speculation become distorted rumors:

"The sun will explode and the world will end on Christmas Eve."

"God's revenge will happen any day. Turn your eyes to the heavens and pray."

"Allah will come to lead all Muslims."

"He has sent a messenger. He is in America, in Wee-oh-mee."

"Miami?"

There is an attitude of sudden reverence among the adults of the world, a sudden disposition to actually respect others and see them as finite, but there is a different reaction of parents to their children, one of grave concern, for the children have not had time to live out their lives, and *they've* done no harm, *they're* not responsible for the evils of the world and certainly *they* should not face the wrath of God.

"I'm not concerned about myself, but my kids. . . ."

"Perhaps, in His infinite wisdom, He will save the children. The faults of the earth are not theirs."

"The meek shall inherit the earth."

"My daughter keeps looking to the sky at night, expecting to see a white light."

Parents must decide how much or how little to tell their

children, for youngsters still at home can be sheltered, unless they hear something from the older siblings.

Some parents comfort and tell their children not to worry. "We will wait and see what the scientists tell us. The comet will probably just be a shooting star crossing the night sky."

This global threat seems to bring out a difference in the sexes: it triggers ancient instincts of care and protection among the females of the planet. Males gather to discuss ways of uniting against the approaching threat. "If this hits, what do we have to do to survive?"

The females bond, make decisions, bring together the family unit.

It is with these mixed emotions that the world awaits further news from Mount Palomar. Meanwhile, more curiosity is directed toward the cab driver who predicted these events, the man who calls himself the messenger of God.

Brucato Planetarium, Palomar Observatory, Mount Palomar, California. Wednesday, September 1st, 3:03 p.m.

Dr. Spencer Tennyson rises from the table of eight astronomers and steps to the podium.

"We'd like to thank the members of the media for going to the extra trouble to set up in the planetarium. There were just too many demands for space and electricity. Then we realized we could use the planetarium to illustrate, by the use of our holotron, the upcoming celestial events as related to the Tennyson Comet. I will have to ask that the television camera lights be turned off and ask that you please refrain from the use of flash photography."

The lights are lowered and the night sky appears; the assemblage murmurs as the stars start to slowly rotate around Polaris, the North Star.

"This is the night sky, as we observe it from this latitude at this time of year. The Tennyson, at this point, is very close to the constellation Leo. Of course, if these points of light were the size of the stars as we see them, at this time the Tennyson would be one ten thousandth the brilliance as shown . . . right . . . here. Only the most powerful telescopes are picking it up. The Tennyson is roughly following *this* path through the sky. Our observations of the nucleus tell us that this comet is most definitely larger, and potentially more destructive, than anything seen since the birth of our solar system. Lights up, please." The lights come up and the silent energy in the room crackles with tension. "But there is *little* or *no chance* this comet will hit the earth," Tennyson adds curtly. "Are there any questions?"

The tension drains, shoulders sag, and there is a collective sigh.

"What do you mean 'little'?"

"What are the chances?"

Dr. Tennyson's right palm stops a cresting wave of questions. "Less than one in a million. We stand a much greater chance of all of us here dying in the same car crash while driving highway S-6 to the bottom of the hill."

The water drains from the damn, the electricity in the room diffuses to bright lights and crowded people.

"Where *is* it going?"

"What was wrong with the original calculations?"

Tennyson turns to his right. "Dr. Cooper?"

The British Dr. Cooper speaks from his seat. "Something perturbed the Tennyson—possibly some large gravitational body with no visible outgassing has passed near it. We were able to record data and put it together from the eight different observatories. A much smaller chance is that there was a collision between the Tennyson and an asteroid; it is passing through the region of the Burke Asteroid Belt. Whatever it was would have diverted it only a fraction, but by the time it nears the inner solar system, that diversion will result in a variation at perihelion of approximately twenty-seven million miles." Dr. Cooper pauses, takes a breath. "You might just be able to see it with a good telescope."

"Another Kohoutek," says a reporter aloud, as much statement as question.

The female astronomer, Dr. Singer, leans forward and speaks. "We told you there was a small chance, and the chance now appears to be infinitesimal. You guys seem disappointed—did you *want* it to hit Earth?"

There is an uneasy silence before the next question. "What if something else perturbs it?"

The Japanese astronomer leans forward to speak into his microphone. "There is that possibility—however, it is minute. The Tennyson Comet has now gone into opposition. We will not be able to see it now for thirty-two more days. We stay here for additional three days, and some very good minds in astrophysics and mathematics will join us here as we employ independent judging of data."

Tennyson, holding the front edge of the podium tightly, asks sharply, "Are there any more questions?"

And no, there aren't any, really. The reporters have what they need to know. As the astronomers leave the room, there remains a feeling of resignation, dismay.

The *Los Angeles Times'* reporter says to his cameraman, "That was like the Raiders last game—they're mounting a winning drive in the last minute, only to fumble the ball on the one-yard line with eight seconds left in the game."

"Hey, I've still got those tickets to the Dodgers-Giants game. If we wrap this crap up quick, we can make it by the third inning—beer and dogs on me."

"Hell, the editor was saving A-1 for me. I suppose he'll still run it—something clever like 'No-Show for Son of Kahoutek'—then I'll probably be back covering the high school riots."

"My wife wanted the comet to come just close enough to light up the sky on Christmas Eve. She said that way we would have known God was there. She made me go to church with her last Sunday."

"Mine too. And our three kids. They didn't know what the hell was going on; they just knew that if they were good, they could go to McDonald's after mass."

"Made for an exciting week. The guy next door to me started building a bomb shelter. Reminded me of the nineteen fifties. I was playing 'Duck and Cover' with my six-year old."

The lady reporter from the *Omaha World-Herald* finishes scribbling some notes and steps into the circle of reporters and cameramen winding cords. "Hey guys, what if they just said this comet was actually coming and ninety-nine percent of life on earth would perish?"

"Ahhh, it wouldn't perish. I saw the shows this week. A year of dust in the sky, a few hot years. We could all be living in northern Canada for fifty years. I hear the steelhead fishing is great at this one little lake."

"Even better if we found out where it was going to hit and put all the criminals in the world on that spot. I was almost looking forward to a new start in some ways. Like maybe it *was* the Second Coming, the trumpets blow, some divine being chases all the evil in the world out."

"They had God on Star Trek once . . . ."

"I know what you're saying. I'm disappointed. It could have hit Houston and it would have been *no* loss. I could relocate to Jackson Hole. I was sent there to try and find that guy. That place is so beautiful."

"There's another story line gone bust."

"Out there in Wyoming, that town will probably string him up."

"No, not in 1999. There'll be an agent on his ass *signing* him up and he'll make three million bucks selling the rights to his story. We'll see him on Cynthia Golden's show within two weeks, guaranteed."

Labor Day, Monday, September 6th, 6:30 p.m.

Taft Vandren, Doj Bolderton and Toby Tiler are sitting around the picnic table in Taft's back yard. Taft gently flips the salmon steaks barbecuing over the mesquite coals, then the emu breast, then the ribeye which he and Doj will share. Doj and Toby are playing their guitars softly, an eight-chord progression of minor sevenths, major triads and major sevenths, each taking a lead after every sixteen bars, background music as the men talk. Taft takes the wrap off his homemade spinach salad steeping with vegetables from his own garden.

Doj and Toby end on a G-major triad and Doj says flatly, "Well,

I got fired as a cab driver and the messenger of God in the same week."

"The cab company didn't fire you," corrects Taft. "They just told you to lay low until the storm blows over."

"What I didn't tell you is that since the astronomers reevaluated their positioning Wilma and Eddy have been getting a lot of sardonic, even threatening, phone calls. Human beings—they pick on an open wound like hens in a pecking party; they should be annihilated."

"Ahhh, brother Bolderdoj, you made people look beyond their walls, and when they had to look back inside, some of them didn't like what they saw."

"What did they see?"

"The end of their fragile lives. You made them see what the end may look and feel like, which made them realize they hadn't got to where they needed to go."

"Where did they need to go, Rastjahmon?" asks Taft.

"The land of worthiness. They needed to feel they were good in heart and soul and they'd done something to make the world a better place."

"Erickson called that a sense of being generative, the final step in the evolution of self," says Taft.

He slides a spatula under Toby's salmon steak and hands him the plate, steaming, succulent with Taft's mixture of herbs and homemade jerk sauce. Then he stabs the emu breast and the medium-rare ribeye and puts them on a wooden platter which he hands to Doj.

"Would you like to try a little slice of grilled fowl or essence du heifer, Toby?"

"Nooo, thanks from you aggressive white men. Give mine to the masses, keep the blood lust," he laughs.

Taft takes a sip of his beer. "Well, everyone is leaving you alone now," he tells Doj. "Stay alert, you may see some backlash."

"But I still believe the comet will come. The prophesy must come true or . . . after they kill me, they will kill themselves. I must get the word out, yet no one will believe me."

As Taft serves spinach salad, potato salad and steaming corn-on-the-cob to the two hungry men, he says, "Well, you have a chance to do that, if you'd like. The cab company's been giving callers this number. Here are your messages." He pulls a small stack out of his pocket. "Talk shows, radio, newspapers, magazines—take your pick."

Doj cuts into his half of the ribeye as he scans the call slips. "Wow—*Oprah, Golden, National Enquirer, People*. Well, this looks interesting: MTV, a show called *Crossfire*. Hey, Rastjahmon, wanna go to New York City and be on MTV?"

"Yeah, mon. We need to practice, go up to that open mike night at the folk club. Very good salmon, Mr. Van Taftdren—did he swim all the way up here from the ocean?"

"Over four waterfalls and three hydroelectric dams, right up Flat Creek before he wiggled the last mile over land to my yard."

"That's great determination," says Doj, pulling at the loaf of whole grain bread. "But perhaps he was trying to get to Two Ocean Lake and over the Continental Divide and failed miserably."

Toby points a half-eaten ear of corn in Taft's direction. "The corn is nibbling *par excellence*."

"Yes, almost out of season already. Labor Day, goodness. That marks the beginning of the fall here in the mountains, I can feel a little arctic chill in the air. Winter is not too far behind. You've got twenty-seven more days before the Tennyson shows its face, so what are you going to do?"

"Toby, I think we should do the MTV show. The Crossfire Hurricane thing."

"Crossfire hurricane was a line from the old Rolling Stones song," says Toby.

"Wasn't their big hit . . . 'Honky Bonk Woman'?" asks Taft.

"No, it's Honky Tonk Woman," replies Toby.

Doj stops chewing. "I Can't Get No Satisfaction."

"Well," says Taft, "perhaps in New York."

Tuesday, September 14th. MTV Studios, New York City. 6:08 p.m.

Doj and Toby follow a thin, long-haired man down the hall

toward the TV studio. Aron is twenty-three, dressed in a vest with an embroidered Aztec design, torn jeans, and leather sandals. He is the show's producer.

"So this is the format: Two parts—*Crossfire the Kind* and *Crossfire Survival.* We'll do *Crossfire Kind* here, then helicopter you out for *Crossfire Survival.* Are you familiar with the show?"

Doj shakes his head. "Never heard of it."

"Yeah, I guess that's because it's only our second week. So hey, things got a little out of hand last week, but only that one guy got really hurt. You want to have Rastjah-dude with you for Kind and Survival?"

"What the hell is it?"

"In Survival you have to take an article—I guess we'd give you a wooden cross because of that Jesus thing you nearly pulled off—and you have to cross this forest with it while the Himbies and the Haties will be firing at you."

"Firing what?"

"Paint balls. Splatball, man, it's the rage. Paint balls only sting, hit pretty damn fast, but you can't really get hurt. Unless, like last week, when that guy took one in the ear."

"I need my ear, Bolderdoj," says Toby.

"Yeah, me too. Do we get paint guns, too?"

"Most major yes. If you make it to the other side before you surrender, you get an extra five thousand bucks."

"I don't want to die in New York City, Bolderdoj. And there's something about being painted I'm not all that happy with. This color is fine."

"Calm your hearts. The director decides when you die. Then the thing is edited. They're *not* going to let it get out of hand like last week—at least that's what they told me. And they're worthy on the idea of having the black dude fighting it out with ya. Ratings went off the *roof* last week and we figure you guys are gonna blow that away. This is gonna be the severest show, man. White-black, religion, Christ figures, and you're both drop-dead gorgeous. Lydia's makeup is nuclear!" He stops at a counter and takes three steaming cups. "Here, drink these."

"What is it?" asks Doj.

"Everything legal. It'll get you up for the show. Ginseng, a lot of herbs good for you, some instant karma."

"Ahhh, herb, there is very good fragrance in this steam. I need to settle this kaleidoscope," Toby sips.

"So you guys still want to do that reggae song to open the show?"

"Yes. Are our guitars there?"

"Yeah. Joobie wired new strings to them and put them through the body tuner. That body tuner is worthy, man. I put my Strat through it and it wails."

They walk up to the door of Studio 6-6 and the producer pulls the plastic security card on a leather string over his head. Doj stands closer to him. "Who, or what, are the Himbies and the Haties?"

Aron looks at Doj in disbelief. "Are you serious?"

"Rastjahmon, do you know anything about the Himbies and the Haties?"

"Medium-sized hippies and unhappy Haitians?"

"Unyes, man. Negatruth. Hey, that's right—you guys are from Wyoming. Where the hell is that? Is that out by Seattle somewhere?"

"Jamaica is where we should be right now, Bolderdoj," Toby mutters.

"Sent by the omnipotent master, I come roaring in on the head of a comet. I'm here to save the planet," Doj tells to the producer.

"Yo! Man! Oh that's *sick*! Keep talking like that during Kind—that'll get the Haties going for sure."

Doj raises his voice. "Who are the *Haties*?"

"Man! OK. Were you guys even able to print your names on the contracts? Do you know what money is? Can I have your five grand? OK. The Himbies, that stands for Heart In Mind — Body In Every Spirit. See, their main thing is that we're all of those things—heart, body, mind, spirit—and they each control our lives to different degrees at varying times. Some people have a higher percentage of, say, Body—a total Body would be some kind of weight-lifting dude. Now you know how sometimes your heart takes over and ya give five bucks to some disgusting street person, some carny-rat guy, know what I say?"

"Got it," says Doj. "*Anything* like the hippies?"

"Not hippies. Himbies! And their whole thing is to not feel any guilt for having done, or not done, something in your life—no fear, no guilt. Say, instead of giving the homeless guy five bucks, you say something sick to him, like 'Quit your heartbeat, man, you're rockin' up my path, agitating my neurons'—that would be the heart seeking vengeance 'cause maybe someone dissed on you, but that's your current emotional state and it's who you are so that would be cool too—know what I say?"

"Got it. Who are the Haties?"

"Jesus Christ! Oh hey, sorry dude, that's who you think you are. I mean, like, Jerry Garcia, man! Dude! The Haties are simply anyone born after nineteen eighty who hates life. They maintain the previous generations left them nothing of cultural, social, physical or even inner worlds to uncover, so they be hatin' life, especially now that the century's chillin' down. They're going to try a human sacrifice at exactly midnight on New Year's Eve, and just as the clock strikes the year two thousand they'd do it. I think we got a good chance of getting the TV rights. It'd be so sweet to produce that, out on a cruise ship in the ocean. We got a volunteer sacrifice already signed. OK, are you guys ready? We soar in two minutes."

"Rastjahmon, you sure you want in on this stuff?"

"I left the Solstice tour to see the world and educate the Rastjahmon. I told you I'd be your shadow, keep your inner eye open. I'll do it."

Inside the studio there are two thickly-cushioned chairs in the center of a brightly-lit, round platform stage. Their two guitars are leaning against the seats. To stage right are twelve kids, none older than nineteen, both guys and girls, in soft, beat-up sofas and chairs. They're wearing torn clothes for the most part, hair styles dissonant, embellished. Small metal objects pierce various body parts and a general snarl curls the corners of their lips. They are the Haties. Camera one scans them as Doj and Toby look past a second camera to the other group at stage left.

"The Himbies," Doj guesses quietly, correctly.

This is a group of twelve as well, guys and girls from about 16 or 17 to as old as 30 to 35, and in varying kinds of dress. A middle-aged male is dressed as a basketball player, a young female is dressed as a cheerleader, next to her is a uniformed postal worker, and seated below him is a man of maybe twenty-five in a neatly pressed gray suit sitting at a black-marble business desk.

"OK guys, thirty seconds to go," says Aron. "Open with your song. Ready?"

The Himbie dressed as the cheerleader says loudly, "I like them. They're cute!"

"You like anything with a twanger," says a Hatie, a black man of perhaps nineteen.

"And you hate anything with a heartbeat," retorts the basketball player Himbie.

"OK! Let's hold it right here!" shouts Aron. "We're not rolling yet. Save it save it save it! After their song we go right into Kind questions. Don't start off mean. Remember, there can be no physical assault during *Crossfire Kind*. OK! Guys . . . three . . . two . . . one. . . ."

The cameras pan around the guests as a woman off-screen at stage right says into the microphone, "Welcome to *Crossfire*! The show where if the questions don't get you, the bullets will! Tonight's Cross Targets: Bolderdoj, who says he is the messenger of God, and Rastjahmon, his smiling naughty-dread disciple."

Toby whispers, "There's an agitated aura here, Bolderdoj. I think we should split, be in Jamaica by tonight, saving dolphin filets instead of the world."

But the producer is pointing to them and the center camera's red light comes on above the lens. Doj hits the e-minor chord and starts the *ker-chunk-a-chunk ker-chunk-a-chunk* rhythm; on the ninth measure Rastjahmon falls in to "Comin' in from the Cold."

When the song ends, they smile at each other and give five fingertips, they'd never played it better, the harmony and the rhythm was perfect and it was national television.

The red light goes off the center camera and the lights come up on the two groups. The producers take their guitars and motion for them to sit back, "Relax!" he whispers.

A Hatie asks, "Which one of you thinks your God?"

Doj replies, "I am his messenger."

A Himbie sits up, "Isn't that a bit pretentious? I mean, so many people will look to you for hope."

Doj begins, "Well, the world's. . . ."

"The world's screwed," a Hatie interrupts. "God would have every right to come to this god-forsaken chunk of rock and kill everything."

Hatie: "Hendrix called it the third stone from the sun. That's all you bastards have left behind you in the wake of ruination."

Doj points at the accuser, "No, actually, where we come from, there are lakes. . . ."

Himbie: ". . . that are polluted; can't drink the water, can't swim in it, can't even eat the fish."

Hatie: "It's a big piss bowl is what it probably is. Did you come from a piss bowl, messiah-man?"

"Jackson Hole actually. . . ."

The Himbie woman dressed as chef says, "The black man is beautiful, look at his face. So expressive."

Hatie: "Say something black man. Are you beautiful?"

"Down in the islands, mon, we have a saying: I'm leaving."

He starts to rise, but Doj grabs him by the belt and the producer motions him to sit back down, giving him a thumbs-up and mouthing, "It's going great!"

Himbie: "Perhaps he is a spirit. Down where he's from, they do voodoo and trance out. Do you have a spirit, Mr. Toby?"

"Does anyone play chess?" Toby asks.

A Himbie woman of thirty says huskily, "But he does have a great body. Do you dance naked for coin?"

Toby turns to Doj. "These people cannot outrun us, and I don't need five grand this bad."

Doj whispers, "They can't touch us. Counterattack, like in chess." Then he says louder, to both groups, "Are you guys pissed off at us or are you just pissed off at each other?"

Hatie: "We're growling at you guys. You get five thousand bucks for this but we have to share five. Just like all your stinking generation, you have to hook the big share. Ya got it all, didn't ya? Well, we're gonna take it all back and twist it the way *we* want."

A Himbie says, "And now you even say you're God. Why does God need cash? Aren't there cash machines in heaven?"

Doj: "No, scurvies, I believe we actually get ten thousand—that's about how much we need to really enjoy ourselves before the end of life, just before the year 2000."

Hatie: "Does that mean you'll be our male sacrifice? Yes! We'll sacrifice God at midnight, kill him just before he is supposed to come back. Worthy!"

Himbie: "How do you figure ten thousand? You only get a five thousand bonus if you get through the forest during Survival."

Hatie: "Not possible. We will hate you to death, all in red paint."

"We'll make it," Doj says calmly.

Toby says to Doj, "Perhaps we could just gig for *Star Search*. Does Oprah still want us?"

Himbie: "Can you do a miracle for us? Just a little one?"

Toby says, "Yes, we could disappear real fast."

Doj: "You *people* are miracles." Then he looks straight into camera 2. "It's a miracle that four billion years of evolution came up with nothing better than this batch of imbeciles."

Aron jumps up and down behind camera 1. "Great!" he mouths.

A Hatie is slowly standing in her seat. "You call *us* imbeciles. Look at the world you've left us. What a legacy. This century has been the most violent in history; your parents and grandparents got to kill one another, and it's still being glamorized. We don't get to kill anyone, except with a lousy paint gun. Let us kill, we already got the hate. Let us experience something!"

Toby: "How about valium?"

Himbie: "And we can't even go to school to learn how to feel. The schools are prisons. My English teacher has bulletproof glass in her car."

A Hatie says, "Hey, God—I'm a lesbian, my family disowned me, I'm in a gang and I knifed my brother. Can I go to heaven?"

Himbie: "You'd have to go upstairs to get to hell."

Hatie: "Shut your rap or I'll come over there and push this pen down your ear and carve my initials on your one lonely-ass brain cell."

Himbie: "Red Rover, Red Rover, send that fat, dyke bitch over. We'll cut off her head and shit down her windpipe. Everything she says is crap anyway."

Hatie: "If you are the messenger of God, go back up there and ask him why there's been so much human suffering."

Doj: "You're the only one suffering. We're all having a great time. We laugh almost constantly. You're the punch line."

Toby whispers, "Doj, your aura is red and black. I have never seen you in this light before."

Doj whispers back, "I'm getting into it. This is almost as good as a bad date on Love Connection."

"We're not doing much to get the word out here. We were supposed to stop hate. You're feeding hate."

Hatie: "What are you salt and pepper shakers whispering about? See, that's just it, ya know what I say? You guys have all the secrets, there's nothing for us to suss out for ourselves. Einstein said the most beautiful thing we can experience is the mysterious; it is the source of all art and science. Where's the mystery now?"

Doj gestures as if he's holding something large. "Check it out. This 40-kilometer wide hunk of ice and rock is coming toward your house at sixty kilometers-per-second. All, or most all, of life on Earth is going to perish—Pffft! You have less than four months to get your spirit right, the spirit you'll spend eternity with."

Himbie, after a pause, "So would both of you like to watch me slowly take off my little cheerleader outfit? Then would both of you like to *do* me? We won't even use a seed-catcher since the world's going to end."

A Himbie man leans back, "What does heaven look like? Is Marilyn there? Will Hendrix be wailing worthy?"

"It looks like your bedroom," Doj says.

When the laughter dies down, a Hatie says, "This dude's righteous. My mom always used to say my room looked like hell. So do I have to share hell with my punk brother?"

Doj holds up both hands. "Rest your tongues, put your lips together for a moment. This is how it is: You are gods, you can give life, make life, or take it away. Your own life—even others'.

You can make this heaven or hell, it's up to you. Yeah, I'll fess I'm somewhat responsible for the degradation of the planet. We are all. . . ."

Toby: "I sprayed insecticide on some pot plants once and am singly responsible for the death of many fish."

Doj continues, "We've all had this unquenchable thirst for more and faster, but more comfort takes more resources. And yes, humankind has explored the farthest reaches of the physical world and the inner workings of human behavior, but there is still progress to be made. Other directions, other realms to investigate, more fun to be had. I, personally, have had a lot of fun."

Toby: "Other riffs never riffed."

Doj says, "You can make this heaven or hell. The consciousness of the planet reflects the consciousness of its individual members, just like your room at home is a reflection of who you are. How you want to arrange it is how you're going to have to live with it, and with yourselves, forever. Do you want dignity and poise? Joy and laughter? Hurt and anger?"

Toby speaks to a silent crowd, "The spirit is eternal, my good brothers and sisters, if that helps. And it takes more energy to have the spirit stay red all the time, even when the bright lights are on you."

There is a long pause, a shifting in their seats, then a Hatie asks, "So does God wear long white robes?"

Himbie: "Is God male or female?"

Hatie: "White or black?"

Himbie: "I shot our neighbor's cat once with a BB-gun. I took it to the vet without anyone knowing, but then I had to steal five dollars a week out of my dad's wallet to pay for it. Will *I* go to heaven?"

Hatie: "Are there rules? Can I wear anything I want there?"

Himbie: "Is there a no-smoking section?"

Hatie: "How many channels do you get in heaven?"

Himbie: "Will my dog Legolas be there?"

Hatie: "Or is it just like we're ghosts or invisible, just floating around smiling all the time and we just kind of meander around because we ain't got no mo' body? That would be so different. I don't know if I could handle it. Heaven might be hell for a Hatie."

Himbie: "Is there sex in heaven?"

Hatie: "Are the streets paved with gold there? Just think, a manhole cover there would be worth three thousand bucks."

Hatie: "If that gangbanger was there that dropped my cousin I'm afraid I'd have to do him again."

Himbie: "Just like we're going to do you guys in Survival."

Doj cuts in louder than anyone. "Every generation before you had the courage to pull the trigger, to make change. You cowards are afraid to pull the trigger."

Aron is signaling cut-in-ten as a roar of epithets directed at the guests becomes an unintelligible verbal barrage. Then the only weapons available to the Himbies and Haties, belts and shoes, come flying at the two men. Doj catches one shoe and hurls it back at the owner, hitting him in the nose, just as the red light goes out on the cameras.

"Fantastic!" yells Aron. "Bouncers, get these kids to stop throwing their clothes. Doj, Toby, we'll come back to wrap things up. Get in something about your sex lives and then we'd better get you the hell out of here, get you rested for Survival. Great job, guys."

Catskill Mountains, September 15th, 9:08 a.m. 'The Weapon Shop'

"A.E. Van Vogt," says Doj, gazing around the large aluminum shed with its equipment for 'splatball' war.

"What about voting?" asks the producer.

"A.E. Van Vogt. He wrote one of the most famous science-fiction stories of all time, 'The Weapon Shop'."

"Right. Well you two can pick out whatever you need. Here's your key; if you were to make it across to the other side, you would put this in the gate, that will start your victory song. What'd you pick? "Zion Train" by that Bob Marley dude. That's cool. Reggae always goes. You got your cross?"

"Right here in my pocket."

"Great. Here's a map of the war zone, drawn to scale. The whole thing's about a mile square. There's all kinds of cool traps out there, twenty-by-twenty-by-twenty pits, you name it. That guy last week tripped on a root and fell face first into a snare and almost hung himself. We've got more cameras in the trees and bushes this week, so that shouldn't happen. Now, there's two of you against twenty-five Himbies and twenty-five Haties. The Haties are in red, the Himbies are in white and blue, those are the colors of the paint in their pellets. They have to make you surrender, hand them your key. Here, each of you take a chamois sash; you've *got* to keep your goggles clear—your dead if you can't see. You're taking rope. That's cool. Daniel Day Lewis does Rambo with a reggae dude as Tonto. The ratings for last night's show were off the roof. I can only pray that you guys could make it, but at least go down in a blaze of glory. Yeah, now those are the rapid fire paint ball machine guns. Take the belt, put in as many rounds as you can. These are the latest in CO_2 cartridges, take a few extra. OK, I'll put these microclips right . . . here on your collars, so you're now miked for sound. As soon as you step inside the gate they're activated. What you do want duct tape for? If you wanna say something like 'Die cocksuckers' as you're going down, that's cool, but you still can't say 'fuck' Jesus, 1999. Maybe the new millennium will bring enlightenment, huh? OK, try the paint pellet guns on that poster of Newt Gingrich. These pellets go sixty miles-an-hour, so for short range you don't have to sight-up at all. And you've got to stay cool at all times, you start sweating in your goggles and steam them up so you can't see, then again . . . you're dead. Got it?"

"Rastjah dude, the reggae colors in your hat aren't going to work. They clash with the foliage. Try this for camouflage. Perfect. Keep your goggles clear. OK, let's head out. You have four hundred yards before you get in the open fire zone. The Himbies start on your right, the Haties on your left. After three minutes, anything goes. Don't lose the key, just in case. OK, stand right here for a moment. Arnie, zoom in for a 'before' shot. Smile, Rastjah dude, be checking your weapons or something. Remember, when . . . if . . . you go down, make it dramatic. Yell a lot, choke on some paint maybe."

Doj unfolds the map. "You OK, Toby, you into this?"

"Aahhh, Bolderdoj, people have been taking shots at me since I got into this country. Now it is my turn to fire back. The machine guns remind me of the spear guns we used in the clear Caribbean waters, young Toby was the best speargun fisher on the whole eastern shore."

"Good thing you've been running with me in the mountains. We may need a little speed of foot this morning."

"For five thousand dollars the Rastjahmon can run pretty fast."

"One minute to go!" shouts the director as the producer ushers them to the gate.

Doj studies the map. "We're going far left, Rastjahmon, into the heart of the Haties; there are cliffs over there, thick woods. We could make this short and sweet. Ready?"

Rastjahmon slings the machine gun strap over his head and pulls out a pistol. "Let's kill some Haties."

Doj smiles, "Rastjah dude, I can't see your aura through all this camouflage, but methinks it is sanguine."

"Go!" yells the director.

They touch fingertips, a bikini-clad model lets them inside the gate, and a loud siren announces the game has begun. In the distance they can hear the whoops and hollers of the Himbies and Haties.

"Follow me!" yells Doj.

They crouch and dart to the left, through the fallen foliage of maple and oak; the sounds of their running shoes make soft, rhythmic crunches in the thick carpet of leaves. Doj notices red lights above the lense of a camera that follows them. Heat-sensitive?

Instincts of hunting and fleeing that were honed for hundreds of millenniums are not absent in these two sharp and strong male primates; Toby unconsciously adjusts the cadence of his steps so his footsteps are in synch with his partner's. Doj raises a hand and they pull up behind a thick oak and stop.

"OK, the boundary is just ahead. I'm sure they're all along the boundary, possibly concealed. We want to make sure we get past the first wave." He looks on the ground, kicking quietly through the leaves until he finds a rock about the size of a large plum. From behind the tree he heaves it in his best first-serve motion far to the right. He hears it land somewhere in the thick brush. Someone says, "Something moving here! Sector 5S!"

"Let's go!" whispers Doj.

They swing out far left, with the barb-wired chain-link fence only twenty yards away. Running at full speed they see their first Hatie, sprinting at a right angle away from them, toward the sound of the rock. Toby drops to one knee and fires while Doj runs toward the startled young man and fires at him four times rapidly, before he reacts. Three of the pellets hit the Hatie and explode bright green on his side; one pellet catches him on the side of his head, causing him to gasp then fall. He starts to yell but Doj pounces upon him, straddles him, then turns him over onto his stomach so his screams are muffled in the leaves and decaying undergrowth.

"Take his gun!" says Doj as Toby sprints up. "Keep his face down!"

Toby holsters the pistol. Doj whips out the duct tape, rips off a four-foot piece and wraps it over the Hatie's mouth. He quickly drags the thrashing Hatie to a birch tree, unwinds three coils of the rope and the thin blue beam flashes from his right hand, severing the rope.

"The light! The Z light from Bob Dylan!" says Toby.

"I am the God of War! Let's initiate some human suffering. War! Christ, this is much better than saving any planet."

They are startled by sudden sound of paint pellets zinging through the foliage; they cannot locate the sound's origin. Rastjahmon takes a hit on the thigh; his leaf-brown-and-stick-gray trousers immediately explode with red paint.

"There!" says Doj, pointing to a mound of leaves with a human underneath. She starts to yell and Doj is upon the girl, dragging her out of the leaves and muffling her scream.

"That bullet stings!"

Toby holds the girl down. It takes less then eight seconds for Doj to tape her and tie her wrists to her ankles behind her.

"You learned something from the rodeo, Bolderdoj!" Toby smiles, crouching to survey the surroundings. Doj jerks his head up, listens, points. "They're coming! This way."

Crouched low, they sprint for a full minute through the leaves, zigzagging, hurdling fallen trees.

"Run on your toes!" whispers Doj, adopting the technique for running in rough terrain. They can hear shouts on either side of them, but the voices are uncertain, questioning. Doj notices another camera pick them up as he runs into a clearing and realizes that the cameras are motion sensitive.

Both men sense imminent danger at the same time. Toby quickly holsters his pistol and whips the machine gun from his shoulder. Doj unslings his gun over the rope coil as he looks forward three steps, looks left two steps, then looks right two steps. A squirrel darts through some leaves then springs to the center of a large oak. Doj shoots it, knocking it off the tree. It rolls; leaves stick to it where the orange paint has hit its midsection.

Then what they see sends a dose of adrenaline into their veins. There is red and white movement ahead.

"Himbie ten o'clock!" shouts Toby.

"Hatie two o'clock!" yells Doj. "I got the one on the right."

He fires, but the Hatie drops flat behind a fallen tree and pellets explode all around the intended target. One misses the Hatie's neck by an inch before she rises to fire back. Doj realizes that the Haties have machine guns as well, and he takes three sixty-mile-per-hour hits on his thigh, his side, and his right hand. He fires back wildly, like a slugger triggering a counter puncher.

Toby comes to a stop and fires from one knee, hitting the Himbie in the shoulder, in the neck, and right on the goggles, knocking them off, evoking a cry.

"Die, blowfish!" Toby yells, then dashes ahead.

Doj and Toby zigzag through the clearing, into the thicker trees, the Hatie in pursuit.

"On on!" yells the wounded Hatie. "Vector thirty-five, heading eighteen degrees!"

"Cut left! Ten o'clock!" Doj hisses to Toby.

They hear voices on either side drawing closer. Their fingers on the trigger, the two trained men weave swiftly through the woods, over stumps, rocks, and downfall, never sure of their next step in the thick leaves. When a pursuing Hatie yells, "Vector three-four-zero, heading-three-four-five degrees," she is farther away.

"Bolderdoj! A road!" Off to the right is a leaf-covered two track.

Doj says in breathless spurts, "It's in the direction we want to go . . . it was on the map . . . let's try to outrun 'em! Damn! The bridge is out over the ravine . . . try to jump it."

It is a full fifteen feet across. Doj accelerates, very slightly lowering his center of gravity in order to launch his weight at takeoff. Just as his speed is at maximum and he's ready to launch, Toby shouts, from three strides behind, "Stop!"

Doj catches a leaf-covered wire at ankle level, and instead of going up he is tripped and flung forward, flying over the rocky creek. He crashes heavily into the roots and rocks of the opposite creek bank; Toby soars above him, landing cleanly on the far side. He hears Doj's painful cry below him as his momentum carries him down the trail. He scurries back to the edge.

Doj is already on his feet, struggling to pull himself out of the ravine. The right side of his goggles are cracked and his rifle is broken at the middle. Toby hoists him up and over the edge and Doj fires the rifle, but the paint bullet goes off at an angle, with little velocity. Doj hurls it away.

"Go! Here they come!" he shouts, limping and grimacing for three steps before he forces himself to run with the pain.

Three blue-and-white-clad Himbies and two red Haties suddenly close in from either side.

Doj replaces the clip in his pistol as they start to outdistance their followers. "That creek is the halfway mark! Let's go for it!"

"Bolderdoj—ambush!"

Suddenly they are in a crossfire from all sides, getting stung on all parts of their bodies from everywhere. The two men instantly turn back to back, but can only fire wildly at the blurred targets. A pellet hits Doj's goggles and knocks them off slightly. They both take ten, twenty shots from ever-closer range, the stinging pellets sometimes landing in the same place in rapid succession.

"This way!" Toby jogs unsteadily to his right, leading Doj past a reloading Himbie.

The Himbie throws his gun at Doj's legs and Doj kicks it with his shin and stumbles forward for three steps. They charge past the constricting circle toward the thick woods as some twenty Haties and Himbies follow closely.

"He's in our forest now!" yells a Himbie. "Why don't you guys return to Hatie?"

"Not until we have the cross!" a Hatie shouts, followed by yelps from his compatriots.

"They've gone to earth!"

"On on!"

"Key to Hatie!"

"Key to Himbie!"

Toby and Doj fire wildly while they run at half speed, flicking paint from their goggles. Doj, then Toby, fling the smeared goggles away.

"You're looking like a patriotic American now, Bolderdoj."

"You have more red than white or blue, Rastjahmon. You look like the six-foot candle from voodoo hell."

They dart and weave, and the yelps behind them fade once again, but they hear voices ahead, from the far side of Himbieland: "Vector one-zero-three, heading two-eight-zero!"

They enter another clearing.

"Stop, Doj!"

This time Doj skids to a stop, not yet seeing what Toby sees. He looks back to his partner's glaring eyes, then follows his gaze until he sees it: The leaves are very flat within a 20-foot square.

"The pit!" says Doj. "Quick, loop this rope around the perimeter, cover it with leaves—fast!"

While Toby runs the rope around the pit, Doj quickly ties a knot in the other end and throws it over the branch of a huge oak. After the knot goes over and swings back to him, Doj sits on the ground and ties it around his ankles.

"Now take that end around the tree there and drag me up."

With all his might Toby pulls him up until he is suspended like a bat, twenty feet above the camouflaged pit.

"Belay me so I don't fall in. Here they come. Climb up that tree and hide. Wait for my signal."

"Easier than the coconut tree."

With whoops and hollers some twenty Haties and Himbies break out of the woods from several directions. When they see their prey suspended above the ground they break into savage war cries and start shooting wildly; only a few of the shots find their mark. As they run to the spot directly beneath Doj, the first two fall into the sheet- and leaf-covered pit; the momentum carries four others screaming into the twelve-foot deep hole.

"Give us the cross!" shout the others.

"Surrender to us, give us the cross!"

"Haties kill!"

The hunters step close to the pit, whooping and hollering as they fire at the man twisting above them. Blue, white and red paint pellets explode against Doj superimposing upon the previous one; he's a human easel and the artist has gone berserk. A blue pellet stings his cheek. He twists around and flings his used pistol at the crowd. When he sees that almost all of the hunters have gathered within the concealed rope loop, he grabs a branch to his right and hoists himself up, yells "Now!" then launches himself with a mighty thrust, diving over another bough. As he falls his weight snaps up the coil, closing it around all but three of the hunters; the roped pack is corralled over the edge and into the pit, like one large, multi-legged, flailing insect.

Toby springs down from his tree and runs at the three already leaning down to pull up their fallen comrades. He dives feet first and kicks two of them into the pit. A girl fires at him, and he kicks her legs from underneath her. She falls backwards, into the mass of Haties and Himbies below, crumbling the human ladder.

A Hatie starts to climb up the rope. Doj quickly unties himself, falling to the ground as the rope slips over the branch—the Hatie falls back into the crowd.

"Go!" Doj yells to Toby. "This way!"

Toby fires off a blast of pellets into the pit before he follows Doj. They run unmolested for four hundred meters until they pick up the two track briefly before breaking out of the trees. Fifty yards ahead is the gate! Just outside are cameras perched high above the producer and a crew who are yelling, screaming, cheering.

"Go rager, go major, go large!" yell two bikini-clad girls at the same time.

But seven more attackers appear from different directions, racing for the gate, trying to cut off Toby and Doj.

"Cover me while I get the key!" shouts Doj. As they approach the gate he pulls the key from his paint-soaked pocket. He wipes paint from his eyes and reaches for the lock.

Toby's machine gun is spent; he throws it at the charging hunters, who dodge the flying weapon, then spray Toby and Doj with pellets. Toby pulls out the pistol he captured and fires, hitting the closest Himbie in the goggles, stopping him. But his ammo is gone after ten shots, and Doj takes pellets in his face at close range, blinding him with red.

"Give us the cross! Give us the cross!"

"Toby put in the key. I can't see!"

As Toby takes it,a pellet hits him in the ear and he drops the key.

"Stand back or die!" someone yells.

Toby reaches down as Doj covers his body with his own. The shots are coming nonstop from two or three feet away, and a Hatie walks toward them, loosening a coil of rope. As the camera crew closes in, Toby finds the key and stabs blindly at the hole; on the third try he gets it in and turns it left, then right. A red light starts flashing and a siren starts wailing and the Marley victory song comes on, but the paint bullets do not stop. Doj and Toby are on their knees, getting pelted, covering their ears and faces with their arms as the rope is raised above them.

"Game over!" yells Aron over a loudspeaker. From a truck next to the camera van four three-inch fire hoses spray the attackers and they roll back from the tremendous thrusts of water.

The two totally painted men rise and wipe off their eyes and simply push the gate open. Aron runs up and hands them towels. "Fantastic! You guys were great! Now don't touch me. OK, camera three, close in. Get the babes in here. OK, hug them. Babes, get painted. That's it. Demeri, your bikini's coming off. OK, audio go! Congratulations to the winning team of Bolderdoj and Rastjahmon. You won! How does it feel?"

"Like Flipper when he was stung by two hundred jellyfish," says Toby.

"Here's your check for ten thousand dollars—unless, of course, you'd like to try for double-or-nothing next week against the cops and thugs?"

Doj and Toby look each other up and down, start laughing and flinging paint at each other. Doj starts a primal victory howl until it crescendos to a piercing scream, ending in an embrace.

Toby holds Doj at arm's length, blinks through the paint and says, "We're the same color, after all, mon, the Bolderdoj and I!"

Sunday, October 3rd, Taft Vandren's back yard, 185 East Hansen, 5:32 p.m.

Taft lifts the lid on the grill and flips the three thick halibut steaks. Toby breathes the aroma deeply and sighs in anticipation as Taft says, "I hope you guys like this jerk sauce I'm glazing the halibut with. My own recipe—just a touch of ginger and a hint of real maple syrup and a few other secret ingredients. I think you'll like it."

"I can't believe they're still showing reruns of our *Crossfire* on MTV," muses Doj. "It's been over two weeks. I wonder if we're supposed to get residuals like those castaways on *Gilligan's Island*."

"I wonder if I'll ever get the last of this paint out of my fingernails and braids," says Toby, picking.

"You've still got a little red on your ear, Rastjahmon," says Taft. "That's a good symbol for your startling vehemence. I particularly loved the part when you went back to the pit and fired off a few rounds for good measure."

"Your aura was red, Rastjahmon, but then, so was most of your body," laughs Doj.

"You looked like a melting flag, Bolderdoj."

Along with the halibut Taft serves asparagus tips with a dilled hollandaise sauce, and sesame fried wild rice with snap peas and shredded baby carrots. For only the second time since June Doj sips on alcohol, Mouton Cadet, red '97. He pours a second glass.

"A little concerned about tomorrow, Mr. Bolderton?" Taft asks.

"Yes, I am. The astronomers have scheduled a news conference for one o'clock Pacific time. I think we know what they'll say; the Tennyson's not coming. But I wonder why they are all still gathering at the Palomar on Tuesday."

"In the paper today the astronomer Tennyson said they were to go over the data one more time. He said there were a lot of variables. It seems some of the astronomers have projected slightly different paths."

"Ahhh, Bolderdoj, the comet would have done away with so many bad people, but some very good ones, too. They're going to pre-empt *Days of Our Lives* for the astronomers. I do so look forward to the unraveling of human lives each weekday."

"Don't forget to bring me your water-sampling bottles, Taft. I've got a Yellowstone tour tomorrow. I'll find out when I get back to town, around seven o'clock. Only if the comet's coming will the pagans bow down before the one who is Alpha and the Essence."

"Pass the butter," says Taft.

Monday, October 4th, Palomar Observatory, 1:01 p.m. P.S.T.

Dr. Spencer Tennyson and his assistant walk out of the door and sit at chairs to the left of the podium at the long table. The television cameras light up the meeting room and the reporters turn their attention from each other and toward the two men.

"Tennyson looks tired," says the *Los Angeles Times* reporter. "Worn out."

"It's not coming, you can tell by his expression," answers the Sacramento Bee reporter.

Dr. Tennyson begins, "Ladies and gentlemen of the media, we'd like to thank you for making the long, winding trek back up to Mount Palomar. Regarding the Tennyson Comet, it has been beyond opposition for approximately forty-seven hours. The eight most powerful observatories have again collected data on its path. At this time there is nothing new to report from our statement of September first. Again, we can say with almost absolute certainty that there is no chance the Tennyson will approach Earth's orbit. Are there questions?"

"There's been no alteration in its path since it went into opposition?"

"No. Whatever perturbed it before caused its path to veer so that it will probably not come closer than Jupiter's orbit."

"Can we be sure that something else won't smack into it again and cause it to come our way?"

"Nothing *smacked into it,*" says Tennyson sharply. "Perturbed means something altered the comet's course by gravitational pull. There is a small chance, statistically—one percent at *p* value of 0.005—that something *collided* with it. But at any rate the eight of us will meet here in three weeks to again compare readouts, employ an upgraded statistical analysis system multiple depression program, chart its precise trajectory."

The female reporter from the San Francisco Chronicle stands. "What is your reaction to the fact that a cab driver in Wyoming predicted a comet would hit Earth late in 1999, a prediction which would fulfill biblical prophesy, and that during the week the citizens of the world believed this prophesy was being fulfilled, crime statistics around the world plummeted? Some referred to the event as the Dawn of Enlightenment and proof of the Second Coming of Christ?"

Tennyson turns to his assistant, Langdon Stofford, the former Nobel winner, now in his mid-fifties, who says, "We do not, will not, and are not qualified to comment on such matters. We are scientists."

"Are there any further questions?" asks Tennyson.

There is a pause as notebooks close, cameras start to be disassembled. "Are you guys pulling for the Astros in the playoffs?"

There is laughter among the reporters.

Tennyson and his assistant rise and Tennyson says, "Well, we'd better not say. It may upset the Dodger fans listening," and they exit.

Tuesday, October 12th. Columbus Day. South Boone Creek drainage, Targhee National Forest. 4:52 p.m.

The Shawnee Indian name for elk is wapiti, which means white rump, from the basketball-sized white patch of fur at their rear; they are the second-largest member of the deer family, after moose. They migrated over the land bridge from Asia during the last ice age and splintered into an eastern species (now extinct); a desert species which grew to 1000 pounds (also extinct); and a rocky mountain species which is concentrated in the Greater Yellowstone ecosystem, some 30,000 animals. They birth in late May or early June. To avoid predators, the vulnerable calves are born with camouflage and no scent. Within hours they can stand. Within two days they can run alongside the herd. Rut is September to October—one male may mate with as many as twenty females in his 'harem.' Wolves were reintroduced into the ecosystem in 1995 as a way of naturally controlling their numbers, because the elimination of predators *Canis lupis* (the gray wolf) and *Ursus arctos horribilis* (the grizzly bear) had minimized the effect of the natural system of checks and balances. Now the elk must also be aware of the hunter, for their flesh is delicious to the primate *Homo sapien*.

Just before dusk a cow elk grazing by Boone Creek just south of Yellowstone Park is alert. In the sparse moonlight the night before, she lost contact with the rest of the harem, but the grass by the creek is green and luscious, and her hunger is stronger than her fear; the rut has drained some of her energy, and the migration off Pitchstone Plateau during the snowstorm two nights previous has left her in need of calories. She does not see the three hunters spread out fifty yards apart from each other, approaching from a cluster of fallen lodgepole pines; they creep up on her from behind.

The hunter in the orange cap in the center silently hand signals to his partner fifty yards up the wooded slope. He points for him to shoot then gestures . . . ten seconds . . . nine . . . eight. . . .

At three, the hunter down slope steps on a branch; the snap instantly sends the elk bounding up the slope, zigzagging for the trees. A staccato blast of gunfire breaks the silence, but none of the bullets impact the frightened animal. She bolts farther into the woods, but just before she is beyond their range, she falls heavily to the ground, as if her legs had been pulled from beneath her. She tries to rise but falls again, then she goes into spasm, kicking, as if she were still running away from the unknown horror.

The hunters let out war cries as they run down the small embankment, jump Boone Creek and scramble up the other side.

"I think I got her right in the shoulder. Keep runnin'. If she bolts, I might have to git her again."

"You asshole, *I* got her from the right. I'll betcha that half-gallon of Jack Daniels."

"You're on, shitbrains."

A guttural growl comes from the men's left and the men stop abruptly at the top of the rise. Wide-eyed, flinching, they jerk their rifles in that direction.

"*Shit!*"

"Look ou'!"

Running toward them, dressed in tree-gray and pine-needle-brown polypropylene, is Doj, a bow and quiver of arrows strapped over his shoulder, his knife strapped at his side. He sees the orange hats and vests of the hunters and skids to a stop.

"Hey!" he cries, putting up his hands. "Me, guy—not elk!"

As they lower their guns, Doj springs by them in four long strides, pulling out his knife as he runs to the struggling animal. He severs her jugular vein in one smooth slice. The blood gushes out and the hunters charge up as the ungulate convulses five times and dies.

"What the hell you doin'?"

"Stop right there, get away from my animal!"

Doj rises, backs up, and puts his hands on his hips. "It's *my* animal. *I* shot her."

"Bullshit," says the oldest of the three hunters. "Just back on up and get out of here. We've put up with. . . ."

"I should just kick your ass right here," says the youngest. "You were the one who threw me up in the statue. You embarrassed me. Just get the hell out of here with your little toy bow and arrow. Go on now. Start backing up," says the youngest of the three hunters.

"Wait a minute. You guys were behind me in line when I got

my permit. What are you assholes doing out here? I heard you tell the ranger you wanted a permit for zone seven—what'd you say? As far away from 'the cab driver devil worshipper as you could get?'"

"We overheard him say this was a pretty active elk route. We registered for zone seven, but we changed our minds," says the middle-aged hunter.

"You know," says the oldest, "hunting can be a dangerous sport, and sometimes people can accidently get shot, especially if they're not wearing the right colors. But of course you know that—you're God."

Doj says, "I do know this zone is bow-hunting only. I believe zone seven is three miles from here." He points and mocks their accent. "Past them thar hills."

"Well we didn't *know* that. Now I'm warning you for the last time, get away from my game."

"If it's your elk, why does she have one of my arrows sticking out of her heart?"

"Bullshit," says the youngest. He lowers his rifle and approaches the animal, which has surrendered to death in a pool of her own blood, assuming its death mask of fright. And sure enough, at the shoulder, broken in half from where the animal fell on it, is a red-quilled arrow.

Doj asks effeminately, mocking them, "Those guns don't fire *arrows*, do they?"

"Son of a bitch, he killed the thing with one arrow and we couldn't hit her once with twenty shots."

"Actually two." Doj points back at a tree where an arrow protrudes. "I'm not perfect, not like you guys. You guys were a perfect zero for twenty."

"You wise-ass. That's all of the bullshit I'm going to take from you," says the youngest hunter. He raises his gun toward Doj. "It was a hunting accident—don't you two see it that way?"

When the middle-aged hunter smiles, the young hunter draws a breath and takes quick aim at Doj's torso.

"Put down your guns, Rotshots, or the Rastjahmon will make you like holes in your ozone." He's pointing a Browning 300 Win-Mag at the hunters from behind a tree. They do not comply immediately, and he fires a bullet into the tree next to one of the hunters, sending splinters flying.

"Ooohhh damn! How *do* you work this thing? Let me try that again."

The three men simultaneously drop their rifles and Doj laughs as he moves to pick them up. "Geez, something stinks around here. Did one of you guys, by any chance, drop a load at the same time you dropped your guns?" He ejects the bullets. "OK, all the ammunition into the Rastjah pack. Don't you just *love* those colors on him?"

"You bastards," says the oldest hunter. "You guys are queers, aren't you?"

"Ammunition in here, before Toby takes a little more practice with that gun. Blow a hole in a grizzly, it would—powerful gun. That's it. That round in your shirt pocket, too. Good boy. I won't throw you up in the tree or anything—that bark scratches fair and sensitive skin—but I don't want you to go away mad. I know that not getting your elk is a bruised male ego thing with you testosterone-ridden, gladiator types, so. . . ." Doj steps back to straddle the elk and pulls out his knife. From the tender backside he makes two crescent cuts and lifts out an eight-inch portion of meat. "Does anyone else like theirs rare?" The three hunters' expressions change to disgust and horror.

"No? Well, *I* do!" Doj takes a bite out of the center and chews it thoughtfully.

Toby says, "Maybe these gentlemen have some jerk sauce with them. Hey, you jerks have any sauce?"

"You guys are sick. You're devil worshippers, aren't you? There's no room in the world for *preverts* like you two," says the oldest, staring away from Doj.

"Oh yeah, we've got a great campsite where we practice voodoo. We piss and shit right in the stream, because that's the kind of netherworld spirits we are. At night we perform intimate, scintillating dances using bald eagle feathers and moose dewlaps. Available on video. Now, hit the trail, little buckaroos. Maybe we can meet down at the Cowboy Bar this Friday, for old times sake. We'll invite Game and Fish. Play some Trivial Pursuit. Do RSVP ASAP. Bye now."

The three hunters turn and stalk down the bank. The middle-aged hunter throws a hand backwards, holding up a middle finger. "Those sons of bitches," can be heard amidst a barrage of curses as they march up the other side, into the trees. Rastjahmon sits on the bank with his rifle, watching in that direction; Doj neatly guts the fresh game while singing a soft song.

Anthropologists study humans. Their customs, origins, and behaviors. They tell us that the primitive hunters who would become humans evolved around the Rift Valley in Africa some four million years ago; fire and tools have been around for about two million years. Eventually fire enabled humans to live in places they otherwise could not. The fire ring became the focal point for safety, warmth, cooking, customs, rituals, storytelling. Now, at the end of the twentieth century, and long after the necessity to do so, civilized humans are drawn to recreate the campfire ritual. Look among the hills, valleys, lakes, streams, forests or mountains across the United States on any summer evening—campfires dot the landscape. Around these campfires ideas and lives are talked about, plans shared; often one simply gazes at the ephemeral fingers of flame as if hypnotized, or they are transfixed by the glowing white center, contemplating the forces of the elements in nature, the forces in the universe, or the forces at play in their lives. The last one to stay up with the fire always feels smugly superior, it is their fire then, they are free to stare into the pulsating white center of their innermost thoughts.

There is a campfire south of Yellowstone National Park, near Boone Creek, on this night. The white man and the black man lean back against thick logs. Doj is alternately reading, for the fourth time, the letter he'd received from Lisen that morning, and scripting his thoughts to her; he cannot seem to convey the emptiness he'd felt after she'd left that summer morning, and the yearning he now has to hold her, kiss her. He writes: "It will take a millennium to share with you all the thoughts I've wanted to since those first sweet but too brief days. You filled my heart and soul with fire and roses, with. . . ."

"This damn smoke!" Toby, arches his back and tries to wave it away.

"I told you smoke follows beauty," Doj laughs. He sets his notebook aside and leans forward, holding out his hands to the four-foot flames; it is a chilly fall night in the mountains, and a big fire was mandatory.

"Third damn time I moved from this seat. They need to make a hammock on rollers for this backpacking stuff. In Jamaica, our bonfire always behaves, because there is always a little breeze drifting onto the beach, and our fingers do not fall off like in this god-forsaken, frigid Antarctica with pine trees."

Doj tosses his down-filled sleeping bag over the flames to him. "The cold air comes down the valley at night and back up in the morning. Slip into that and take a few hits off that Rastjah-herb. I think you're still a little jittery from those hunters."

"Aahhh yes, this is better." Toby wiggles deep inside the lofty bag until he is comfortable. "Yes, for a moment today I forgot those were not paint pellets."

"Good thing we borrowed Taft's Browning. You thought it was for the big grizz."

"It's staying here by Rastjahmon's side. Rastjah never go into the water without a spear gun for the shark. These grizzlies are like some giant, mountain-shark."

"There used to be many when the first trappers got here. They called the grizzly Old Ephraim. The largest had a jaw eighteen inches across and weighed a thousand pounds. They're only a few left in this entire twelve million acre wilderness ecosystem now. Our odds are pretty small."

"Ahhh yes, but once I dropped a bar of wet soap and it landed on the small edge. Do not worry. The Rastjahmon is a great and famous killer. He is not frightened. Today I killed three vicious trout. Wait till you taste the young succulent fishes cooking in the lemon and red onion and garlic and kind herbs."

Doj rotates his elk steak, sizzling above the fire and turning brown. "You'll join me for a little wapiti filet, yes?"

"No, Bolderdoj, meat makes one too aggressive. I stay with the fish, brain food." Toby leans forward and quickly flips the aluminum foil-wrapped fish.

They stay up long into the night, talking, eating, laughing. Since Doj got his elk, there is no reason to wake up early. Throughout the night Doj sips on Maxiciser, a concoction of Taft's, a drink of vitamins, minerals, amino acids and glucose polymers that supplies replenishment to the muscles and minerals to the brain, and Rastjahmon occasionally puffs on a thick cigarette of *Cannabis sativa*, which inspires a round of flute playing, during which Doj fades in and out, intermittently singing or playing his harmonica.

"Ahhh, Bolderdoj, we play in so much harmony. Perhaps we need some dissonance so that Old Ephraim does not come to listen."

"I can play and draw all the animals of the forest in if you'd like—maybe two of each, like Noah waiting for the flood."

"Bolderdoj, my good new friend these three months, perhaps now, with only the trees and flames of the fire listening, you can tell the Rastjahmon how you came to call yourself the son of the white God; and how you can look into the future and past, and how you make light with the flick of your finger."

Doj pushes a burnt-through log back toward the center of the fire, but he hits one of the supporting logs with his pusher stick and the structure collapses, sending sparks spiraling upwards into the night air.

"Prescience. Knowledge of things before they happen. I look toward the future and I worry. Without intervention it will get very bad in the first years of the next millennium. The thin little shell which supports seven billion people cannot do so much longer. Goodness, beauty and honor will be trampled by the sheer numbers of carbon-based reasoning intelligence here on planet number three."

Doj holds his hands to the warming fire and looks up at the star-filled night sky. "My message was simple: with cooperation we could start a new, balanced world filled with dignity and respect; we could understand the role of every life form. I had a chance to do my part, but it looks like I am alone again in this unsettled world. My cataclysmic vision is being replaced by glimpses of a more fearful and somber life. My hope and faith are being replaced by doubt."

"And what is it that you now doubt?"

Doj selects another branch, breaks it in two. "Toby, can I tell you something?"

"I am two ears. One for Ephraim, one for you."

"You are the only friend I've ever had."

"Ohhh, how can that be true?"

"It's true. I lost my parents. When I walked out of the desert I focused all my energy in training to compete because I never wanted to lose anything again. I am the culmination of what's evolved from two million years of human development. Like civilization, I was always striving to know more, to win once more, to conquer more. I thought if I could know everything and win at everything I would be at the top—above pain and loss. I have never harnessed my quest for knowledge, or for victory over those more or less strong of mind and body than me. That is why I never took the time to form a lasting alliance with another human, and why I cannot share the ganja with you—it clouds my brain from concentrating on the game, it makes me not want to compete."

"Then give up the competition, Bolderdoj. There is no need for it. You come back to Jamaica with Rastjahmon and we play the music at night at my Uncle Jenolee's club and snorkel all day and be strong and send our cares out to the ocean, where the sharks wait to feed on them."

"That's what I'm best at—running away. As soon as I near completion of something, as soon as I am about to make my world a better place, a place where joy and reasoning may triumph, I stop—then go on to another project, another world. Completion means a fulfillment, an ending. But life never ends and civilization is never fulfilled. The closer I get to the top, the more frightened I become, and the harder it is to look down, or look back. This time, finally, I must finish what I am destined to complete."

"What is it you need to complete now, Bolderdoj—and why should the Rastjahmon help you?"

Doj lays a new branch on the fire, lays a smaller one crossways, then stares into the fire for several heartbeats. "Will you trust me?"

Toby gazes away from the fire, looks at Doj, says quietly, "I have seen your aura and know you speak truly, from the very marrow of your heart bone. You have questions and doubts now. The Rastjahmon has been very close to the spirit, and close to you. I will stay by your side, perhaps together we can discover the correct path through this present life. If your worldly existence was to end the Rastjahmon can tell you—your next one will be beautiful if you keep your spirit in the same good light. I will trust you, Bolderdoj."

"Then know, Rastjahmon, Toby Tiler, my friend and blood of my blood, genes of my genes we shared so many years ago, that the things I say are true. I *am* a messenger and I was brought here to let the world know of the imminent destruction of life."

"Why would God want to destroy the life on this planet? There are many good souls."

"The good is being smothered by the sheer numbers of humanity. Forty thousand children die every day on our planet, mostly to starvation. Evil is finally overwhelming the good, who must stay behind locked doors, huddling together with other good souls; so often now even family cannot always be trusted. Police are frequently worse than those they protect, government officials are corrupt, church leaders are dishonest, and the environment and its resources are being depleted. It would get very bad in the first years of the next millennium." He holds his hands to the warming fire and looks up at the star-filled night sky. "But it looks like the master has changed his mind anyway. Perhaps he believes as you do, that if there's one good spirit, one newborn child, there is always hope; if we could survive and learn how to coexist with each other and with the forces of nature, then he is forced to hope as well. Perhaps that is why you have been sent to me. You embody that hope."

"Ahhh Bolderdoj, it is very kind of you to see the Rastjahmon in that light; he tries to keep it pure. But the Rastjahmon found his spirit when he saw the bright light. Tell me about your light, and the master who means to change the world."

"Words came to me; and the words spoke of compassion for *all* of earth's creatures. The masters—there are many—hold an admiration and wonderment for *all* living things which evolved here; even if they are aggressive and hunt and kill other entities to survive, the masters can understand this. One hundred-and-fifty million human beings have been killed in wars during this century; and many more from crime, hate, and revenge, made easier because weapons were invented so the murderer did not have to see the expression of the victims. It's the fact that humans are trying to play God which initially sent the comet. The masters' hope was that those who survive would start anew and treat the earth and all of its inhabitants better than before. His hope was that we would grow up after the comet."

"Tell me, Bolderdoj, will the Rastjahmon go to heaven?"

"You've been there once—why would you want to go somewhere you've already been?" Doj holds a serious gaze for only moments before he laughs, then Toby laughs with him and looks away.

"Tell me more, my good Bolderdoj. What does God look like?"

"The starlit night sky and this ant crawling on my leg, the mountains and the oceans, the sun which gives everything life."

"Aaahhh yes, the light. Always the light. The scientists said the comet would make a cloud, a cloud which would block the light. The sun gives you power and that we share too. But there is something you're not telling the Rastjahmon, it is more evident than the orange light on your face. The Rastjahmon, he knows your many shades now, Bolderdoj."

Doj leans forward, crosses his elbows over his drawn-up knees, puts his head on his arms and gazes into the flame.

"Aaahhh, that is it, Bolderdoj. Not often lately have I seen the peace color. Now, finally, your light is not agitating."

Doj looks Toby in the eye. With discernible effort he says, "Do you remember our chess match?"

"Of course. A brilliant sacrifice of your rook, right when the spirit of Rastja had surrounded you."

Doj stares into the fire for five slow heartbeats. "Yes . . . well . . . I was having a difficult time discerning a way out of that position. You had played brilliantly. Do you remember? . . ."

Gunshots shatter the calm. Fired from behind Toby and Doj in rapid succession, different guns with different reports. Doj twists until he is lying down behind the log he had been resting on. Bullets whistle through the woods, hitting branches and trunks above them, the ground around them.

"Get down, Toby!"

Rastjahmon rolls over, to the ground, looking like a giant green caterpillar wiggling frantically in his sleeping bag, trying to scoot behind the log. Just as he is about to duck, a bullet slams into Toby's back, near his left shoulder, and blood flies from the impact point. Some of the drops land in the fire, the blood hisses and disappears in a tiny red flame.

"Toby!" Doj screams.

"I got one!" comes from somewhere in the night forest. "I got the nigger!"

Toby cries out but his expression shows only shocked surprise, as if a unicorn had just walked through their camp.

Doj starts to crawl around to his friend, and to the loaded rifle by Toby's side, but bullets explode all around him and he realizes fire is coming from at least two different angles. Another bullet hits the ground inches from his ear; he rolls backwards, away from the fire. As bullets continue to impact nearby and whiz over him, Doj darts away from the fire, grabbing his bow and quiver of arrows from a branch as he crouches and sprints blindly into the darkness.

Now there are fewer shots, and a longer time before the bullets go zinging through the woods.

"Jesus God!" Doj prays under his breath. He finds a lodgepole pine he can hide behind; he can make out the three hunters from earlier that day appearing in the firelight.

Toby pleads frantically, "Doj, help me!"

One of the hunters shines a bright light in Doj's direction so he turns sideways to the log, barely concealing himself.

Doj hears a drunken slur. "Ya got the nigger, Frankie. You have the honors of finishing him off. Well, look at this—he's got some of this devil weed."

As the black man writhes on the ground beneath him, the older hunter picks up the joint, lights it with a burning twig, then extinguishes the joint and the twig in Toby's gaping wound, causing him to cry out in agony; then Toby passes out. Just as the hunter stands to light the twig again an arrow whistles through the air, but misses its intended target: it goes through the thick clothes and pierces the left shoulder of the oldest man, just below his clavicle. He falls backwards.

"Son of a bitch!" yells the youngest hunter.

"Shine the light! Where is he?" The other hunters shoot wildly into the night, their spot light illuminating the surrounding forest.

The man jerks out the arrow, grabs Toby's towel, and presses it to his shoulder. "I'll live. We got to kill that other bastard. Keep your light shining out *there*, Chris. Tie the nigger up and we'll finish him off later. We'll make his death a slow one. Weren't you old slave boys happier when we chained you up at night so you wouldn't run off? You voodoo worshippers like to smoke that devil weed and get stuck with the pins, don't you? We can arrange that. Not too tight, Chris, no rope marks. This can still look like a hunting accident. That's good. Don't get cold, nigger. We'll put your rifle in the fire. We'll point it right at that red spot on your jacket. There, that should keep you warm. Now, let's go get that other slimy, long-haired bastard."

The other two hunters turn on their microspots mounted above their rifle sights, brightly illuminating the woods in any direction the guns are pointed. They take ten steps into the woods. Doj bolts from his place of concealment.

"There he is!"

"Bring 'em down, Chris!"

Doj darts back and forth, the light illuminates the pine forest, and though the bullets land all around, none find their target. He sprints to the right, then remembers he left the penlight in his chamois shirt. He pulls it out. Though the light is weak, he is able to leap over the deadfall and rocks. He runs until the lights and sounds of the hunters are faint in the distance behind him.

A million thoughts race through his mind, but one salient image pervades: his only friend lying tied up by the fire, possibly bleeding to death. Doj hooks his hair behind his ears and listens, hears them coming from afar.

"Master lord God anyone. I need you now."

Before he can determine a plan of action a weak light appears just above him. He ducks. The light sweeps to his right and Doj runs again, finding the creek. He follows it down for two hundred yards then runs back up into the woods.

Perhaps if I could circle around and get back to Toby. . . .

"Here's a footprint! He's over here this way!"

I'm still wearing my knife!

If I could circle back quickly I could cut the rope and carry Toby out of there. . . .

My eyes are adjusting to the night. Turn off the penlight. Don't let them see me. They're maybe 150 yards away.

"I'm going back to the fire in case he cuts back. I'm still bleeding like hell out here. Kill the bastard."

Doj can see all three lights in the woods to his right; one of the lights turns and starts back toward the campfire. He finds a large Douglas fir to hide behind; as the light passes his place of concealment, he darts fifty yards to a large Engelmann spruce, where he can see the campfire. As the spot swings by again he ducks then goes up the tree, climbing the sturdy lower branches until he is thirty feet high with a clear opening. He draws an arrow from his quiver, one of only three left, and fits it to the bow. He tries to control his breathing; his heart is pumping so strongly he cannot keep steady aim. The hunter will pass within forty yards of where Doj is perched. The hunter steps toward Doj, who can only make out a silhouette behind the bright light. He breathes out slowly, focuses in on a point, and releases the arrow. There is an abrupt "Aarrrggghhh!" and the spotlight is suddenly pointing up; the arrow has found its mark.

"I'm hit!" comes out in a low gasp, but loud enough to warn the other two hunters.

"He's got Harvey!"

"We're coming! Hold on!"

As they reach their fallen comrade their bright microspots reveal that Harvey has been shot through the heart; blood pulses from the pressure of the aortic valve, a foot-high arc, the thickness of a man's finger.

"Keep your eyes open! Shoot the bastard!" says Chris. He slings off his coat, then grabs the shaft of the arrow. He puts his foot on Harvey's torso to brace himself then jerks on the arrow, but it does not come out; the oldest hunter rolls on his side and winces in excruciating agony. The largest hunter pushes the arrow back in forcefully until it is pointing out of Harvey's back. He steps around, grabs the shaft just behind the arrowhead pulls it out cleanly through his heart and out his back. He lays his dying companion down and puts his wool jacket over the gushing wound. "Relax, Harvey."

"I don't see him unless he's behind one of those trees," says the youngest hunter, his shaky tone revealing a frightened tentativeness behind drunken courage. "Ya want me to go look?"

"Wait a sec. Ole Harvey's gone into shock. He'll be dead in a second. Nothing we can do now except find that son of a bitch and kill him like a mad dog."

Archery is a sport for those with calm nerves and motor/neuron control; as Doj slows his breathing his aim becomes steadier. He does not aim for the heart of the youngest—he has a heavy wool coat on over other layers, and the angle from above offers a different target. Doj sights carefully, then releases the taut string. The arrow whistles through the night and hits its target, it goes into the left eye socket and into the brain of the young hunter. He falls backwards, convulses on the ground.

He flings his gun skyward, then grasps at the arrow lodged in his eye, in his brain. His screams pierce the night and his crying words are unintelligible. He tries to jerk it out once but screams out in horror. On the second try he succeeds in pulling out the arrow, but his eyeball comes with it. He looks at it with his good eye and starts shaking uncontrollably, his trembling hand unable to stop the flow of blood coming from the deep socket.

Chris, the middle-aged hunter, sees that both arrows must have come from somewhere above him and he points his gun higher in the tree. He sees the outline of a bow . . . moving!

"Drop it right there!" he shouts, shooting as he advances toward the tree, the painful wailing of the younger man behind him.

"Chris, don . . . lea . . . me. . . ."

As the hunter approaches the big Engelmann spruce Doj appears on a branch above him, brightly lit, crouching, loading his last arrow and firing, all in one smooth movement. But Doj is blinded by the bright spot, so the hunter has time to duck behind a thin lodgepole; the arrow misses its mark. The hunter starts to fire at him and Doj moves behind the tree. The hunter's footsteps are approaching. Doj's mind flashes a million thoughts-per-second but he can come up with no plan of action. But then he hears a sound that brings a smile to his lips and some small joy to his heart: the sound of hammer striking the barrel without a cartridge.

Doj drops down to two lower branches, then swings off the third to drop twelve feet to the ground; he sprints toward the bright light.

The hunter has already taken a spare magazine out of his belt and with surprising speed and accuracy, faster than he's ever done it in his life, he places the new one in the chamber. He looks up and is startled to see the man that close, running at him with a knife in his hand with the look of a wounded, cornered animal. Chris does not raise his rifle and sight it, but simply fires from the waist. The first shot goes too low, then the hunter overcompensates and the second shot is too high; a third shot hits the upper part of his assailant's left leg.

It doesn't stop him.

Doj is upon the hunter. He knocks the rifle out of his way with his left hand and with the right hand he plunges the knife under the rib cage and up toward his heart and he gives it a quarter twist before he yanks it out, does it again. The hunter yells, not the ranting, piercing screams of the hunter shot through the eye, but more visceral, quieter. He falls back onto the ground, somehow still instinctively clutching the rifle he weakly tries to refocus on his attacker. Doj runs his knife across the inside of the wrist of the grunting hunter and wrests the rifle from his grasp. He holds the end of the barrel of the gun one inch from the man's left kneecap and fires. The man screams then, piercing the night louder than the echoes of the gunshot.

"Don't go nowhere," Doj says with a sneer.

Doj sees, feels that the bullet which hit him just grazed his leg; he ignores it. Shining the microspot, he walks fifty feet to where the youngest hunter is lying, still shaking, whimpering like a freezing animal, now with a red bandana pressed against his eyeless socket.

In a low, guttural growl Doj says, "Anyone around here missing an eye? Oh? You? Well, don't let it go to your head!" He leans down to pull the hunter up by his wool coat. "Listen, you son of primordial soup, you shot my friend, the only friend I've ever had. I'm not going to kill you yet because if he dies, your death will take a very long time." He drags the babbling young man through the woods toward the campfire. "You know, I hear hot rocks work well as replacement parts. We could paint a little pupil on the rock, no one would know the difference from the original, which *was* a tad bloodshot."

Doj drops the hunter when he sees Toby lying unconscious in a large pool of blood, snapping him back to the immediacy of the situation. Doj runs the last fifty yards, tosses two more logs on the fire, props up the rifle so the microspot beam shines on his injured friend, then presses two fingers against Toby's throat—the carotid artery still has a pulse. Weak, but there.

"Toby, I'm gonna get you out of here, brother."

He cuts the ropes; Toby still has breath but it, too, is weak. The immediate concern is the blood he has lost. Doj swiftly cuts, fashions, and applies a tourniquet, with square patches over the entry and exit wounds, at the least the bullet must have hit a major vein. He knows he will have to carry Toby two miles back to the Rastjahmon, then pray he makes it to the ranger station and wouldn't they have blood there? If not, another hour to Jackson . . . or a helicopter. . . . Doj then becomes aware of his own bleeding. He quickly cuts through his jeans and the layer of polypropylene tights and tapes a patch over his thigh wound.

"Doctor . . . please . . . God," comes from one of the hunters in the night.

"Chris, come get me!" screams the younger hunter.

"Hey, you two should get together," says Doj, "have a little party for old time's sake. I'll send a doctor, but the only doctor I know's a psychologist. But then again, you guys could tell him about your problems, because right now you guys have some *major* problems. You know, your inner child has really. . . ."

Doj stops; he hears a sound in the woods. He grabs the gun and points it at . . . a large gray wolf, which retreats behind a tree, looks back, then trots off into the darkness. Doj hears another sound to his right and shines the light on a second wolf, then a third; each, in turn, retreats. But not before Doj notices that all three are foaming at the mouth . . . they are rabid.

"Well now, you guys *do* have some problems. I hope my doctor friend gets up here before it's too late, because, you know, wolfophobia can be a very *real* fear at times."

Doj hoists Toby onto his back. Bending at the waist he lashes Toby's hands around his chest, then lashes his feet together, ankles crossed in front of him, so he carries his unconscious friend like a backpack. He flings the sleeping bag behind him, over Toby's back, and anchors it between their bodies, knowing that keeping him warm will help his chances for survival. He picks up the rifle again and shines it quickly around, noticing that the three wolves have moved closer.

"Well, Harvey's going to be rude and not say goodbye, I guess, so buenas noches to you. Hey Frankie, did you ever hear that country song, "Don't it Make My Brown Eye Blue?" You should learn it. Maybe Chris will hum a few bars for you. You're gonna have some background harmony in a minute or two. Bye, guys."

When he is gone, and with the firelight dimming the surroundings, the three wolves move in closer, drawn by the smell of human blood.

Although the rifle is cumbersome, Doj keeps it in one hand while holding onto Toby's hands with his other. Besides providing protection, the microspot illuminates the forest far better than Doj's penlight, so it is worth the weight. He sweats profusely by the time he reaches Boone Creek and the trail out, but he keeps on at a slow jog.

Although it is an estimated two mile trek, Doj is back at the van in less than twenty minutes. As his physical strength is nearly spent and his knees start to buckle a logical thought of true horror crosses his mind: where is the key?

He says a silent prayer as he unties Toby's feet and hands, and gently lets him down. He pushes the sweat-and blood-soaked sleeping bag away, stills his own hard breathing, then checks the carotid artery again—the pulse is weaker, and the breathing shallower, than at the camp. He checks the front left pocket of

Toby's pants—no key. He checks the front right pocket and his fingers surround something flat and solid—the car key!

"Thank God!"

He unlocks the side door, slides it open, then lifts Toby inside and lays him on the mattress. The Rastjahmon's head turns and he calmly babbles several syllables, something about Annie. Perhaps he feels some comfort in familiar surroundings.

As Doj backs out, then drives down the dirt road, he notices the first lighting of a new day.

All that training, and I'm not prepared for the most important game.

"We're gonna be all right, Rastjahmon, you just hang on back there."

Doj must reach back and steady Toby when he goes around the gravel turns, lest he rolls off the mattress. Twenty minutes later he pulls up to the ranger station at the south entrance of Yellowstone. Lights are on in a residence. Doj comes to a screeching halt at the front door, honking the thin, whiny Volkswagen horn with one hand as he reaches back with the other. Toby has no pulse.

Doj gets out. "Help! I need help!" he yells at the cabin. As he reaches the van's sliding door, the ranger opens his front door, casting an orange light in the predawn stillness. As Doj breathes two quick breaths into Toby's lungs and starts to push down on his sternum, the half-dressed ranger appears at his side.

"He's been shot, lost a lot of blood, no respiration, no pulse."

Fourteen minutes later they are in a park service helicopter heading for Jackson. The chopper lifts off to meet the sun's first rays over Mount Leidy while the ranger and Doj continue CPR, fifteen thrusts for every two breaths, but Toby does not respond.

The helicopter tilts due south at maximum velocity, and in only twenty minutes the descending craft finds the St. John's Hospital emergency crew awaiting them by the helipad. Toby's symptoms have been radioed ahead; it's not the first hunter shooting they've ever seen. In seconds Toby Tiler is on a gurney and disappearing through the large swinging door.

The helicopter pilot switches off the motor and the blades start their long deceleration. He crouches and walks under the chopper blades then puts his arm around the man whose name he doesn't know, who's displaying symptoms of shock.

Doj watches the swinging door come to a halt before he realizes that Toby is not in the arms he is holding out. The ranger walks toward them and Doj becomes aware that the pilot has been speaking right next to him.

The ranger says, "Come with me, Mr. Bolderton, you've got a wound that needs looking after, too. We need to get you lying down, and you've got to try to relax a little." The ranger escorts Doj through the swinging door. "Now, why don't you tell me what happened out there?"

Doj relates the macabre events of the previous afternoon and early morning. The ranger leaves to call in the location of the three hunters. Doj is alone.

"No. This cannot and will not happen. There can be no more loss. If you leave me powerless and helpless I will make the world pay."

Still in his blood-soaked clothes, he starts to walk down the hall when he sees the nurse disappear into the emergency room three doors down. He follows her in, but she turns around and with no hesitation ushers the dazed man out of the room.

"We're doing what we can," she says. "You need to get looked at yourself, let me call."

"I'm OK right here. I won't leave. The Rastjahmon is hurt. . . ."

"Then you have to wait right here. Promise me?"

"I'll wait."

Doj leans against the wall, staring blankly through the emergency room window swinging back and forth in front of him, but he can only see the profile of a male attendant looking down, then up to a machine next to him. Doj turns to a drinking fountain and suddenly becomes aware of the incredible dryness in his throat; he is not aware of how much he sweated, or the last time he drank liquid. He drinks deeply now, visions of the previous night flashing before his closed lids. He remembers the wolves and finds some gratification in hoping the hunters each had died a justifiably horrid death.

Then Doj sees a phone and instinctively starts dialing the only number he knows to dial, 555-6608, the number of his neighbor, his landlord, Taft Vandren.

"Hospital operator, can I help you?"

"I'm trying to dial out."

"You must first dial nine and wait for a dial. . . ."

Doj dials and Taft answers after one ring. "Toby's been shot."

Doj briefly describes what has happened.

"I'm on my way."

When Doj hangs up he is startled by the sound of an electric 'whhhooommmppp!' Doj knows the sound: The doctor is electro-shocking Toby's heart in the hope that it may beat on its own again.

Minutes later he hears the ugly jolt again and he starts to shake—from fear, or from the tension of the only friend he's ever had being gravely injured, or is it the physical fatigue after a superhuman effort? Just as his sobs accompany his uncontrollable shakes, Taft comes in, momentarily takes a wrong turn, then sees Doj leaning against the wall.

As Taft approaches Doj rises and throws his arms around the elder man.

"Doj, you're injured. We need to. . . ."

The emergency room door swings slowly toward them; two doctors and a nurse step outside. The doctor takes off the gloves as he looks Doj in the eye.

"I'm sorry, he didn't make it."

A wail, a growl that is like nothing human wells up from inside Doj Bolderton. As he raises his arms above him he seems to grow. He turns and marches away, his shrill wail growing louder and more discordant. Taft and the doctor follow him. It is weird, the inhuman wailing, Doj's arms rolling in the air above him, as if he is in a strange trance. Doj does not hear Taft say to the doctor, "Did you try everything?"

"We tried electro-shocking him, and he's had almost a total blood transfusion—he'd lost over five pints. He'd been without oxygen for probably ten minutes and his core temperature has dropped to ninety degrees. We tried everything we could."

"I'll take care of Doj," says Taft.

"Get him back in here. It looks like he's had a leg wound."

Taft walks up behind Doj, who's leaning against a plate glass window. Taft is startled when he puts his hand on the young man's back—he had expected tears and more uncontrollable emotion, but he sees a face so set in resolve that he steps back.

"I want to have a little talk with God," Doj states tersely.

Taft does not reply but simply nods; Doj can see the reflection of Taft's lined face in the sterile hospital window.

"And I want to have a talk with the people of this darling little valley. Let's go."

Doj walks off, Taft following. "Wait a moment . . . that man has a bullet wound. . . ." trails off behind the two men as the automatic doors come to a mechanical stop.

As they make a right turn onto Broadway a car with Sheriff Clark turns into the hospital parking lot followed by a cruiser with Police Chief Nuxhall.

"Where to?" asks Taft.

"KJVI studios—the local morning news comes on in eight minutes. I think it's time they had a guest speaker. They will learn."

Taft is silent as they wait for a light at the town square. Taft glances at Doj whose jaw is set with firm resolve. When the light changes, he says, "How would you like to speak to the whole country?"

Doj turns to him. "How?"

"They've got uplink capability now, they broadcast to Cody, Driggs; they can transmit. If a colleague at CNN will receive, you'll be nationwide."

Doj leads Taft into the second floor television studio. Bill Francis, the station manager, is looking over the shoulder of his morning newscaster—she's frantically typing. He looks up and does a double-take. "What in God's name . . . what happened to you, Doj?"

"Billy, you need to help me."

"May I use your phone?" Taft heads straight to the phone in the station manager's office before the startled newscaster can reply.

She says, "You have to hit nine first."

"Doj, what happened?" Bill asks. "You're bloody."

"My best friend was murdered last night. It's time to catch the perpetrators. We need to get an all points bulletin out. Will you let me on?"

"What, are ya nuts? The last show you did was the most-watched thing we ever aired—we're *still* getting calls. Our topic story for this morning was how alfalfa is up eighteen cents a ton from last year, so it's all yours, brother. Two minutes to go. You want to get cleaned up?"

"No, let them see the *Sangre de Christo*."

"Ten . . . nine . . . eight. . . ."

As Doj steps in front of the world and weather maps, to the left of the news desk, Taft steps between a camera and a light bar and says softly, "You're linked, Doj."

Doj nods slightly and his jaw set in determination.

The red light comes on and the camera focuses in on the pretty, dark-haired newscaster, with her perfect makeup, perfect lips, perfect self-esteem being exuded through perfect political correctness.

"Good morning, and welcome to the Jackson-Hole-Hold-Onto-Your-Coffee-Cups Wake-Up Show. This morning we are deviating from our normal format to report on a murder which has just occurred here in Teton County. With a special report we go to a man who brought nationwide attention to Jackson Hole earlier this summer when he claimed to be and then appeared to prove that he was a messenger from God, heralding the end of the world. Doj Bolderton, you were at the crime scene. Can you tell us what just happened out there?"

Camera two's light comes on. Doj peers into the lens, seeing his reflection, seeing the faces of hundreds of thousands of people on the other side of the lens. He raises his head, then looks straight into the lens.

"There is no God. I lied." He turns and paces between the camera and the world map, pauses, then looks into the lens again. "You remember me—everyone reads *USA Today*, watches the evening news—I said I was the messenger of God. I lied. I am a messenger, but I have come here to prove to you that there *is* no God. Because if there was, twelve million people wouldn't have died from AIDS. A God with any power would not have let

Courtney Segal, the girl from Florida, be kidnapped, tortured and murdered last week; she was seven years old and was still clutching the ear of her favorite teddy bear when the police found her. If there was a God we wouldn't have been under the misguided notion that humans hold dominion over every other plant and animal on the surface of the earth, and used that justification to plunder, subdue, control, enslave, kill, mount, burn or destroy anything that got in our way these past two thousand years—and more so in this blood thirsty and greediest of centuries known to man. A true god, a fair god, would not allow this. Nor would he or she create all men equal, then allow them to become so unequal these past hundred years.

"Yes! It is true. There is *no penalty* for the kinds of lives we've led—lives of greed and selfishness and the subordination of every other living thing. It's human nature, and it will never change. There is no hell, so you can just go out and take what you want, there are no penalties. If you have enough money, you can get away with murder. What do you think, that you're going to sink down into the surface of the earth and there's a guy with a pitchfork and big red ears and you spend eternity sweating like a freaking *PIG?*

"There is no hell! If we are here to live out a struggle between good and evil to see where we'll spend everlasting life, why do we need the Grand Canyon? a flower in bloom? a full moon over a . . . Caribbean sea? A barrier reef, northern lights? Hummingbirds? No, life is not a morality play! These are results of natural phenomena, successful adaptation and survival of the fittest! If hell was a possibility, why should there be moments when you turn your body and soul into the grasp of another body and soul and say from the heart, 'I love you?' No! Neurotransmitters in the hypothalamus produce a reaction in the brain which give us pleasure, so making love feels good, and propagation of the species continues, a species which has won the race! We win the gold medal, we're king of the mountain, the top of Olympus. We've been up Everest and we can't get any higher. This is the only heaven you're going to get to because we're not going anywhere else. There is no heaven above you and we sure aren't doing a damn bit of good at making this spinning chunk of rock, earth and water anything even faintly *resembling* heaven—in fact, it looks like the ruins of a dying civilization."

Doj paces again. The three members of his live audience are mesmerized. He thinks of Lisen for a moment. Could she be watching? Is she safe? He sees blood on Taft's shirt and it startles him, but then he remembers that it is his blood, or perhaps that of his dead friend.

He looks back into the lens. "Would a god be so cruel as to make all of life a test, where we constantly have to choose between fulfilling biological needs and adhering to morality? If there was a moral and just god in heaven, would Hitler have killed innocent millions? Would the effects of a senseless Viet Nam war still be manifested? Would Richard Speck, Charles Manson, John Wayne Gacy or Jeffrey Dahmer be allowed to fulfill their sick fantasies?"

He shows anger now, like that first day in the newspaper office when he seemed to grow in size just before the beam of light appeared.

"Instead of making us all in his image did He decide to introduce us in different flavors just as a test? Just to see if we can overcome prejudice? Guess what—the melting pot idea is not working. It's the Law of Raspberry Jam: The wider any culture is spread, the thinner it gets. Cultures are not combining. We're different! We can't be forced *not* to be different. Rather than blending, our differences are becoming more accentuated. So we still draw lines and do battle, physically and subtly. Would a god allow killing and slavery based solely on skin color? No! Its called ethnocentrism. 'Our group is the focus of everything good and true, the center of the social universe.' The opposite is xenophobia, the fear and hatred of strangers and that's natural for survival. It's never going to change. There is no God, no grand puppeteer.

"And Mary was not a virgin! Reproduction just doesn't work that way! God is an invention of humans. The nature of god is only a shallow, simple mystery. The deeper mystery is in the nature of humans and our nature is dark and violent. We live to serve ourselves. Greed, fear of loss, and hard-wired biological drives motivate the human race. We are selfish. At the best, clanish. We only want those around us who share our greed and our fears."

Doj takes a deep breath, Billy zooms in for a close-up. Doj is calm again, his arm gestures stress the reasoning timbre in his voice. "The planet will be here at the end of the *next* millennium, but we, in all likelihood, will not. The coming years will be hard times for many people. We are not fulfilling some prophesy of two thousand years ago written in order to keep the masses in line and looking upward, waiting for divine intervention. The year 2000 is simply a number describing how many times the world has gone around the sun since one of history's many orators was estimated to have been born."

His voice rises. "Orbits, chemicals, reactions, gravity, energy, empty space, cause and effect. That's all there is. When the clock strikes midnight on December thirty-first, nineteen ninety-nine, don't look to the heavens for angels and trumpets, look to the people of the world, the people you're with. You are only what others perceive you to be. So everyone else is a clear reflection of you, of God.

"This planet can't support all these people, all these gods. It is simply a matter of numbers. The smart, resourceful, wealthy and powerful may survive, that's natural selection. This could have been, if not heaven, a great place to live, full of wonder. But we've overrun it, overwhelmed it.

"The trumpets are not going to blow and the meek are not going to inherit the earth. They will continue to be eliminated by wars or starvation, because why should the next century be any different from the last one? Just because the earth reaches some finite point in its orbit, it doesn't pull in for an oil change. It goes on.

"Religion is no more than legend and lore which should have been outlawed at the beginning of *this* century. Religious faith and trust in the established order of politics and religion has given us false hope when common sense, clear thinking and scientific method needed to prevail. Our moral faith in religious leaders has deserted us as their human and sometimes inhuman desires have been made public.

"God is not going to replace the forests of Madagascar and Brazil, or the hundreds of thousands of plant and animal species we've eliminated in just this century. Put down your frosted flakes and sugar water fruit juice and look around. Are you comfortable? Does that make it fulfilling? What's next to you is your heaven and hell. That's all you're gonna get. You still need gods and devils? The thoughts and actions of everyone in the world is evidence of the collective consciousness of God and the Devil. The newspaper under the bread crumbs and coffee stains is called the Daily Mirror. Does anything look familiar? It should, we're all contributors.

"So this is my prophesy to you: The end *is* coming for life on Earth and how fast that end arrives is in your control. You must fortify now. Those who are the most prepared will survive the longest, so quickly take what you need; there is no penalty for greed. Avoid pain and suffering at all cost. There will be no moral reckoning the moment after your final breath."

Doj is calm again, looking into the camera, into homes across America.

"Will those who survive the longest feel blessed by God? *Is* there a god? Because if there was an omnipotent, all-seeing, forgiving God watching over us, Martin Luther King, Mohatma Ghandi, and Meredith Wellard would have lived longer lives. So would a man that was on earth to bring pleasure. A good, happy, simple man, a man named Toby Tiler."

The red light goes off on camera two, the light bar fades to a dull orange. Billy Francis switches the live feed to camera one, where the pretty morning newscaster is gaping at the bloodied man to her left as if he just beamed down from the Enterprise. The station manager is bringing his hand up and down, pointing to her, "You're on!" he whispers.

"I've got to go home and check on my cat. Billy, do you need anything from the grocery store?" she asks, absurdly.

He points emphatically to the red light and the digital clock above the lens. Her eyes focus in from some far place, and she realizes where she is; her years of training and degree in journalism take over.

"The weather in your hole today . . . I mean the hole weather .

. . I mean the *weather* for Jackson Hole today . . . will probably be taking place outside, which is where I'm going. Tune in tomorrow, when our guest will be . . . who was that . . . I don't know, some asshole politician. I'm outta here."

There are fifteen seconds left, so camera one follows her offstage, then focuses on the world map, in front of which Billy Francis is rolling the credits and, today, a disclaimer. Per the usual format, he closes in on the continent of North America, then the United States, then Wyoming, finally the northwest corner of the state, where lies Jackson Hole.

"Wow," he says to Doj, "helluva show. It was strange, but normally we get only five minutes to do the ABC insert, then I have bay one programmed to stay on the CNN feed. But today the feed monitor broadcast our show, so I couldn't figure out what was the matter with bay one."

Taft Vandren says, "We uplinked the signal to the CNN repeater, then bounced it to Comsat, then to the Atlanta studio. Homemakers packing their kids' lunches and the getting-ready-for-work force around the country were watching your show."

Doj asks, "Do you think anyone got the message?"

"Oh yes," nods Taft. "You rambled some, but that fit in well with your bloody torn clothes—the effect was just right, I think."

"For sure, someone got the message," adds Billy Francis. "This will make me or break me with the affiliate. Might as well go out in a blaze of television glory. So why don't you bring that Rasta-dude back and play a few songs for *The Whole JaHo Show* Saturday?"

That changes the feeling in the room, Doj drops his head. Taft puts his hand on his shoulder.

"He was my friend. They shot him and had no remorse. A Roman philosopher Lucius Seneca said, 'Revenge is a confession of pain.' The pain of hate was theirs, those hunters—they knew pain and hate in the end."

Taft replies, "And Milton said 'Revenge at first though sweet, bitter ere long on itself recoils.'"

Doj gazes at Taft Vandren as the newscaster comes out of the office, her eyes still glazed as she wiggles into her maxylene coat.

"The phone lines are going crazy in there," she says. "But one call was the hospital. They told me to tell you to get Mr. Bolderton down there. You've been shot."

Taft shakes hands with the station manager as he pushes Doj toward the door, where the light is still blinking On the Air. "Thanks, Billy. Call me if there's a problem with your affiliate. I'll handle it."

"Billy," says Doj walking by, touching fingertips.

As they drive out of the parking lot they pass Sheriff Clark followed by Police Chief Nuxhall just turning in. Taft watches the Chief's cruiser bottom out over the speed bump and says to Doj, "May bad luck follow us the rest of our lives. . . ." Doj looks at him with a quizzical expression. ". . . and never catch up to either of us."

When Doj walks into the hospital, he finally gives into the physical, mental and spiritual exhaustion. He looks at the soaked bandage over his right thigh and, for the first time, winces from the sting of a metal projectile slicing through his flesh.

A nurse with a manila folder sees him. "Thank God you're here!" she says, then pushes open the swinging door. "Dr. Worham, he's here!"

Doj's proud carriage droops to its lowest, a depression he hasn't felt in sixteen years. It gives him a headache and makes him want to sleep right there. The nurse and the doctor each take an arm and guide him toward the wide door. When the doctor puts his hand on the door Doj resists and leans back in their arms, not wanting to go where his best friend had just died. But the doctor and nurse pull him through the door, and two steps inside Doj stands straight up and gasps. The doctor and nurse release their grips.

"Bolderdoj, so nice of you to stop in and see the Rastjahmon! They tell me you went on the TV without me. I could have been the next Paul Schaffer."

"Rastjahmon!" Doj runs to the bed and hugs his friend to him, eliciting a groan of pain before the nurse pulls him back. Doj takes Toby's hand. "You were dead. . . ."

"I went to the same place, Bolderdoj. I walked out over the sea toward the bright light. I told my uncle about you and our game. Queen to bishop four is what I should have played! I had to come back and tell you. I want a rematch."

"We had given up on him," the doctor admits. "There is no reason he should be here now."

Rastjahmon holds out his fingertips and Doj matches them with his bloodied left hand. "This time, Bolderdoj, when we were walking out over the lovely turquoise sea again, my uncle and father and I, we walked farther than the last time. A man came running up from the sun on the horizon and you told me of your mission. Now I understand and I finally see how important your destiny is. That destiny must occur, Bolderdoj."

Doj looks at Taft, then turns back to Toby. "I'm thinking about your offer to relocate in Jamaica," says Doj. "Tell me again about that bar. They wouldn't, say, get television down there, would they?"

The doors swing open. Sheriff Clark and Chief Nuxhall storm into the room.

"Doj, we need to talk to you right now," says the sheriff. "There are three hunters up in Boone Creek who have been shot, then eaten by wolves. Start talking."

The doctor steers Doj toward a gurney. "He can talk while I'm treating him."

Sunday, October 17th, 1999. 3:39 a.m.

Doj drives past the opened gate onto the tarmac as Jake K. Solstice's Private Lear jet taxis to a streamlined stop in front of Jackson Hole Aviation. He ponders the jet for a second. He recalls Taft's story of the first settlers coming into Jackson Hole a brief one-hundred-and-fifteen years ago on wagons, dragging logs behind chained wheels—the brake system for coming down Teton Pass. The passengers in the jet have streaked 2000 miles in less than four hours.

He waits by the door of his van, until the jet engine props slow to a stop and the door opens. Aisha walks down first, sees Doj, then runs to him, hugging him. Then Lisen emerges, looking radiant and concerned. He hugs both women at the same time.

When the pilot hands Aisha a piece of luggage Doj kisses Lisen.

"I've missed you tremendously," whispers Lisen.

"Toby's all right now," Doj assures them. "He's resting in Taft's cabin. He's gonna be all right."

Doj knocks on Taft's door. "Toby?"

"Come in."

Aisha leads Lisen, Doj and Taft into the dark cabin.

"Toby baby darling!"

She runs to him and a wail breaks down into sobs. She takes his hand in hers, kisses his cheeks, forehead, lips. The others surround the bed and Toby holds Aisha to him with his good right arm.

Lisen asks, "Can you tell us what happened?"

"Everything?" says Doj.

Aisha says, "You can leave out the television show, Doj. We've seen the replay. Well said."

Doj starts uneasily. "I won't tell you all the details, but Toby and I were hunting. . . . "

Three minutes later Taft changes the subject: "Doj, I think it might be a good idea to take that two-day camping trip you were talking about." He turns to Aisha and Lisen. "In the four days since Doj's speech these three cabins have been the target of passersby heckling and taunting." He holds up a wooden devil's mask with "Doj" scribbled in red on the cheeks. "People have been hurling more than insults. There have been supporters as well, and the night before last the police had to break up a skirmish between the two factions."

Doj tosses a second sleeping bag into the back of his VW van and shuts the door. It seems loud in the predawn solitude.

As Lisen slides onto the front seat she wraps the goose-down coat tightly around her to keep out the early-morning chill. Doj says, "At least we're leaving before the taunters show up. Taft had to change his phone number. Since the TV show there's been a lot of stuff in the media debunking what the religious right has called the 'anti-sermon'."

He starts the microbus and they pull quietly away.

"I've been scanning the Internet," says Lisen. "Reaction has been mixed. Everything from hatred to sarcasm, from appreciation and idolatry to humor. Jay Leno performed a skit with an actor that looked just like you. What did police say?"

"I was interviewed first, then Toby. They admitted the evidence points to self-defense. All three of those guys were criminals. Felons. There were warrants out for two of them. I'm released pending further investigation. Would you mind running in here and grabbing a couple of bagels? The counter girl thinks I'm the anti-Christ."

Over the next two days Toby's recovery progresses remarkably through Aisha's application of various salves and herbal ointments, seven different aromas, and tender, loving massages. Taft enlists the services of 24-hour security for the cabins; things eventually quiet down. Three days after Aisha's and Lisen's arrival Toby is able to accompany them, Doj and Taft to the airport. The sleek jet rolls to a stop in the predawn, the steps are lowered, and Jake K. Solstice steps down.

Toby walks forward. "Brother Jake, I did not know *you* were coming."

The dread-locked reggae star says, "Toby, brother Rastjahmon, I am sharing in your pain. The Solstice family misses you and we want to know when you'll come back. We hope before we see your name on the country and western charts or mounted on some cowboy's wall next to a buffalo."

"Brother Jake," smiles Toby, touching fingertips, then hugging the taller man, "my destiny is clearly here now. We will break bread and make jam again when the master shows us the light. We both understand. Jake, meet our brother, the Bolderdoj."

Two minutes later Doj and Lisen have one more moment together as the jet is refueled and the props rev up. "Lisen, there's something you haven't told me. Something's on your mind."

She takes both hands in hers and looks into his eyes. "You *are* perceptive, messenger or not. Walk with me—"

"Let's go!" shouts the pilot from the top step. "I have a commercial flight on final approach and there's a storm southwest of here. Load 'em up!"

"What is it Lisen?"

"Doj, what do you think about . . . if the world didn't end . . . well, I love you and. . . ."

"We'll call them from London," says Aisha, pulling the reluctant Lisen away.

As surreptitiously as they arrive, Lisen and Aisha depart; the Lear jet whisks them over Sleeping Indian mountain, toward the land of monarches and Greenwich Mean Time.

At the least, Doj and Toby are celebrities. The tape of the morning show is replayed across the country many times, even by the Trinity Broadcasting Network, where Pat Robertson refutes 'each and every blasphemous statement.' Some networks use clips from *Crossfire Survival* to depict the events of the night with the hunters. *The Globe* runs a cover story. But Doj and Toby hide themselves for two weeks. While things simmer down they recuperate mentally and physically; Doj wins the chess tournament nine games to seven but Toby wins backgammon nine to three. From Taft's living room they speculate on the purpose of the visitors to their cabin while Taft secludes himself in his laboratory downstairs.

Saturday, October 30th, 1999. 8:23 p.m.

Nearly three weeks after the night of the hunters, Toby has almost recovered. Toby and Doj sit across from each other in Toby's cabin, playing the jingle they wrote for the new business they're thinking about starting, Rent-a-Friend; for two hundred dollars a night—with a discount for poor, lonely people—Bolderdoj and the Rastjahmon will be your friend, come and play music, tell stories and jokes, cook, or just listen, whatever the client needs. Enough people have requested interviews, and so many have asked for Doj's cab—tonight's his first night back, by popular request—that the idea formed three nights ago over good wine, kind ganja, and a few Tylox, the pain medicine prescribed for Toby.

A quick slide up the guitar brings Toby discomfort.

They stop and start again. They rehearse a song about the night of the hunted, when the wolves showed up, a symbol of nature's revenge for all the one-sided hunting and poisoning that their wise breed have had to endure, and how Doj was exonerated:

'Cause I had told the cold cold truth
If you'd like to know the end
I stabbed him with my sharp sharp knife
Call up and Rent-a-Friend!'

Rastjahmon laughs loudly at the end, swinging his bracelets, hitting the E-chord three, four times, shaking his dreadlocks. "Irie! Irie!"

"People will never even have to leave their houses in the year 2000," says Doj. "They have satellite TV, FODDER, the Internet, telephones and faxes; we'll come over to supply them with the human contact they need, and pick up a couple of bags of groceries on the way, party like salamanders."

"What's FODDER?"

"Films on demand, day/evening rental."

An airy mechanical static from Doj's two-way precedes Wolfmeister's voice. "Hey Schwarzbo!" The Wolfman's new name for Doj is a cross between Schwarzenegger and Rambo.

Doj ponders answering the radio for a moment—they were just getting into their song—but it is the night of the big Halloween 'Prelennium' costume party and with things getting underway at nine, the Wolfman knew it would get busy.

"Go ahead, Wolfmanmeister."

"Where're ya at?"

"East Hansen."

"You're at home. Ya probably won't get a lot of walk-on business with the cab sitting in your driveway. Listen, pick up at Teton Village. Thirty Morley Drive. Said she was Marilyn

Monroe, going with Bogart to the big costume party at Snow King."

"Got it Wolfmeister; on my way." He says to Toby, "I don't know, maybe I should just go on some of those TV shows, like that one that phoned, *Hard Cover*. I could make a bunch of money. Convince Aisha and Lisen and we'd all move to Jamaica, open our own bar."

"Do you think that is your destiny in life, Bolderdoj?"

Doj stands. "No. Driving a cab is my life. I love it so."

"I'll stay here and watch the Discovery Channel and play with the song. We need one more verse in there. How about this:

'When you rent a Rastjah-friend

You also get the Rastjah-blend.'?"

Over those next hours the creatures come out in Jackson Hole: maidens and monsters, politicians and stars, tables, an ostrich, a moose, genies, and then someone going as a cactus. Besides the Snow King gala there are costume parties at both the Mangy Moose and the Cowboy bars, and at the Wort Hotel children are ushered by parents through the Haunted House.

It is the night before Halloween, 1999.

A roving eye beholds the lives of these sentient mortals scattered over the 8000-mile-diameter blue-green-white orb.

In Albany, New York it is Mischief night, and the Mischievers are on the move. They are 'cranked up', and out to 'Pain the Town'.

"Hey, don't get edgy with me tonight, OK?" says Lonny.

"Whole damn city's edgy, man, since that cop got plastered by the Porch Monkeys last night, know what I mean?"

"How you know it was a Monkey?"

"I got ears. Keep those guns ready, there's going to be some bad shit go down tonight, know what I mean, if anybody starts nothin'."

Just then a large sedan turns the corner toward them, and the driver recognizes it as a car of the Centrals. "Cock your guns, we're right on each other's boundary, so don't start shit less you see a tool."

In Detroit they call it Devil's Night, and Munson Lawrence, eight years old, slips out of his apartment. He knew the fight between his parents would get loud, it always did. It was Saturday, as usual they were drinking, and the arguing was about the same old things.

He walks down the long apartment building hallway and knocks three times on the wall, just behind the rack where the fire extinguisher used to be. He can hear Timmy's parents yelling, but he can also hear the loud roar of a football game on the television.

Timmy opens the door in just a few seconds. "Where do you think you're going?" shouts the father.

"Down to Munson's to play Virtual Vacuum!" yells the kid.

"No you're not!" The door slams shut. "Get back in here!" is muffled as Munson and Timmy charge down the hall way and through the door to the stairwell.

They spring down the steps two or three at a time but they both know they won't be followed now, they are on their own, their parents will continue to fight and drink and Timmy's dad might even screw his step mother right there on the living room sofa. But tonight they don't care. Tonight is exciting. They had discovered a little crawl space in the basement behind some old furniture that had been boarded up. They pried the wooden planks open and crawled inside. Then they came back with candles. Then last night they stashed an old stack of newspapers and Timmy took a gallon of gas from his dad's back seat and all their friends meet them because that older kid from the tenth floor said gas was the coolest way to make a good blaze.

Twelve minutes later fifteen boys are tossing newspapers in a big pile then the older boy sprinkles a little gas over the stack. Munson tosses the wooden match and a bright blue flame jumps up.

"That's cool."

"Watch this," says the older boy.

He pours more gas and the flame instantly crawls back to him, up to the spout of the can—then explodes.

The incendiary combustion traps and burns six of the boys

before the rest escape. The fire quickly spreads into the old building. People are trapped. Some jump to their death. Before it's over forty-eight lives are lost, the building and every home is destroyed. It will be the headlines in the next day's local paper.

In Los Angeles tiny concealed video cameras are mounted high on power poles in neighborhoods of high crime, because so many grocery stores had been looted in the past three weeks. At Police headquarters a sergeant watches a screen showing an armored car cruising slowly down a long street. But he recognizes the armored car as the new one belonging to Crimecast Network for their *Prime Time Crime Show*. The heavy-plated machine cruises high-crime areas with video cameras peering from the turrets.

Moskoto Mondoran in Lima, Peru, has never driven a car before and this one is old, it sputters, and he is not used to working the brake and accelerator. And in the back seat is a bomb.

Moskoto Mondoran is a Bolivian Indian from the high country, Cochabamba. Unable to farm in a country that no longer requires his limited skills, he, like tens of thousands of displaced rural people, is forced to the cities. There he is hired by the terrorist group, Sendero Luminoso. The Sendero Luminoso movement specializes in car bombs.

As he parks the car at the front of the hospital Moskoto realizes he will make more money than he ever has before. He walks quickly away and disappears into the night. Two minutes later a bomb at the back entrance of the hospital explodes followed by distant gunfire. When the Bolivian ambassador is wheeled out of the front door the car bomb explodes next to him; the killing is a success. In a dark building overlooking the scene a man smiles and asks if Moskoto would like to make even more money by simply taking a package down to San Paulo.

Moskoto envisions food and new clothes for himself and his mother, a chance to buy the cerveza for himself. Perhaps then he would not be *desclasados*, a person without class, as he and other Cochahamba Indians are referred to in the city.

Moskoto sees a chance for a life away from starvation and nothingness. He simply nods and says, "Yes, I will do this thing you ask."

In Lubango, Angola, a nineteen year-old army sergeant walks toward his battalion. This will be the first night he is in command since Sergeant Ngugi was shot the previous night. What did Ngugi just tell him, there in the hospital, before he was wheeled away to have his leg amputated? Make something up that the enemy did, something heinous to make them seem like the unscrupulous barbarians they are. Make them worthy only of cruel death. Then give your soldiers guns and never let them see the faces of the Zambian dogs they must slaughter.

At Scotland Yard a detective punches in a code on a computer. A flashing dot on an adjacent map reveals the location of Jonathan Ludd, one of thirty-seven habitual criminals in the London area who have had electrodes implanted under their skin which sends out a signal, recording their whereabouts at all times. The detective takes a sip of tea then checks a readout of Ludd's location the last twenty hours, for there's been another rape in the Hackney district which has Ludd's signature all over it.

In Seoul, Korea, a young male smiles. He and another graduate student in chemical engineering have perfected a silicon/zarcon compound which can be injected into a lock as a liquid but instantly solidifies; with refining any lock in the world might be opened. They experiment on their professor's locked file cabinet, and the two smile at each other as they pull out the final exam.

"We can make a lot of money with this invention."

"We should take it to that American firm. The man Dupree bought Ling's design for the plastic mini gun."

"We will be very very wealthy."

Near Bolzana, in northern Italy, Francesa Botelari, waits in the trees, concealed by the night, far away from the lights of the city. He waits for Dr. Cominelli to step outside the astronomical observatory. Dr. Cominelli has been much despised by many in the village since he had told the residents, confirmed what the papers had said, that a comet may come, and yes, having an underground shelter was a good idea. Francesa spent all his money to protect his wife and family, then he was laughed at by the people of the town and his relatives in Milan. The money he spent was supposed to be for the new butcher shop he was to open with his sons. Now, instead of a new shop he had a half-finished pit. "What is this, Francesa, an open air market!" said the mayor's body guard as he walked by two days before.

The astronomer strolls out, lighting his pipe, and Francesa fires his shotgun, striking him. Francesa walks closer. He reloads and fires into the astronomer's chest, then walks away, satisfied.

In Oslo, Norway, a crew of whalers unties the last of the knots holding the boat to shore. There is more excitement from bow to stern today. Their legislature has once again defied the International Whaling Commission, and the crew is going whaling for Minkes. The way of life shared by these young and old crew members' fathers and forefathers is in their blood; they stand into the wind and salt spray and grasp each other's shoulders in a gesture of camaraderie. Life is just like it's supposed to be.

Jack Weatherford, a professor of anthropology at Macalester College in Minnesota, looks over his notes for Monday's lecture in Savages and Civilization, a 501 course.

Discuss:

> True borders rarely exist in nature. Humans go to great expense and effort to create them, and having done so, they go to even greater efforts to make them real and to protect them. Physical borders make so little logical sense, we build great ideological arguments about culture, nationality, race, and ethnicity to support them.

Satisfied, he falls into the easy chair and leans back. He hits the power button on his remote and scans through the channels.

Nothing catches his attention until he stops at channel 85. It is his back yard. The camera pans once, and he hopes he correctly adjusted the motion detector so breeze would not activate the light and the alarm. He wonders if he should upgrade and get the camera that is interfaced with the VCR—the model that starts recording as soon as something activates the motion detector.

Dr. Weatherford presses the up channel to 86. His son and daughter are playing in their room, playing with the toy soldiers, using the pillow for a mountain. He wonders how old they should be before he tells them that the left eye of the mounted whitetail buck is not an eye but a camera. The twins are six now. Maybe he'll wait until they no longer need baby-sitters.

Doj pulls up to the costume party at the Snow King Convention Center.

"That will be nineteen dollars, please, sir."

"Here's twenty. Keep it, pal."

"Thanks, pal."

There is not another fare waiting for him. So, Doj dons a simple face mask and takes a slow walk around the costume party, marvelling. Everyone is wearing a costume that night, frightening, humorous, magical, or serious, and he sees many different characters. They mingle, talk, laugh, dance, drink, adjust their costumes and practice their poses for the costume contest. The band is just into their third song, and the revelers do not yet face the music.

Article in USA Today, Monday, November 1st, 1999:

ASTRONOMERS MEET

Eight members of the International Astronomical Union will meet at the Palomar Observatory on Wednesday to discuss the Tennyson Comet, named after Dr. Spencer Tennyson, head of the Palomar Observatory and president of the IAU, and the comet's discoverer. The Tennyson

Comet, once predicted to come very close to Earth's orbit by the end of the year, is now expected to come no closer than Jupiter's orbit, but it may be visible with high-powered backyard telescopes, according to Tennyson.

Other items on their agenda include the discussion of the NASA launch of an IAU-designed satellite with a powerful radio telescope, a telescopic camera, radar, and an experimental laser, which will be used to destroy man-made satellites whose orbits are decaying.

"This should avoid disasters like last year's Comsat satellite," said Tennyson. The Comsat crashed in September of 1998 into a village near Talca, Chile, killing two and injuring three others.

The astronomers will be mourning the death of fellow astronomer Bordin Cominelli, who was murdered by an unknown assailant outside his observatory near Bolzano, Italy on October 31st .

Monday, November 1st, Taft Vandren's cabin, 1:14 p.m.

"Come on guys," says Taft, emerging from his laboratory. "Doj, Toby, it's a beautiful Indian summer day out there. Since *All My Children* you've read *USA Today* twice and scanned 57 channels six times each—there's nothing on. Everything's on *outside.* You've got fifteen minutes to pack the Aerostar with whatever you need for three days. We're going on vacation."

They drive out of Jackson Hole, over 8,400-foot Teton Pass and into Pierre's Hole, Idaho potato farm country, and they pass the Spud Drive-In, where a flatbed truck holds a twelve-foot plaster potato. They drive over rolling, golden country, gazing up the foothills to the backside of the Teton Range. They turn right in Ashton and approach the Yellowstone Plateau from the west. In the tourist town of West Yellowstone they turn north and drive along the Gallatin River, through Montana canyon country, where high mountain streams get a good running start in their push to the sea. Then on to Bozeman, home of Montana State University. Taft visits with a biology professor there, an old acquaintance. Toby finds the music department and a flautist to jam with. Doj sits in the student union and writes a letter to Lisen that will go along with a poem. That night they stay at the Gallatin Gateway Hotel outside of town, a regal place with tiled floors in a stone lobby, a place with history.

Then on to Chico Hot Springs Hotel, where they stay two nights. Taft spends his days wandering about in the woods near the springs, looking for thermal seeps. Doj studies the topographical map and runs new trails. Toby nurses his healing shoulder in the large hot thermal pool, "The closest thing I've found to my home seas in this country. I'm never leaving!" He is able to swim a little, mostly the side stroke, leading with his healthy right arm.

But Doj is pensive. After dinner Toby and Taft resume their backgammon battles but Doj leaves quietly, to walk outside under the stars.

Toby says, "It is soothing to him, like the warm water is to me, like being amongst the trees and plants is to you."

In the morning Doj is not in his bed. Toby and Taft find him on top of the Aerostar, in a sleeping bag, in the wire-mesh luggage rack.

"Orion is in the sky," Doj says.

Taft knows that means Doj stayed up late.

Toby knows Doj is ready to face his problem.

Then they drive back through Yellowstone. Ten miles north of Old Faithful Taft leads them through the lodgepole pine forest to a thermal spring with perfect temperatures where they soak. In the distance they hear the surreal bugling of male elk, though Taft must convince Toby that the high-pitched trumpeting is not the sound of wolves stalking them.

"I wish I had my bow and arrow," says Doj, gazing in the direction of the closest shrill bugling.

Then down the volcanic plateau, along the Lewis River Canyon. There are hardly any cars on the roads this time of year; the first heavy snows could come any day, and they pull over when they please. Taft spots things the others do not: the beginnings of a beaver dam, a patch where he secretly planted some aspens following the fires of 1988, old claw marks seven feet above ground on a lodgepole pine where a grizzly scratched the boundary of his territory.

They travel back past Jenny Lake, beneath the Teton Mountains. They complete the Loop at the Lame Duck Chinese Restaurant in Jackson. Doj and Toby get comfortable in a private tea room while Taft hands the chef bundles of his homegrown herbs, spices, and dried morels, and describes how to use them in three different wok combinations. They share appetizers and jokes and hot saki. They share the different dishes, the shrimp-fried rice, and stories of adventures and characters they've met.

When the bill arrives they divide the cost and each take a fortune cookie nearest to them that tells them nothing about the future or what they're really like.

Thursday, November 4th, 1:08 p.m.

"Doj, come in!"

Doj finishes twelve-bar riff on his harmonica before grabbing the two-way and pressing the transmit button. "Go ahead, Eddy."

"Got a pickup at 35 Aspen Lane. Guy is in a hurry. He's going to the supermarket."

"Got it, Eddy."

Doj circles the town square before heading down Cache Street to Aspen Drive. He yawns, looking out the side window, watching the falling wet snow accumulate on the still-green grass. He doesn't like the day shift, all the hustle and bustle of work and time orientation and efficiency which characterizes day movement. And winter is coming. He wonders if he should leave this cold, gray Jackson Hole. He could go back to school and finally write that master's thesis, but he is so tired of school, learning more and more, yet all the knowledge does not make him happier. Maybe he should just do what his heart tells him and go with the Rastjahmon to Jamaica, play music, snorkel, run in a place where no one knows, or cares, who he is.

But there's at least one good thing about daytime driving: The customers are almost always ready to go—they're waiting, instead of drinking—and before Doj comes to a complete stop a man bolts from his short porch, opens the passenger door and jumps in.

"Grocery store at Albertson's. Step on it before the rush gets there."

"What rush? It's mid-afternoon in the off-season. There's not going to be many people shopping now."

"You didn't hear the news just now, did you?"

"No, man, what I heard was the blues—key of A sliding blues with a twisted e. What's happened now?"

"The comet! The Tennyson is heading to Earth!"

Doj swerves over to the side of the road, skids to a stop, and turns to the man for the first time. "Say that again."

"Hey, you're the guy who predicted this—you've been on TV. You predicted this all along!"

"The Tennyson is coming?"

"The astronomers just had a news conference. They said something made it move, altered its course. It's heading toward Earth. Go, go. Everyone's going to be thinking the same thing: Stock up!"

Doj peels out and takes the right turn on Flat Creek Drive, his mind flashing on a light year of thoughts. He looks through the cracked front windshield to the sky above, "Hello! You're coming! I knew you wouldn't let me down!"

"Who are you talking to?"

"God. The master. The big fisherman with the big net who will save you and everyone like you who stocks up on Sun Chips."

"How'd you know I like Sun Chips?"

Doj pulls up to the store. The man hands Doj a ten as the radio crackles, "Doj comes in!"

Doj puts up a hand. "That's OK," he says to the fare, "this one's on me."

"Doj, come in!"

Doj turns around and jets out of the parking lot. "Go ahead, Eddy."

"The phone's ringing off the hook in here. The *News* and the *Guide* have both called, they want you to call them right away. Your comet is coming!"

"It's not my comet, Eddy, my boy. It's going to smack this

planet so hard, we will all bask in the glory and share the wrath of one who is wise."

At 5:37 p.m. Doj parks his van in the near-dark grayness at the top of Teton Pass, 2200 feet above the valley; the snow falls heavily, accumulating on the slope, and a breeze comes from the west, the Idaho side. He walks straight up the fall line to the top of Telemark Bowl. There he falls to his knees and reaches up in supplication.

"May we do the right thing, master and mentor. May the world be a better place. I know I must be respectful now. I will tell the people of the hope for the future and the better world which will evolve. Yes, I know that many will be hurt, and I know that I may even die. Yes, I know there will be ruination, but I do believe life will be better for *all* who live. Now I will pray.

"Our father, who rides on comets, hallowed, haloes be thy coma. . . ."

Friday, November 5th, Palomar Observatory, 1:08 p.m.

Once again the Brucato Planetarium is filled to capacity, and the buzz of human excitement is at a near-fever pitch.

Tennyson's assistant leads in the astronomers. They take seats behind their name tags as the lights come up and the cameras start their searching hum.

"What's Langdon Stofford doing here?" whispers one reporter to another.

"Which one's that?"

"The man sitting behind Tennyson."

"He's been at every conference as Tennyson's assistant. Why? Who is he?"

"He won the Nobel prize in physiology in '97. He teaches at Delta University."

"What does he teach?"

"You name it. Philosophy, biochemistry, physics and astronomy, physiology and sociology. He's run with people like Buckminster Fuller, Isaac Asimov, David Attenborough, Carl

Sagan, Ann Druyan, Arthur C. Clarke, Evelyn Vasquez that crowd. Some of the first things I ever read were his science-fiction novels."

"Well, the last time we were up here, the whole shebang turned out to be science-fiction. If this thing's coming how much damage could it do?"

"Ladies and gentlemen," Tennyson begins, standing at the podium, his shadowed eyes and gaunt face revealing a man that looks as if he'd been cramming for exams every night for thirty years. "We would like to make a brief statement, then field your questions."

"Is it coming?" comes a voice from the sea of media.

"A brief statement will be *followed* by your questions. Dr. Singer?"

She rises. "The Tennyson is *definitely* coming into the inner solar system and *will* impact the planet Earth. We expect this event to occur sometime between the twenty-ninth of December and the third of January."

"What's going to happen?"

"Why did it change course?"

"If we could have the camera lights off, please."

The planetarium lights dim, the sound diminishes.

"Thank you."

The holotron produces an image of a galaxy. The word 'sun' hovers above a point of light two-thirds from the center of the galaxy to its edge. The spiral starts to slowly rotate.

Dr. Singer speaks narrates, "The sun is a star which orbits the center of a spiral galaxy, the Milky Way. In recent years we've learned that it also oscillates above and below the galactic plane of the galaxy at the rate of once every thirty million years or so—it bobs up and down. As we near the top or bottom of the plane, the gravitational attractions of interstellar gas and dust and stars in the plane reverse our direction so we bounce back the other way. Extinctions on Earth have also been occurring at the rate of every thirty million years, though probably more like thirty-three million. The ages of fossils and craters on Earth reveal a time scale of almost thirty-three million years; the dinosaurs became extinct sixty-five million years ago from the impact of a comet. We are now about thirty-two million years above the galactic plane, but we may be close enough to the top of the oscillation to cause fluctuations in the Oort Cloud. We believe this is the beginning of a flurry of activity within the Oort Cloud. These gravitational forces are causing perturbations which are diverting the Tennyson from a consistent, elliptical and predictable path."

"So, won't these interstellar gravitational forces continue to cause fluctuations? Couldn't the Tennyson be perturbed again?"

"No," says Dr. Singer firmly. "The Tennyson is a captive of our solar system now. We reconfigured our data just two days ago. After initial input we got a reading which would take it back out to interstellar space, but then we added the orbits of the planets and found that Jupiter's close propitiation to the Tennyson will divert the comet into the inner solar system. That gravitational pull will cause it to enter relatively close to the sun, what we call a sungrazer. The Tennyson will swing past our sun, then impact Earth post perihelion."

A cacophony of human discord follows. After five seconds the loudest, most resonant male voice rises above the barking. "What kind of damage will it do?"

Dr. Tennyson looks to his right. "Dr. Cooper?"

The British astronomer leans toward his microphone. "This comet has been very hard for us to study because it is coming at us from the other side of the solar system, behind the sun, so we've only had glimpses of it. It appears to be a long-term comet, its aphelion was probably some thirty-two million years ago. That aphelion probably took it to the middle of the Oort Cloud."

"What is an Oort Cloud?"

"The Oort Cloud is the sun's collection of comets, loosely bound to it by gravitation. The Oort Cloud is huge, a hundred thousand Astronomical Units across, or about halfway to the nearest star. We, by comparison, are one Astronomical Unit from the sun, or ninety-three million miles. There may be as many as one hundred trillion comets in the Oort Cloud. The Tennyson is what we refer to as a dark comet. It does not appear to have a comet's usual amount of dirty snow, and there is very little outgassing as it is approaching. It could have passed close to the sun its last time around, some sixty-four million years ago, and burned off this material."

"Can it wipe out Earth?"

"The best we can predict at this time is that the nucleus is about twenty-five kilometers wide."

"In miles!"

"About fifteen miles in diameter. If we compare it to, say, Halley's comet, Halley's was about five kilometers across, or three point one miles. The recently discovered Chicxulub crater off the east coast of Mexico was from an asteroid 6 to 12 miles in diameter. Seismologists believe that impact eventually led to the extinction of the dinosaurs sixty-five million years ago."

There is a quiet rumble of voices as the reality of that statement passes like a flood wave. The rumble echoes off the domed roof of the planetarium; each person experiences the sensation that the chattering din is directed at them.

The tone of the next question reveals the sudden feeling of meek vulnerability. "Does this mean it could destroy Earth?"

Tennyson defers to his left. "Dr. Hoyle?"

Dr. Hoyle leans toward the mike. "Of course it will not destroy the Earth. And perhaps not even all of its inhabitants—at least, not at first. An impact of this size would be equivalent to one hundred and fifty megatons of TNT, or about that of an earthquake of magnitude twelve on the Richter scale. The Earth will buckle, and even four hundred miles away, the surface will create waves some three hundred feet tall. Fifteen million billion tons of excavated rock and vaporized cometary nucleus will be launched some sixty to seventy miles in the air, from a crater which would be approximately thirty to forty miles in diameter and seven to eight miles deep. An impact in an ocean would cause tidal waves that would propagate at four hundred to five hundred miles per hour, probably two to three hundred feet tall, and would flood the closest coastlines. If rock and vaporized comet lands on the ground, which it almost certainly would, it will cause fires. If it impacted on land, it would immediately incinerate trees and buildings within a radius of some five to seven hundred miles and start massive fires, perhaps worldwide. I believe Dr. Cooper can comment on long-term effects."

"First the dust cloud and debris will block out the sun, halting photosynthesis, more so in the hemisphere where it will hit."

"Where's it going to hit?"

"Well, it's winter in the northern hemisphere and more of the southern hemisphere is exposed, so there is more than a fifty-percent probability the comet will hit in the southern hemisphere. Besides the impact that created Chicxulub and wiped out the dinosaurs sixty-five million years ago, another body of this magnitude impacted the earth approximately two-hundred-and-fifty million years ago, at the end of the Permian Period; that impact directly or indirectly killed off eighty percent of land animals and ninety-six percent of marine life. A similar effect will occur this time. Our preparedness and collective reaction will dictate what percentage of life will survive. After initial warming due to fires and vapor, the tons of soil and rock dust thrown into the atmosphere will circle the globe for perhaps five or six decades, blocking out the sun, halting photosynthesis. From these dust clouds a type of acid rain will fall. The clouds will reduce solar radiation and trigger an ice age. The effect will be the same as that of a nuclear winter."

"Can't it be stopped?"

"The International Astronomical Union recently launched a satellite that's supposed to explode or divert decaying satellites. Can it be deployed?"

Dr. Tennyson shakes his head. "That wouldn't work for a body of this size. In fact, even if we *could* laser it or, perhaps explode an atomic bomb near or on it, we would not want to. The comet may even break up on its own as it enters our atmosphere; we do *not* wish to experience that scenario. Many fragments would cause more damage, as the destruction would be spread farther out. And besides, when it enters the earth's atmosphere, it will be travelling at approximately sixty kilometers per second."

"In miles per hour!"

"About one hundred and thirty thousand miles per hour."

There is another rumble of excited voices filling the room and a cameraman looks up to the ceiling of the planetarium, as if the Tennyson could come crashing through the roof any second.

"When will you know exactly where it will hit?"

Tennyson continues. "After perihelion it will come from behind the sun and we will have about ten days to predict exactly where it will land. There's a lot of ocean in the southern hemisphere, if that's indeed where it lands, and our hope is that it lands mid-ocean, somewhere deep. It may help that this comet is in prograde motion, as opposed to retrograde, so it will be going in the same direction as Earth. . . ."

"When will we see it in the sky?"

"You won't. Not until it enters earth's atmosphere. As Dr. Cooper has explained, it doesn't appear to have the usual snow and dust and whatever it does have will be burned off at perihelion. Properly it may be called an asteroid after perihelion, as it heads toward earth."

"But can you be absolutely certain it's coming this time and will not be perturbed into another orbit?"

Tennyson says, "Dr. Hoyle?"

"The satellite we launched two days ago, the International Ultraviolet Explorer, is equipped with a new Infrared Astronomical Receiver, as well as a Barger radio telescope and a 1.3-meter Fuller Telescope. The satellite has verified what our ground data from eight observatories have told us, including our newest and largest telescope in Cerro Paranal, Chile, as well data from the Hubble. Our statistical analysis program is showing a *p* factor of 0.001. The Tennyson is most definitely Earthbound."

There is another pause, cameras which beam images around the world peer in; the eyes and ears of millions. The media members are nearly at a loss for words.

"Who will survive?" the *Los Angeles Times* reporter asks.

Tennyson looks out over the assemblage. "We would like to have Dr. Langdon Stofford answer that question. Dr. Stofford?"

Stofford, 55, is a man of imposing physical presence and charisma. He shuffles a few notes, then lays them down in front of him. His gaze quiets everyone: deep blue eyes in strong, sharp features and a large cranium; he makes eye contact throughout the room, as if drawing everyone into an intimate conversation. In the charged silence he begins.

"Jesus Christ was born of a comet." He takes another pause and the silence deepens. A light bar buzzes and is quickly turned off. "So was Buddha. So was Mohammed." He pauses. "So was Dr. Tennyson." He speaks softly, with crystal-clear diction. "As were all of the members of this panel, including myself." He scans the wide-eyed faces slowly, quietly. "So were all of you. The comets which carried the first organic materials to this rocky wasteland, billions of years ago, brought the initial building blocks of life. The comets brought water, carbon and nitrogen when they landed amid this hydrogen-rich atmosphere. From those beginnings ultraviolet light and radiation were added. The mixture was warmed gently, more water was added, some lightening, and life was formed. We've created life in laboratories by assimilating similar conditions. The comets have given life and now one is coming to take life away. It will not destroy Earth. The planet will go on. Life will go on. Us? Humans? That's what you want to know? We will have to work together; every one of us on the planet. If we try to compete, if we get greedy and try to secure just for our own future, it could very well mean the end for all humankind. We have the technology to survive this. Not all of us will make it. Perhaps not I, but I will try. I share the survival instinct with every living thing, with all of you.

"I plan to meet with several of the major sociologists in Stockholm in three days. We will discuss human reaction. Dr. Singer will meet with a panel of select nutritionists in Washington, D.C. Dr. Tennyson will meet with the other members of the International Astronomical Union, the American Astronomical Society, and the European Space Agency and we will confer with several geologists. We will look again at the Chicxulub, Meteor Crater in Arizona, the 1908 Siberian asteroid, the recent discovery off Florida, and establish a most-likely scenario so the citizens of all countries may prepare.

"Now I would like to address not only the media assembled here, but all peoples of the planet. Dr. Tennyson and I have just finished a conference call with the President and several Heads of State of the countries of the United Nations. We'd all like to emphasize that the world must go on. From the kid who rents shoes at the bowling alley to the CEO of a corporation. From farmers to store clerks, from policemen to school teachers. A breakdown in the work force at this time will greatly lessen our collective chances for survival. If the economic network collapses right away, we will guarantee our doom. We have all agreed that what we don't need at this time is a great military influence, so these various Heads of State have agreed to mobilize their military forces in preparing emergency measures, food and shelter. And we'd better get good at canning and freezing very quickly. When we know where the comet will hit, we will have a week to ten days to mobilize the greatest evacuation in the history of humankind; we could be successful if we all cooperate. And in deference to Dr. Tennyson, we will no longer call this comet the Tennyson, but the Millennium Comet."

"Does this comet prove the existence of God?"

"Is this the prophesy of the Second Coming of Christ as foretold in the Book of Revelations?"

Stofford pauses again, and the imposing man seems to draw himself even larger. He takes a deep breath before he starts. "I look inside myself and cannot answer that for you. The great minds here at this table cannot answer that for you, nor can the President or Pope or head of the United Nations. To answer that you must look inside of yourself. Thank you ladies and gentlemen. Now let's get to work."

Through television, radio, Internet, telephone, fax machines, and even remote travel via foot and horse, the word of the comet—the Millennium Comet—spreads throughout the world in mere hours. While one can see fear of the unknown in the faces of Earth's people, they also have a look: I am mortal; suddenly, startlingly, I am aware of it—and I haven't done everything I want to. What should I do if these are the last days of my life?

And reaction is varied across different cultures.

The Christian community immediately rejects any notion of astronomical cause and effect; for them it *is* the Second Coming. The way must be prepared for entry into the kingdom of heaven. At the lofty-towered Mormon Tabernacle in Salt Lake City the vigil is ongoing, the parade of devotees endless. The Christians affect a joy, a sense of deserved brotherhood—they were right all along. Standing, kneeling, or sitting in pews, in cathedrals, churches and chapels around the world a curious laughter breaks out. It starts slow, as a nervous laugh, then becomes uncontrollable and often the man or woman loses motor control and collapses into a quivering, uncontrollable laughing fit, often punctuated by "Oh thank you, God!" or "Praise the Lord!" or "Thank you Jesus!" They call it The Laughing Revival, or The Toronto Blessing, from where the phenomenon originated.

Some of the most soulful singing ever, anywhere, is going on in the Baptist churches, particularly in the southeastern United States, with more spirit and brighter harmony that at any time since the Emancipation. "Get it right this time, choir, 'cause we might not have a whole lot more chances. The Lord is *coming!*"

A rural church in Antogafasta, Chile, is overcrowded; word there is that the comet will hit very near them, because the southern hemisphere is more exposed, and they are near the coast.

The heads of state, presidents, prime ministers, kings, premiers, all employ their citizens to maintain the structure of the workplace and economy. But after work, weekends, spare time, communities start to work together to prepare basements, rectories, schools, old bomb shelters, anything which could establish a survival center. Leaders emerge; their authority is not questioned, and often embraced. Ideas are respected, ingenuity and efficiency integral, adaptation welcomed.

People stroll the streets, walk their dogs around their neighborhoods, walk through a park, hike down a forest trail, or just sit on a beach at night; they occasionally glance skyward weighing matters in their minds. They learn about comets, about themselves.

In Perth, Australia, two women who have just finished a match of lawn bowling talk under an umbrella, out of the summer sun.

"I never knew Earth and all the other planets were formed by all these things running into one another."

"They say the moon formed the same way, debris from a meteor or something striking Earth. You know how the moon looks to be about as big as a nickel held at arm's length? Well I heard that when it was formed, the moon would have been as big as this saucer held at arm's length. All those craters were formed by meteors and asteroids; the sky is just full of them. It is simply our time, I suppose."

"They say it may hit close to here, maybe even Australia. How are we going to get eighteen million people off this dried up old rock?"

"If it hits in the ocean, we can all have a big party atop Ayer's Rock. If it's heading for the mainland I'd think the cruise ships will be pretty heavily booked."

"The word 'comet' comes from Greek for hair. I think that's rather nice."

The President of the United States and the Joint Chiefs of Staff are in a conference with Spencer Tennyson and three other astronomers.

The President asks, "So it might actually be possible to blow up the comet with a nuclear weapon, or several nuclear weapons at once?"

Tennyson shrugs, "Our best prediction of that scenario is that it would simply spread the damage and make it worse. If it were a tenth of its size, perhaps we could pulverize it into very small pieces which would burn upon entry, but that's not the case here."

Chief Seward counsels: "Mr. President, I think we ought to prepare ourselves and have weapons in position. We can launch four nuclear bombs from space."

The President is not convinced. "I think, like Dr. Tennyson has stated, that not a whole lot is known about comets and certainly this event is unprecedented, at least in the annals of recorded history. I agree that we should have these weapons in position, so in the event it appears they could be of use, we would have that option. I'll tell NASA. Dr. Tennyson, will you help establish launch and interception coordinates?"

"Certainly, Mr. President."

"I've talked to the Russian premier and the Japanese Prime Minister and their space agencies are prepared to assist in any way."

"Yes, Mr. President."

Slowly, people migrate back to their families, back to their roots, back to their homes. Hugs and long looks say, "We need each other now, I need your support." Past injustices, grudges, and trespasses are forgotten, or they are talked through and forgiven. Help is offered, given and returned. Love is affirmed or reaffirmed. No one wants to be alone now, so bridges are built or rebuilt, hands extended, and neighbors introduce themselves to one another.

In Jackson Hole, on Sunday morning, the seventh of November, the weather is brilliant. Snow fell on the Tetons three days earlier and the western horizon is a backdrop of blue mountains with white frosting and dark green pine forest trimming under a clear, cloudless mountain sky.

Doj and Toby are singing and playing outside of a small chapel; far too many people have gathered for them to perform inside. Over two hundred people are sitting and standing around the historic Chapel of the Transfiguration and the old Menor's cabin marking an early homestead. Television cameras broadcast the gathering around the country. The last two lines of their song are also its title:

> "You kept me warm this winter
> And it lasted thirty years."

"Praise Bolderdoj!"

"Praise the Rastjahmon!"

Televangelist Jude Brooks sits in the front row, his entourage around him. "Brother Bolderton, will you give the Christians of the world a glimpse of what the new life will look like? Will you give us an idea of the everlasting happiness which is about to reign over us? A small sample of His glory?"

"You want us to play another song?"

"We want to lay witness to your miracles. You are the messenger from God, are you not?"

"That's me. You want me to turn the Snake River into blueberry Kool-aid and make it flow uphill? Well, let you who are free of sin get stoned first . . . or however that goes."

"If he's God's messenger then I must be the blessed Virgin Mary," comes from a Scandinavian accent on the right. The female belonging to that voice emerges from behind the willows. It is Lisen. With her is Aisha.

"Lisen!" shouts Doj.

"Aisha!" Toby jumps from the stage, slings his guitar to his back, runs to her and hugs her. "Irie sister love! Praise Jah! What are you doing here?"

"Lisen's pregnant," announces Aisha. "God's going to be a grandaddy."

Everything stops. Jaws drop. Doj runs to Lisen and grasps both hands. "Is it mine?" Doj asks, eliciting a collective gasp from the crowd.

The blonde nods her head and searches Doj's face for his reaction. He breaks into a huge smile, then hugs and kisses her passionately.

"The rest of our fall tour is cancelled," explains Aisha, as the guys step back on stage and the girls follow. "The Millennium Comet. . . ."

"I wasn't sure when or how to tell you," Lisen says, gazing up into Doj's eyes, her dark blue eyes reflecting the sparkling mountain sky, her face radiant, lips parted. "What do we do now?"

Doj looks at her, at the crowd, then at Aisha and Toby.

Toby smiles. "Aaahhh yes, Bolderdoj! I can read your aura so well now. How 'bout Zion Train in four-part harmony? I'll take tenor."

They position their guitars and start strumming. Rastjahmon sings the lead on the Bob Marley song, while Doj and the women harmonize with great emotion, pulling the notes, milking them. Some of the crowd close their eyes and start swaying.

The televangelist fidgets as some start dancing and some start leaving. Two repainted Colorado school busses honk on their arrival, stopping across from the chapel. The graffiti spray-painted on the busses announce that the Haties and the Atheists have joined forces.

"Never! Never! Never-No-Way!" chant the Haties, streaming out and toward the gathering.

"A comet comes from outer space!" chant the Atheists, "God wil *not* save the human race!"

Park rangers form a line between the ranting protestors and the stage.

Doj rotates his guitar behind him, raises a hand, and waits until the clamor dies before he shouts, "Deep inside, you say too clearly that you have come here because you *want* to believe there's more to life then a few years of consciousness followed by nothingness. You've come here to see proof for yourselves—and I will show you. These will be the last miracles I shall perform, and they will prove once and for all who I am. No more will the master allow people to suffer from AIDS: within three days I will show you the cure. Come back to this spot three nights from now and you will see this come to pass—then I will show you the hand of God."

Extinction, throughout the evolution of life on Earth, is the rule. Survival is the rare exception. Life is a series of mutations, almost always to the organism's detriment and the organism perishes, but occasionally the mutation allows the organism to adapt in some positive way, perhaps filling a new environment. In the last decade of the twentieth century, nearly one hundred species a day became extinct; they could not adapt to change.

Some nine million species have adapted and survived to occupy some niche, these are the present-day victors.

Blue whales, the largest animal remaining on Earth, emit sounds hundreds of miles in an attempt to find a mate. Great white sharks, growing to thirty-six feet, are able to sense mere ounces of blood in miles of ocean, for survival means eating—and eating means attacking and killing. The milk of female elephant seals has twelve times more fat than that of domesticated cows, for it is essential their pups grow quickly to be able to defend themselves only six weeks after birth. Only three weeks after birth their weight is four times their birth weight.

Young chimps emulate the dominant males, aping every nuance and gesture-they are looking for heroes to worship, longing for signs of acceptance from these heroes.

Leaf-cutter ants live in complex, disciplined colonies of up to five million in which workers cut leaves to carry to gardens, where they are 'processed.' An edible fungus grows on the processed leaves. The way the young are fed determines which of six different castes they will mature into. Unfertilized eggs become males which fly out of the nest to start new colonies.

A virus is a microscopic infectious organism which reproduces in living cells and can be transferred from one organism to the next. In the twentieth century, new strains of viruses have adapted to spread to every part of the planet.

HEADLINE IN USA TODAY, WEDNESDAY, NOVEMBER 10th, 1999:

SCIENTISTS DISCOVER AIDS PREVENTION

Dr. Vanya Landis, head of the AIDS research division of the Institute of National Health, has announced the discovery of a microbe which prevents an HIV gene 'vpr' from causing AIDS. The new microbe is the culmination of years of biogenetic research. The microbe was discovered in a remote thermal pool in Yellowstone National Park, existing in water far hotter than scientists previously thought possible. It prohibits the gene called vpr from producing a protein, known by the capitalized abbreviation 'Vpr'. The presence of Vpr enables cells to produce new, infected viral particles that can, in turn, infect other cells.

Dr. Landis noted that the target date of the end of the

millennium had been met for the ongoing project and lauded his research team. Calling their work "one of the great medical finds of the twentieth century, maybe the most important. We cannot yet cure AIDS, but we believe we can now stop the HIV virus from becoming AIDS. People infected with HIV will put the virus on hold indefinitely."

By Wednesday the Park Service had revoked the special use permit granted to the members of the Church of the Millennium: Toby Tiler, Doj Bolderton and Taft Vandren; they would not be able to use the Chapel of the Transfiguration again. Too many people were making the pilgrimage as word spread that the son of God, Messenger of the Millennium, would perform a miracle. However, a permit was granted for Bridger-Teton National Forest.

At sunset there are over six thousand people gathered in Antelope Flats, in groups around large bonfires. There is peace in the camps, except for the those of the Haties and Atheists where one hears cries of protest and barks of defiance; they are on the farthest periphery of the gathering.

Under a clear mountain sky, with the sun safely tucked away and with the stars just showing through the chilled late fall air, Doj, Toby, Taft, Lisen and Aisha stroll from camp to camp, playing guitars, flutes, tambourines, and singing harmonies, in front of the roaring bonfires. At Fairy Camp (for gays and lesbians) there is a new found joy. The HIV suppressant will be ready for the public in less than two weeks.

At Media Camp they play "Don't Talk Now," a James Taylor song from 1969, to a staccato of flashes. They finish to a chorus of questions:

"What miracle will you perform?"

"Do you believe God speaks to you?"

"What sign were you born under?"

In the Christian Coalition camp, Doj and friends perform a Cat Stevens song. As they finish they ask what every group asks,

"When will you show us the presence of the Lord?"

Doj says, "Behold the magic as day turns to night, the sky is painted and a hundred thousand stars come out—we call it the heavens. But what you want is a little pizazz, a little zing. A little bit of that old time 'OK the comet's coming and this long-haired hippie predicted it and he's pulled off some pretty neat stuff, but I travelled all the way from Pocatello Falls, Idiot Flats, Spudland or Backwater, Oklahoma. . . ."

"Stillwater, Doj," corrects Taft.

"Whatever. OK. Here we go. Watch closely." Doj hands his guitar to Lisen, then steps toward the campfire. He grabs an unburnt end and pulls a stick out of the fire, the tip is a burning torch.

He taps the end of the branch on a rock at his feet, it breaks into three pieces, then he bends down to pick up a baseball-sized glowing coal. He tosses it quickly back and forth in his hand, blowing on it, making it glow brightly. After ten seconds he tosses it high in the air above him, grabs his guitar from Lisen and swings it from the neck. He hits the coal with the back of his guitar, sending the coal spiraling above and beyond the crowd, casting small sparks into the night. All the Christians turn to him with looks of, "Is that it?"

"Hey, come on!" Lisen calls. "That wasn't bad. Try that with your smoldering self-righteousness sometime."

"Show us proof!"

"Give us a sign!"

"What will heaven be like? Show us!"

At Cowboy Camp Aisha and Toby harmonize the lead on an old Hank Williams song, "I'm So Lonesome I Could Cry," but there is only restless silence and cold stares at the end.

"Ahhh, I hear the sound of one hand clapping," Rastjahmon says. "What would you suppose that rope is for?"

Aisha says, "When we were in Houston a guy said the latest thing was dirt rap. Or dirt trap. Something like that. He taught me one called Psychowboy. It's in b flat if you think that might work."

"This is a tough room," agrees Doj. "Go ahead, we'll fall in.

Just sing it with a southern English accent and we'll try to come up with a line dance at the same time. Clap your hands every eight beats."

In Rainbow Camp they get the spirit going; forty other drummers join in to pound a mesmerizing rhythm as the old and young hippies dance; fourteen other guitars join in and everyone seems to know exactly when to come in with the chorus in John Lennon's "Give Peace A Chance."

In the Haties/Atheists Camp "The End" by the Doors goes over big.

In Generation X Camp a "Crowded House" tune goes over pretty well, but not as well as Rastjahmon getting in a hacky sack circle and showing his mastery at kicking the luminescent foot bag.

At Senior Camp Taft nods to Doj: It is time. Rastjahmon sounds the flute, which calls in all the groups to gather around the big Seniors' campfire. Six thousand people move quietly, showing both awe and fear in their faces; their expressions reflect the orange flicker of the flames. Doj stands in the sage at the top of a small rise, the other four sitting by his feet.

"Welcome to purgatory. I'd like to thank everyone for coming out tonight, especially the gays and lesbians. Only kidding. In a moment we will be passing around baskets—dig *deeper into* your pockets until the spirit *moves* you . . . no, that's not right either. Ummm, let's see. . . . In a moment, we're going to bring out four young men from England, the Beatles! . . . I'm sorry, I used to be able to *do* Ed Sullivan. How about some classical music? Bach? Does anyone know Bach's organ works? Yeah, he had twenty-three kids! I see the Mormons are well-represented. Toby was very honored when the Tabernacle Choir asked him to sing tenor—sure, ten-or-twelve miles away! Oooh, tough crowd. Well, it's great to be here in the West. Some western animal humor, perhaps. What did the doe say when she came out of the woods? That's the last time I'm going in there for two bucks! Yikes. Oh, here's a good one. Wait, you'll like this one. What do you call a heifer that's had a hysterectomy? . . . Decaffeinated!"

"Cut the crap!" comes from the crowd.

"If you're the son of God, prove it."

"Show us the Hand of God!"

"OK!" shouts Doj, quieting the crowd. "Nag, nag, nag. OK, now let's all shake out a little, loosen up, get some *air* in those lungs! Now, look . . . there!" He points behind him to the east.

All stare, some using their hands to shield their eyes from the glow of the fire.

"I don't see anything!" voices chorus.

"It is God!" Doj says.

"Where?"

"The constellation Orion. It is the shape of God."

"How do we know?"

"Because God is a warrior. We are all warriors to have survived all of life, and we did it by conquering the plants, the animals, and other people. God is Zeus, Ajax, Achilles, Thor, Orion, and Hercules, the God of strength."

"But God being a warrior in the night sky proves nothing," shouts a man.

Doj replies, "Well, God's also a lover—the three stars which angle out, and the three which angle down, represent sex, when He is and when He's not aroused. Besides fighting, loving and sexuality are most important in our history. See that in Orion. See the miracle."

"Then where is woman?" someone at Feminist Camp yells. "There is more than one sex in the universe."

"The constellation Cassiopeia—there! It looks like a W. That stands for Woman. That's why Cassiopeia is always near Orion. See the miracle. Witness it!"

A restless stirring grows in volume for long moments until the Hatie/Atheist Camp begins a chant of "Bullshit . . . bullshit!"

"OK!" shouts Doj. "All right!" He waits until the jeers die. "I told you I'd cure AIDS. There is proof!"

"You did nothing!" says a man from Fairy Camp. "A protein was discovered which prohibits the triggering of HIV—and it's just a little late, if life on Earth is about to perish. There are many suffering now—cure AIDS tonight if you're God!"

"C'mon, gimme a break here. I had a lot to do with discovering that protein, and that's way better than turning water into wine. Now you *should believe* me; I perform miracles."

"Biogenetic research using microbes has been going on for years," retorts someone from College Camp. "It was a quantum leap, but a logical step in a series of biogenetic laboratory experiments."

"And a little too late!" cries an angry voice from Fairy Camp.

"God bless Doj!" comes from the Christian camp. "I believe . . . I believe. . . ." comes from the Christians on Doj's right, followed by "Bullshit . . . Bullshit. . . ." from the Hatie/Atheist camp at far left.

"Then get a load of *this!*" Doj says.

He whirls to his left and points into the night. Blacktail Butte, a mile away, explodes in three consecutive huge flashes, followed by three thunderous shockwaves which blast through the crowd, causing moans, screams, and calls of "Praise Doj! Praise God!" and "The Hand of God!" Three rumbling echoes reverberate from Shadow Mountain behind them.

"God has shown us!"

"It is portent of events to come!"

A fire storm of rock and flaming debris falls; small fires glow on Blacktail Butte.

"Not bad, huh?" yells Doj.

"It is Him!"

"Bow down before the son of Man!"

"It is a sign from God Almighty—He has come back to save us!"

"Bullshit!" yells a loud voice from the Hatie/Atheist camp. "Pyrotechnics! That can be done with dynamite! Bullshit . . . *Bullshit* . . . *BULLSHIT!* Crucify Doj . . . *Crucify* . . . *CRUCIFY!*"

Doj replies thunderously, "The last seven weeks are your test! Prepare your spirit for ETERNITY! BEHOLD THE HAND OF *GOD!*"

Doj stands by himself; his 'disciples' no longer sit at his feet. He tosses his pale green sweat-shirt hood over his head, casting his eyes in shadow, then raises his right hand and points to the Tetons, looming behind the crowd. The blue laser-light emits from his fingertip, shining across the valley, fading into the night.

For ten seconds there is total silence, then comes "*CRUCIFY! . . .CRUCIFY!*" as the Haties and Atheists start to push toward him. A six-foot two-inch red plastic cross is being forced toward Doj; people are getting shoved and are falling beneath the surge. Some get stepped on and their cries and wails can be heard above the crowd noise. A rock flies past his ear then a second rock which Doj avoids by ducking at the last second. A muscular, bald-headed, bearded Hatie stalks up the hill to loom over Doj. The Hatie growls; his hands move toward Doj's neck.

"I told you to *BEHOLD*!" Doj shouts again.

A thick beam of light comes from some point far in the night sky, then two, three, four more beams come from that same point and crisscross. When the beams converge, the Tetons explode with the power of multiple nuclear warheads.

Six thousand people turn to face the massive conflagration of rock and fire which decimates the once-calm night. The mountains explode into different colors, beautiful and terrible. Those massed together are both awed and terrified. For twenty seconds lights dance and destroy.

When they turn back, Doj Bolderton is gone.

The fire blazing in the river-rock fireplace warms the small mountain cabin. The firelight and the glow from the three candles cast orange ripples of light on the naked bodies of Lisen and Doj.

He runs his hand up her thigh and stops at her belly, above the embryo which evolved from his seed. He whispers, "You are the woman I've searched the cosmos and waited an eternity for, aren't you? We were meant for each other, weren't we?"

"Does this all mean our child has to be born in a manger?"

"Not if we get married before New Year's Eve."

Slowly, Lisen starts to sob. Doj does not know, does not ask, if her tears are from happiness, love, or a sense of loss. He simply holds her tightly, pulling the goosedown comforter over them both.

During the days leading up to Christmas, most people's conversation vacillates between the season's customary good cheer and the anticipation of news from the Palomar; the astronomers say they will soon emerge from the observatory and detail when and where the Millennium Comet will strike planet Earth.

All around the globe, "Merry Christmas," and "Happy Holidays," is also dotted, like Christmas cookies, with "Good luck," and "Who will you comet with?"

"I will wait to hear where it's going to hit," is the customary reply. Around the world, in so many different languages, the last thing said in a conversation between men and men, women and women, men and women, young and old, is "Don't hesitate one moment if there's anything at all you need, anything we can do for you."

Around the world lovers, in the deepest expression of heart felt emotion, exchange vows, "I will stay by your side no matter what."

The children of the world will open toys, and dolls, and train sets, the things kids get. There are not a lot of gifts for the house, or vacation trips planned, for people don't know if the house or the vacation spot would be there in another month. Water purification systems sell well, lots of canned goods, and generators, warm clothes, fire extinguishers and anything fire resistant. Fire-resistant bibles are a high-demand item.

The general consensus among parents throughout the world is that if their children are old enough to learn about Santa, they are old enough to learn about the comet.

The NCAA cancels the Bowl games scheduled for the holidays and the NFL Player's Union cancels the playoff games. The comet's imminent arrival postpones the debate whether or not to require the players to use Airpads and Posimotion Casts for the upcoming Pro Bowl, there were so many more injuries that season, and something had to be done.

There will be no Macy's parade Christmas Day.

Throughout the world military action reduces to virtually

zero, no jihads, no counterattacks, no assassinations or acts of terrorism. Temporary truces are declared and papers signed. Soldiers, politicians, revolutionaries, generals, privates and terrorists are home with family.

Violent crimes—robberies, rapes, murders—fall to almost nonexistent.

On Christmas Eve morning the astronomers announce they will make a statement later that afternoon. Throughout the day regularly scheduled programming is interrupted by remotes from the eerie, quiet entrance of the Palomar Observatory. CNN stays live on the air at that spot, but no one appears for hours, and only the security guards peer back at the assembled media, and at the millions of worldwide viewers.

The world waits.

It gets very quiet.

Suddenly the networks interrupt "The Year-in-Review" (Fox), "The Century-in-Review" (CBS), another special on comets (ABC), and a rerun of "It's a Wonderful Life" (NBC) with "Let's go live now to the Palomar Observatory. . . ."

The guards at the Palomar open the doors and stand to the side, so the media can file into the planetarium and set up under the dome-shaped roof.

Before all the media is settled the side door opens. Langdon Stofford leads Spencer Tennyson and the other astronomers to the table. Tennyson stands at the microphone at center, and a pin-drop silence blankets the room.

"Thank you ladies and gentlemen of the media, thank you ladies and gentlemen of the world. We have just completed and confirmed the data from the Schmidt Telescope, the Hubble, space-stationed radio telescopes and ground-based telescopes. If you will turn out the light bars. . . ."

After the fluorescent house lights dim the lights of the cameras dim and a holographic earth spins slowly above the assemblage. On the opposite side of the dome the sun appears.

"The Millennium Comet will strike the earth in seven days. This is the orientation of the Earth to the sun, as it will appear at that time. We had thought that there was a greater chance of the comet hitting the southern hemisphere, but this will not be the case. The comet will strike in the northern hemisphere, approximately here. . . ."

A laser-produced 'comet' materializes from behind the sun and follows a slow path across the room as the holographic Earth rotates. The comet impacts graphically, vividly, in North America, in the desert of the southwestern United States.

"The coordinates of impact will be thirty-seven degrees, twenty-eight minutes north latitude, one-hundred-fifteen degrees, forty-five minutes west longitude—about seventy miles north-northwest of the city of Las Vegas, near the Pintwater and Pahranagat Mountain ranges, state of Nevada, in the United States. If there are no questions, I recommend we all get to work evacuating a wide area."

"Seven days from today is New Year's Eve! What time?"

"In the daylight hours. Between three and five o'clock this time, Pacific time. If there are no further questions we will leave evacuation procedures up to the various governments."

"How far away does everyone have to get?"

"Every scenario has been discussed, there are no changes. Most everything in a six-hundred-mile radius will be destroyed. We recommend a one-thousand mile radius, but that is now up to the President and other leaders—and, of course, everyone within the circle."

People and possessions are evacuated with the efficiency of soldier ants. Lines of Ryder and U-haul rental trucks, school busses, Greyhound busses, Army and National Guard trucks, personal vans, flatbeds and cars file out of the six-hundred mile area now known as The Ring of the Millennium. Within the next seven days areas in and around Los Angeles, Flagstaff, Phoenix, and San Francisco are evacuated.

When the refugees show up in communities outside the Millennium Ring they are welcomed in homes, in churches, in gymnasiums, in community centers, in campgrounds and in state parks. The churches become centers for locating a home if one is displaced, or in need of food, or seeking a place to share spirituality with others.

"We've got room for you!" becomes a national slogan.

People from around the world send supplies of food, clothing, and medical supplies. Civil war in Africa stops while seven-and-a-half tons of canned goods are shipped to the U.S., some with foreign labels, some which had been sent from the U.S. originally.

"Do you have everything you need?" resounds across the land.

A journalist in USA Today writes: "It is interesting to witness, with a great religious prophesy seemingly being fulfilled, the religious peoples of Earth physically preparing for the Comet, and fleeing their churches within the Ring; the secular and religious are joining forces in a way that unites the family of humankind as never before.

"Those of little previous religious sentiment now share in a universal spirituality, complementing the belief that 'We shall overcome!' Is it the clan reuniting, fighting together to stave off the saber-toothed that lurks outside the cave? Are we the Family of Man after all?"

December 31st, 1999. New Year's Eve Day

The bottles of wine, whiskey, vodka, etc., are available for the drinking, along with the necessary additives. The beer is cold in the refrigerator. After all, it is the king of all New Year's Eve's parties, the last one of the 1900s, and falling on a night traditionally reserved for fun and frolic; it is Friday. But on this night the eagle is not flying, contrary to the old blues song. There's just not that much drinking going on—little sips here and there, little bites from the tray or plate, or tin or wooden bowl. Nibbles. Sips. Not a lot of eating. But a lot of touching, as if tribe members are verifying one another's presence, reassuring that they are ready to help them face the celestial enemy. Some recognizable degree of apprehension settles over the sentient intelligence of the planet, like that in a courtroom awaiting a jury's verdict in a murder trial. Families in their own living rooms speak in hushed tones and walk quietly around the house, as if one might be able to hear the comet coming and duck into a hallway closet or basement shelter.

It's the television or radio that has everyone's attention.

The eight astronomers are part of a team of thirty-six men and women who stay at the Palomar. By one o'clock p.m. Pacific time they are able to announce 4:03 p.m. Pacific as the time of impact. They say they will stay until three then retreat to a prepared shelter.

"Hopefully we will be able to monitor radiation and initial fallout."

The President of the United States and Chairman of the Joint Chiefs of Staff have not yet decided whether to launch bombs at the comet. The decision will not be made until all possible information is gleaned.

Robotic television cameras, what the television stations were calling 'sacrificial lens lambs,' dot the area where the comet is predicted to impact, following the occasional commands to turn their lenses skyward. The sacrificial uplink dishes look like huge white plates awaiting a serving.

At 2:59 Pacific time, one minute before midnight Greenwich Mean Time, Universal Time, in western Africa and in England, one minute until the year 2000, a light appears in the sky over North America. The world takes a deep breath. The cameras pick up the white point. Over the next hour the light grows brighter, a larger dot on the television screens around the world. People watch it breathlessly, holding hands, sitting very close.

At 4:03 p.m., Pacific time, the emphatic, controlled voice of Dr. Spencer Tennyson grows louder as the light grows bigger and brighter. "Ten . . . nine . . . eight . . . seven . . . six . . . five . . . Four . . . THREE . . . *TWO* . . .***ONE!"***

A great white light fills the screen.

Book II

The Book of Revelations

Seven months earlier, May 30th, 1999. Delta University, California.

Doj Bolderton abruptly halted his cross-campus trek. It was too beautiful a day to hurry. Besides, someone had left a chair under his favorite tree, a 230-foot sugar pine, and he had his dulcimer in his leather shoulder pouch. Classes would break in a few minutes. The coeds would parade down the walk and cross the green. He slipped the leather pouch off his shoulder and sat down on the chair, slid out his dulcimer, tuned the strings into the perfect 5th interval, three high d's and the g bass string, then began twanging through Richard Farina's song, "Pack Up Your Sorrows". It is a song of joy. Three people who knew him, and a coed who didn't, stopped to listen. The coed *did* know the high harmony on the chorus—her mother, she said, had been a hippy.

With his day pack and dulcimer on his back Doj continued his jog through campus, inspired by the lovely spring weather, the feeling of *primavera* in his heart, the excitement of meeting the pretty coed, a voice major, and getting her phone number, and the anticipation of spending some time with Langdon

Stofford, his closest friend, his mentor, and for the last seventeen years, his surrogate father.

Doj was sad that he hadn't spent much time with 'Stoffy' the past year, but ever since Stofford had won the Nobel Prize in Physiology two years previous, his dance card had been full with lectures and symposiums. Now the genius with so many interests was leaning toward astronomy. That Stoffy asked Doj to meet at his office and not over dinner was curious. The tone of his voice had portended something good. He bounded up the steps to the third floor of James Day Hall.

"Sorry I'm late, Stoffy; there was this beautiful alto—" Doj stopped mid-sentence.

Stofford had company, a thin man with large eyes, academic-looking. The man was appraising Doj even before he came to a stop.

"Excuse me, Stoffy . . . Dr. Stofford."

"It's OK, Doj. I'd like you to meet Dr. Spencer Tennyson. Dr. Tennyson is head of the Palomar Observatory. Dr. Tennyson and I have known each other for years and he is a part of the reason I asked you to come. Sit down." Stofford poured Doj a cup of 'team', tea with supplement 'M', which Stofford had invented in 1998. "Dr. Tennyson and I have a project you may be interested in. We've discussed your potential role in it, but I would like your permission to fill him in now on your background. I think it will clarify why I consider you to be the best candidate for this project."

Doj took a sip of the fragrant tea blend, scrutinizing Stoffy, realizing he had a few more gray hairs now in his . . . what . . . fifty-five years next week—remember that—and that he no longer resembled a younger Marlon Brando. There was less hair above the large cranium, but Stoffy was very fit physically and still exuded charisma and magnetism. But that day he had computer eyes, something was on his mind.

Doj nodded slowly, "Of course, Langdon. You know I trust you. You raised me. Where would I be without you?"

"Probably out of school, at least. OK. I'll start at the beginning. Doj, when your father was the head of the European Southern Observatory in Cerro Paranal, Chile, Dr. Tennyson knew him.

But Spencer, what you don't know is that Doj's parents didn't really die in a car accident." Stofford paused, started to take a sip of tea but put his cup back on the saucer. "They were murdered."

He sipped his tea then continued. "The observatory in Cerro Paranal was not doing well financially; the country was in turmoil and there was no money to support it. And, to make matters worse, the observatory was near coca fields, which Doj's parents were aware of. The family that owned the fields offered them eighty-thousand dollars and protection if they would do a simple favor for them; bring twelve kilos of cocaine to the states when they left in August 1983. Doj's parents decided to take the chance. His mother, Gabriella, a botanist, was always bringing plant specimens into the States; the boxes had ceased being searched ten trips before. The observatory needed the money. But when they got back to the U.S., they couldn't do it—they knew what cocaine did to human lives. Doj's parents told the police, who contacted the Drug Enforcement Agency. The DEA set up a bust.

"But the bust backfired. The drug lord had some soldiers that the police had not accounted for. The car was riddled with bullets and the car's occupants, including Doj's parents, went off a cliff."

Stofford sipped the tea, looked at Doj then back to Tennyson. "The whole matter was hushed up. And why not? There was no benefit in implicating Doj's mother and father, since they decided to do the right thing. We all know Emory Bolderton as one of the preeminent astronomers in the world, as Gabriella was a renowned botanist; they were dead as were the people they had turned in. The cash was recovered—do you remember the eighty-thousand dollars the IAU received that September as an anonymous gift, Spencer?"

"I've always wondered where that money came from. It saved two programs."

Stofford nodded. "So the newspapers did not mention foul play, nor the two officers who died with them. But the Bolderton's had left behind a son, Dojen. As their best friend, I became his guardian and set him up in his own place, since he had just graduated from high school that summer."

"I was angry," said Doj. "Remember how angry and cynical I was? I wanted to defy everything and everyone."

"You got that from your mother."

Doj told Tennyson, "I had just finished third in the California State High School Singles Tennis Championships; I graduated with a 3.8 G.P.A., though hardly studying; I was president of our chess club, and ran a pretty good 5K in cross-country. So my future was bright, but I tried to throw it all away. I got a Volkswagen van, started smoking pot and running in the mountains. I just wanted to escape from the world which had killed my parents. But there was no one to vent my anger at, so the anger consumed me. My parents had been my best friends, but it took a while to come to terms with the realities that I would never play chess with dad again, that Mother and I would never stroll through the woods, shooting pine cones with our bow and arrows, sharpening our aim as we sharpened our wit. So I fled into the Nevada desert, prepared to end it all. So I'm out there, running a hose from my exhaust system into my tent so I could get even with the world, when Stoffy drove up."

Stofford gestured with a wave of dismissal and said, "I had taken a transmitter beacon from one of the condors that died and stuck it under Doj's car; his action was predictable, and I felt I should know where he was. Well, we spent three nights together in the desert. I guess we got as close as we could get, separated, as we were, by age and background, but drawn together in that we shared the grief of Doj's parents dying. Well, eventually I talked Doj into enrolling at Delta, studying under my tutelage. . . ."

"And I've been here ever since, still not accepting the real world, or any world beyond the borders of our little academic island—that's what Stoffy would say if he was telling the whole truth."

"It took Doj nine years to end up six class hours short of a degree—and that was in physical education. He used up four years of varsity competition running cross-country in the fall and playing on the tennis team in the spring. Dojen played for the University Chess Club and has been top-ranked for most of fifteen years. He's got . . . let's see, what did I do with your transcripts? Here they are. Forty-eight credits in philosophy, thirty-seven in religious studies, twenty-eight credits in sports psychology, thirty-two in exercise physiology, twenty-eight-and-a-half in biomechanics of sport. You have one-hundred-twelve credits in music, with four in special musical studies—the Dynamics of the Hammer Dulcimer?"

Doj smiled sheepishly. "That was a tough program, Stoffy. Have you ever tried to *play* a hammer dulcimer?"

"Thirty-seven hours of archery?" Stoffy asked with a raised eyebrow.

"That was worth it! I got really good. Stand fifty yards away with an apple on your head and I'll prove it to you."

"Three credits in US Geography?"

"I know my state capitals. Try me."

"How about Wyoming?" said Tennyson.

"You've got thirty-six hours in psychology, including a three-hour course called Studying Faces?"

"Lines in one's face are the road map of one's life. Lips, for instance, reveal a lot. Tight lips means a tight anus, means a tight disposition, someone who's usually cheap, like this guy on our chess team that was so tight we tricked him into thinking WD-40 was underarm deodorant."

"You've got eighteen hours in sociology and forty-two in anthropology."

"Mankind *interests* me! I'm just not very fond of many of them. Womankind is more attractive. For instance this alto had perfect lips, which reveal. . . ."

"As soon as you near completion of something you tend to stop and go off in another direction," Stofford said sharply.

"A behavioral psychologist professor told me that's because my parents and I were so close, that when they died, a crucial part of my development never got finished; therefore, I can never finish anything for fear it will be taken away. Except this tea—could I have a tad bit more, Stoffy? I have a feeling the excrement is about to hit the oscillator." Doj smiled at Tennyson.

Stofford poured more tea, then sat back and looked at Doj for five beats before he said, "Doj, how would you like to be the son of God?"

Doj laughed at first, choking on hot tea, a good, deep, belly laugh. "Wonderful choice *there!*" When he saw the other two were not laughing, he set down his tea and said, "OK, sure." He waved away the notion, chuckled and shook his head. He leaned forward as if to wait for the punch line. "That's good, Stoffy!" Then he leaned back, extended and crossed his legs and took a sip of team, but the other two just stared at him. Doj shifted again, laughing at their expressionless faces, he pointed at either of them with his right hand, then crossed his arms.

"Stoffy, fill me in here. I have a feeling that this time I'm not just a guinea pig for a class you're teaching next term."

"Doj, have you ever heard of Mensa?"

"Of course. The high I.Q. society; Only those with the top two percent of all I.Q. scores are eligible to qualify. You're a member. I guess I could have been. I passed the test but then spaced out sending in the processing fee. I believe that makes me a Densa. I know, I actually bought this dulcimer with the money I'd allocated for Mensa. Want to hear a tune?"

"Doj, I know you're getting nervous; reality's coming—you knew it would come eventually. When would you like to stop winning at games which don't mean anything and play one which counts for something, besides fortifying your lofty self-image?"

Doj squirmed uncomfortably, took a deep breath. "Right now, it looks like."

He flashed back to those three days in the desert and his dialogue with Stoffy as they walked over sand washes and salt basins: "We're going to have to grow up now, Dojen," he'd said then, "both you *and* I. Doj, a time will come when you will leave me and pass on to mankind what you can. You will have a destiny." Doj now echoed his adolescent voice from sixteen years earlier: "Go on, Mr. Stofford."

"Have you ever heard of the Sigma Society?"

"No."

"The Sigma Society is a rather secret membership of the American Mensa—only the top percentages of the I.Q. scores of the *Mensa* members qualify for Sigma. Dr. Tennyson and I are both members."

"This is getting good. More, please."

"There are thirty-six of us, men and women, who are Sigmas. Besides Dr. Tennyson, seven other astronomers are members. Among the others are a sociologist, a television executive, a biogeneticist, two NASA officials, a surgeon, a CEO of an entertainment conglomerate, an ambassador, and a university president. Last August one of our members, Garland Stein, was murdered."

"I remember that."

Tennyson said. "At the time Stein was president of the International Astronomical Union, a brilliant man, who was deeply loved; we had made great strides under his leadership. He was at the Livingstone Observatory on Mount Lusaka and came between two warring tribes. They held him and his wife hostage, turned his observatory into a stronghold, before it was bombed. Arlene Stein, his wife, also a Sigma, was paralyzed. His death shook the very foundations of those in the astronomical fraternity, as well as in Sigma Society. We were shocked. He was a charismatic and happy person, our spiritual leader. We could make no sense of it."

Stofford continued, "Our September, 1998 meeting, hosted by Dr. Tennyson, was at the Palomar Observatory. Stein's death was all we could talk about; nothing on our agenda was addressed for two days. It was then that we began to realize there was nothing really unusual about his death, certainly not on a global scale, but not even the media took notice. It was just another paragraph on page three which washed into the violent history of this century. The world went on, and nothing changed. We kept asking ourselves who was responsible, and after three days we came up with the answer: We were responsible. All of us. And if someone did not take the initiative, the next century would continue in the same fashion as the twentieth, with more decadence and displacement, with more hopeless life and senseless death. We talked, some of the greatest minds in the world, late nights around a campfire, mornings hiking in the mountains, afternoons locked in a room. Something had to change. We determined that if people actually saw that the human race was on a path to destruction, they might wake up to face reality. Warnings of inevitable environmental and societal destruction were going largely unheeded. We felt the people of the world needed to see, actually *realize,* that destruction was imminent, that we were passing a point of no return. Only in that way would people react, make some change."

Doj is wide-eyed. "So how are you going to make people see we humans are on a path to destruction and . . . uhhh . . . where do I come in?"

Tennyson said, "We reasoned that society would never self-destruct totally. Humans would simply continue to blame one another, while violence and territorial greed continued. But if there were some outside force on the verge of destroying Earth, and people believed the end was near. . . ."

Stofford continued, "We have to stop the wars, the violence in our streets, in our homes, the degradation of the planet and its resources, xenophobia and ethnocentrism. . . ."

"So you want me to dress up like Spiderman?"

"We are going to predict that a massive comet will impact with Earth and end most or all of life on the planet."

"Sweet Jesus."

"No, that's where you come in," said Stofford.

"Our sociologist said, and many of us agreed, that it would not be enough to simply say this comet is coming," said Tennyson. "The announcement would fulfill biblical prophesy for many around the world, but for others it would simply be an act of nature. A logical reaction would be for people to hoard. Promoting greed is not the goal of this quest."

Stofford said, "The Sigmas believe that the appearance of a religious figure at the same time, predicting these events, performing apparent miracles, could move the denizens of the planet to get their houses in order, so to speak. We want to teach the world a lesson."

"This is . . . so much, my mind's going a million miles per second. How would people react?"

Tennyson said, "Doj, an airplane crashed outside Chicago last week. The last thing the pilot said was 'Oh God, help us!' The pilot was a member of a group, Atheists Perpetuating Evolution." Tennyson paused until the import dawned in Doj's eyes. "In time of great crisis, people turn to spiritualism, and to each other.

They look inward for strength and reach out for support. Reaction to imminent disaster and catastrophe is universal and predictable ever since our primal ancestors banded together to defend and attack. Indeed, that's how mankind came to rule the world in the first place; the ability to cooperate. But at some point in our development, there were too many of us to cooperate, so we started to work apart. We, as scientists and doctors, can no longer stand by and watch the fabric of human society unravel any longer. The scientific community has done so much to supposedly make life better in this century: curing polio, and other diseases, introducing computer technology, but also building the atomic bomb and developing biological and chemical warfare."

It got very quiet in the room, then Stofford spoke. "If humankind can be rudely awakened to face sudden and grave peril. If, for three months, three weeks, three *days*, the brotherhood of man can ignore walls or erase boundaries, can be coerced to work together, relearn cooperation and, of their own volition, establish worldwide peace. It will be worth the risk."

Doj gaped at both men. A songbird in the fan palm outside the window caught his attention for a moment before he said, "So I am to be the predictor, the messenger of God. How do you propose to pull this off?"

Tennyson and Stofford let out a breath and almost imperceptibly nodded to one another before Tennyson said, "Have you ever heard of Jackson Hole, Wyoming?"

June 16th, 1999. 5:18 a.m.

Doj slowly, groggily woke up in his hospital room at Delta University Medical Center. Stofford and Tennyson, the doctor who performed the operation, and a woman he didn't know were standing around his bed.

"How do you feel?" asked Stofford.

"Can I get another shot of whatever that was? I feel like I'm having a slow-motion orgasm."

"How does your right ear feel?" asked the doctor.

Doj slowly sat up in the bed, rubbed his eyes, then blinked. "I can't really feel anything—maybe just a little ear wax."

"Good," said the doctor. "The micro-eustacian transreceiver is in your left ear, right up against your middle ear. Let's get a volume check on it. Dr. Stofford?"

Stofford stepped out into the hall and walked twenty yards down the darkened vacated corridor. He whispered, "Doj, the woman standing in front of you is Dr. Singer. When we met at her first IAU meeting, she and I ended up in a Jacuzzi until quite late that night. Ask her if she remembers what happened after that."

"Dr. Singer, what happened after you and Stoffy got out of the that first night?"

The woman blushed slightly. "I'd say the micro-eustacian transreceiver is working perfectly." She opened the door and called into the dark hallway, "Stoffy, dear, get your maximus back in here."

Stofford returned. "Welcome to the SigNet, Mr. Bolderton."

June 17th, 8:50 a.m.

Doj turned from his packed '71 Volkswagen van in front of James Day Hall, and Stofford, Tennyson and Condesca Singer stood next to him as bells rang close and far, signifying the end of the first period. Stofford shook Doj's hand, hugged him, then stepped back.

"In this envelope there are five thousand dollars in traveler's checks and three hundred in cash to get you going."

"Stoffy, you don't have that kind of money."

"The Nobel Prize and its subsequent benefits have paid well. Don't worry, we've got more. Think of the money as an investment. You'll stop in Las Vegas, go to Caesar's Palace, and ask for George Greystoke. He's the owner. He's also a Sigma. If you tell us when you walk in the door, he will find you. He will have something for you. Stay away from the casino; I know you like to gamble."

"Only when I win, Stoffy, you know that. This fifty-three

hundred just about covers your chess losses over the last twenty years."

"You got lucky. Now pay attention. We've eliminated any link between you and us. There's no paper nor electronic trail. We're linked only by the SigNet now. You *will* be investigated, and they *will* know you went to school here, but they will not establish a link between you and me. Your legal guardian has been your deceased maternal grandmother. I will keep my name out of the comet thing for as long as I can. I'll be in the background as Spencer's assistant. The comet will be Dr. Tennyson's puppet."

"You will make your prediction on the 25th," Tennyson told Doj. "That's in eight days. You must obtain as much media exposure as you can. We will follow with an announcement three days after that."

"We will be in contact through your transreceiver," said Stofford. "Pulling your earlobe will activate it, but don't make it too obvious—brush that hippie hair behind your ear and pull your lobe. That's it. If you don't want us to hear what you're saying pulling your lobe again will turn it off."

"Don't be kidding me about my hair."

"It looks good," Dr. Singer said. "You look like the picture of Jesus on my grandmother's dining room wall, only more handsome."

"If one person says I look like Peter Frampton, I'm going to smack them."

"Now don't get into any trouble," said Stofford. "When you get to Jackson Hole, find Taft Vandren. He's our Sigma there. He's lived there on and off for fifty years. Listen to what he says. He's working on some crucial biogenetic research in the Yellowstone area. You can help him, but be careful in everything you do. Remember, when you're talking to us, anyone around you will be able to hear what you're saying as well. And about the hand laser: We're not sure about that, so don't get carried away with it. The laser is physical evidence you might not be exactly, shall we say, of divine influence. Use it only if you have to. If you're threatened maybe those thirty-six hours of karate, aikido and tai chi will prove of some use. Our network of Sigmas throughout the world will support you in ways you probably wouldn't think possible. Taft said Jackson Hole has artists, writers, and lots of outdoors types, but also cowboys and rednecks, so don't let your mother's gift for cynicism get you killed, Dojen."

Stofford took a deep breath then grasped Doj firmly by the shoulders. Stofford sighed and his expression changed, softened. Over the past sixteen years Doj Bolderton had come to be his only son, his only family. He's loved the brilliant young man as any father has loved any son, and he is now worried about his young charge, the only thing he has ever devoted himself to besides his work. "Is there anything else I need to say to you, Dojen?"

"I love you, Stoffy."

"I love you too, Doj." Stofford blinked several times, then turned away to wipe his eyes. "God, we've never said that to one another."

"Now, how do I get to Jackson Hole?"

"Where's your map?"

"I don't have a map."

"Oh lord," moaned Stofford. "We're trying to save the human race and we can't even figure out how to get to Wyoming. Condesca?"

She flips her purse open, hits several keys on a lap top, waits a second, hits a couple more and says, "Take 210 to Route 2. Then 2 to 138. I-15 north to exit 39, follow the signs to Caesar's. . . ."

"I just hope I don't enter into a stretch of bad luck at the craps table." Doj smiled. "Only kidding, Stoffy."

"Then back on I-15 to Brigham City, Utah, exit 362, pick up 89 through Logan, stay on 89 and around thirty miles out, Taft will pick you up on the SigNet, direct you to his cabin."

"Is there anything else, Dojen?" said Stofford.

"You know, I was thinking about this. I've never actually even read the bible."

"We'll net you the highlights," said Condesca Singer. "You may need some words of faith while you're driving through Utah."

"Do you think I could squeeze a master's thesis out of this, if it works?"

June 21st, 1999, Jackson Hole, Wyoming, 8:47 a.m.

Wilma Tackitt, the owner of Conestoga Cabs, and Kaela Welch, her 8-year driver, were sitting on stools at opposite sides of the counter when Wilma's day manager walked in holding the dispatch phone in one hand and the two-way radio in the other.

There were two raps on the wooden door. . . .

Doj *had* read the classifieds in the local papers when he got to Jackson Hole. Except for teaching tennis to undergrads and being a research assistant, he'd never had a job. He was able to eliminate executive secretary, carpenter, waiter, busboy, town planner and bartender, so the cab driver ad sounded the best—he would get to see the countryside, get the lay of the land, and the ebb and flow of this mountain resort town. Taft Vandren knew most everyone and everything which had happened in the valley for the last fifty years, and he would be Doj's ally and his relay to other members. He could talk to Doj directly, patch him to the SigNet, or arrange a conference call with any or all of the other Sigmas, all through the micro-transreceiver in Doj's ear.

Their first test was easy—Doj's cab test—"Where's Jackson Lumber?" was the perfect question. Taft Vandren had built his three cabins himself, as well as the small laboratory, so he was well acquainted with the lumberyards.

On the second test, Doj just got lucky. Taft had written the science column for the *Jackson Hole News* periodically for thirteen years, mostly covering local ecology. Had Kathy even remembered that staff party at the cabin in the woods when they'd all ended up in the hot tub? She was younger then, and wild, and drunk, and probably wouldn't remember having told the story about her grandfather getting attacked, then putting her butt in Taft's face to show him her grizzly bear tattoo.

Doj spent about three seconds being tentative about the project when he got to Jackson Hole. "Check it out! There are *people* outside the world of academia! This is like another planet!" Doj told Stofford over the SigNet.

There he was, in the middle of the mountains, the majestic

Tetons. In his time off he started running mountain trails, getting stronger than he'd been since winning an intramural 5K nine months before, and in this environment his confidence swelled.

Doj knew full well the state of the world. He *had* travelled some, but mostly with the tennis team or the cross country team or the chess club. And there were the three bow hunting trips to New Mexico with Stoffy, but those forays were into the world of nature. "Nature is the only real, true dimension," said Stofford, and a younger Dojen Bolderton smiled, and looked around, and nodded.

When he travelled with his various college teams he stayed at pretty nice places, but he was there to win, that's where his energy was spent. The chess club trips showed him there was a separate reality out there, especially the 'unofficial' trips down to the Santa Monica International Chess Park at Venice Beach to play speed chess for money. For Doj, that was great sport and easy money for just using his mind, competition that didn't leech his abundant physical energy.

In Jackson he was able to challenge his mind and body, and he had the support of the SigNet. When he walked into the *Jackson Hole News*, Doj expected he might have to use the laser. It had worked fine off of the Granite Canyon trail. He'd extended his right arm and the ingenious set of tiny pulleys jettisoned the tiny flesh-colored tube to the edge of his index finger; the silent laser beam needed only three passes to cut off a four-inch branch. It took him four tries to draw for accuracy and hit the pine cone. A squirrel tried to run off with it while it was still smoldering.

The whole thing in the newspaper office went pretty well, though Doj didn't know that the Dylan poster had been autographed and was worth money.

He was less sure at the town square. Neither he nor any of the Sigmas could be sure what the reaction would be when he predicted the comet. That would be a huge step, and the SigNet would be listening. It was unfortunate that he'd thrown the cowboy up on the statue, but Taft had vouched for him.

"He deserved it, Langdon," said Taft, "Doj is right where he should be and we look forward to hearing the International

Astronomical Union's announcement in a few days. Then we'll see how well the limb we're out on holds up."

If Langdon Stofford had taken the place of Doj's father, Taft Vandren was taking the place of a beloved, caring uncle. At sunset they would walk through the woods; Taft would identify the flora and fauna, telling Doj the remarkable history and ecology of Jackson Hole, the Tetons, and Yellowstone.

Veronica, the beautiful but suicidal woman he picked up in his cab, had been tough for him. The SigNet had nothing on her, and all Taft could come up was two DUIs and her big credit card balance, so Doj had been on his own.

The class he'd taken, Reading Faces, showed there was hope. Her face showed she experienced much laughter and joy in her life; her large and wide-open eyes, generous and slightly parted lips and forward facing mannerism indicated that her and probably her mother's trust in people were her greatest asset and biggest liability.

There was much to be admired within this young woman; Doj made her feel that. His only regret, which he expected, was that she soon lapsed.

The hardest part of dealing with Veronica was leaving her warm, yearning, glistening body there on the bed, for Doj was a healthy male in his sexual prime. His relationships with Delta coeds lasted a year or two, maybe three, but finally it was always his refusal to leave campus and graduate to the real world which ended them.

He knew he couldn't let himself get involved with Veronica.

For once, he owed it to himself, to Stoffy, and to the world to see the Millennium Project succeed. He came to realize then, too, the power of his amazing gifts, a natural intelligence and insight honed under the tutelage of one of the most eclectically brilliant humans on Earth. Doj's fifteen years at Delta University, the Harvard of the west, where he immersed himself in psychology and sociology were invaluable. He studied human behavior, scrutinized and classified postures, gestures, soma types, clothes, faces and eyes—so important were the eyes—the entrance way into the mind. His ability to foresee complex lines of possibilities in chess play crossed over to an ability to see possible behaviors in people. He could *anticipate* what people were going to do before they did it. Analyzing situations was another game to Doj—and, with the help of the Net, he was good at it.

"I am the new prophet. I am prescient," he privately told a roiling Snake River, then publicly repeated to a reporter.

For Doj, shooting the deer was an act of submission into the world of nature. Edgar Rick Burrough's *Tarzan* books were some of the first he'd ever read, handed down from his grandfather and father. Doj became that noble English lord turned king of the jungle. He reenacted Tarzan's ritual of killing and immediately eating the flesh of his prey. Part of the animal *became* him.

When the first news release came out, merely mentioning that a comet was to pass by the solar system, Doj was confused. He'd thought the Sigmas would make a definitive announcement.

Taft just nodded and said, "I expected that." He suspected a few of the Sigmas were not convinced they should go through with the project. When Taft and Doj conferenced on the SigNet with Stoffy, that turned out to be the case; three members thought they should call it off—it was taking too many chances. The whole thing could backfire and lives could be lost; any blood shed would be on the hands of the Sigmas, despite their philanthropic intentions.

"At any rate, the dissenters agreed to announce the comet was *out* there," Stofford told Doj. "Let's see the reaction. Taking this cautiously is a good idea. You're out there farther than we are, but you need to be—the prophet needs to appear before the prophesy. And pawn to queen's bishop four. By the way, remember to turn off your transreceiver when you're giving a massage."

Doj was actually quite confident in the July 4th 10K running race. He felt just brazen enough to predict he would win and break the course record. His PR—personal record—was 30:58, a minute and a half faster than the course record. What he didn't take into account, however, was the altitude, the thin air. But Doj hated Jason Land's overbearing arrogance and that motivated him to disregard the burning pain in his legs and lungs during the mad sprint. Doj *did* have some pride, he *was* a NCAA Division IIA All-American and even though that was ten years before he never stopped training. He still had 60-second quarter track speed.

With the help of the micro-transreceiver, Taft guided Doj through the interview with Sheriff Clark and Chief Nuxhall. Taft remembered when Jed Clark competed in cross country for Jackson Hole High School, also Taft had access to the *News* CompuFiles at his fingertips.

Through the SigNet Taft accessed the law enforcement personnel files of the State of Wyoming. It was no problem. For Doj, bantering with Chief Nuxhall and Sheriff Clark was fun. It was a verbal tennis match, and Doj thought of himself as the game master.

But Doj's world came to a cul-de-sac, a high-mountain cirque, when he drove the parents and Herbie, their dying child, to the support group. There was nothing in his experience that could help him, nothing Taft or the SigNet could say, and Doj lost his composure. He had no answer to give to Herbie, or any of the parents of those sick and dying children. No hope to offer. There was no one to direct his frustration toward. He went into the mountains, to the only place he knew to go, to ask for an answer. He looked to the setting sun, and he looked to the heavens. But it was Stoffy he pleaded to, and Tennyson, and three other Sigmas who were on the SigNet at the time. They were his Gods, and they were powerless as well. They reminded him that the Project's purpose was to show people that if they could work together, instead of spending so much time and effort working apart, they'd have the resources to find cures for some of the diseases that inflicted humankind. The Herbies can be cured. Doj's contribution was essential if there was any chance.

Doj felt helpless and hopeless, but the episode finally served to strengthen his resolve.

The chess tournament diverted his thoughts from Herbie and the suffering in the world. Diverted indeed, Doj infused all of his immense powers of concentration into the task at hand. The challenge of 'if I' and 'then he' and 'then if I' played to the nth degree was the forte of the game master—it exercised neural pathways that hadn't been stimulated in seven weeks, since he beat Tennyson the night before he left. Playing Kaiser was most rewarding, for Kaiser was a good player, a classic player. Kaiser knew all the openings, but in the middle game Kaiser's powers of imagination were inferior to those of Doj's. He made Kaiser squirm. Kaiser should have exchanged queens when he had the chance; but Kaiser didn't know Doj became impatient with the banality of end games.

Doj recognized he'd met his match in Toby Tiler. Doj refused to use the SigNet, even though one of the Sigmas was a grandmaster, and they could tie into the Chessomputer. Doj refused, that is, until the Rastjahmon played knight to bishop 4. The Jamaican didn't psych Doj out, he simply had the ability to look one move deeper into the board. He played better. Ordinarily, Doj would have let the Toby win graciously, but Doj knew he must not lose credibility, not if he was to be known as the son of God. The people following the tournament, the residents of the valley, the world, needed to see he was flawless. Against his moral judgement Doj went on the SigNet, stated the position of the pieces, and the grand master and the Chessomputer came up with the same move, rook captures knight, a brilliant sacrifice, an eventual winner.

What blew Doj away was the fact that Toby *recognized* his demeanor had changed, his "aura went to yellow." He recognized in the Rastjahmon a kindred spirit; they were on the same wavelength but a different frequency. Toby's spirit was dark but a brightness shined from inside. In Toby's presence Doj felt stiff, empirical. But for the first time in his life—besides Stofford—Doj experienced friendship. Teammates were friends, but they were also obstacles in the path to victory. Doj had to be number one on the team, any team. He recognized in Toby an exuberant soul, neither offensive or defensive, who thrived in the present tense, and vibrated with a zest for life.

The Rastjahmon was the brother that perished *in utero* when his parent's car fell off the cliff.

The day after he met Toby Doj recalled a Sigmund Freud quote: "How bold one gets when one is sure of being loved." Toby emboldened him. He absorbed Toby's outlook on life that everything is irie (wonderful). When they appeared on *The Whole JaHo Show*, Doj was at his best.

Taft Vandren was known as a renowned biogeneticist and a chemist. For the show he laughingly concocted a compound Doj slipped into the water glasses of the hostess and guests, a drug he called SPEECH. For *S*odium Pentathol—also known as truth serum—; *P*rozac; a designer drug called *E*cstasy; *E*lavil; *C*odeine; and *H*alcion. "Right past the R-complex, directly to the subconscious," said Taft. "Their most secret and unconscious desires will be exposed. It should be fun. With this drug, if you get a SPEECH, it will be the truth."

Rastjahmon's story of his near-death experience even made Doj wonder about life and afterlife, for Doj had lived his life in academia where there was a cause-and-effect, a logical explanation for everything that occurred, and he never really contemplated what happened after death. He had taken classes, even religious studies, but Toby was someone who believed in afterlife because he had *been* there, and everything about Toby seemed true and honest. Toby made an afterlife inviting, his account of it made Doj's life seem richer and, perhaps, destined for some higher plane.

Doj had never witnessed such venom as when everyone verbally attacked one another during *The Whole JaHo Show*. And such tightly woven pieces of moral fabric within the community! Taft thought the dosage was perhaps a little too strong. But all ended well, according to Taft, who later heard that Regina and Dannette turned out to be quite an item.

What next opened Doj Bolderton's eyes toward a new direction was when Taft guided him and Toby to, and told them all about, Yellowstone National Park. Doj felt drawn here. He was mesmerized by the primordial hot springs, geysers, and mud pots; their close proximity to the seething interior of the Earth made him feel a new relationship with earth: symbiotic.

Doj felt he belonged among the wolf, moose, and herds of elk and buffalo, for he was a hunter, and there he was in the land of plenty. At least the land of plenty of ungulates.

When Taft led them beyond the Grand Canyon of the Yellowstone and into Pelican Valley, where one of the few grizzlies in the lower forty-eight roamed, the three went unarmed, and never were Doj's senses so keen. The grizzly was an adult male and they followed his six-inch-wide prints. He was the last of his kind that were once kings of the Rocky Mountains for so many years, and that bear had mauled a hiker the summer before.

The second morning, in Yellowstone, when Doj and Toby Tiler ran to Lone Star Geyser, the geyser erupted just as they came out of the woods and saw the strange cone. They screeched and shrieked and postured like apes. At that point Doj felt predestined to complete the task set forth for him, for he had evidence now, tangible, solid evidence, that the planet Earth could indeed be heaven and that this Yellowstone Park—primal, raw, burnt and (nearly) untampered with—was the crown jewel in a planet's tiara of wonders.

The eruption was an awakening for Doj. Because there was a Yellowstone Park there was hope and just as Lone Star erupted, he no longer wanted to do this for Stofford, but now he wanted to do it for anyone who might ever have a chance to see Lone Star Geyser erupt by themselves, or with someone close. The powerful eruption of hot water and steam was a mental, spiritual, and physical climax, and a self-actualization. It was a message to him from the heart of the Earth.

When they got back to the Old Faithful Inn they showered then joined Taft in the dining room and Taft showed them the USA Today article: Tennyson announced to the world the comet was coming closer than predicted. The next step was taken. Doj and Taft exchanged meaningful glances. The IAU meeting scheduled for August 23rd would be the moment of decision, but they did not verbalize that, for Toby was there, and Doj and Taft agreed that Toby needed to be kept out of it. If the whole thing blew up there was no need to implicate someone innocent.

So the FBI showed up and Doj was 'requested' to do Yellowstone tours. He would get paid to meander around one of the great wonders of the world and tell stories about it.

Toby said, "Aaahhh, Bolderdoj, the Yellowstone makes your aura a richer color than I have ever seen. The Rastjahmon likes the Yellowstone so much, the color of the Silex Spring and the

Morning Glory is so much like the waters in Jamaica when the mother sea is being kind."

The annual International Astronomical Union IAU meeting was, in fact, a meeting of all the Sigmas. They were there or on the NetScreen, as was Taft Vandren. The resolve of the three dissenting Sigmas was eroding, for they marked the one-year anniversary of the death of Garland Stein with a video of his life and work, and when the lights came up in the planetarium his wife was there, in a wheel chair. Shrapnel from the explosion that had killed her husband fragmented one of Arlene Stein's vertebra as she tried to shield him, leaving her partially paralyzed. She dropped out of the Sigmas after that, and this was her first appearance since.

The effect in the planetarium was astounding, as if the comet itself came crashing through the roof. Arlene Stein had been a writer and eloquent lecturer, and her impassioned speech supported the Millennium Project:

"The Chamber of Horrors that society has become, in so many pockets of the world, we *know*, in our hearts and in our minds, will continue into the twenty-first century. Your own projections tell you the planet will pass its sustaining capacity in the year 2012, just from the sheer numbers of humans. Fortunate citizens, prepared citizens—the powerful and wealthy and resourceful—will support those that aren't for as long as they can, until they come crashing through our doors. If the Millennium Project is a success we may save lives. If we don't attempt *some action,* can we as easily share the burden of malingering decay, followed by an agonizing death without honor?"

Two of the dissenting Sigmas affirmed the plan and still the last one, Dr. Cominelli, was reticent.

"If we are successful we will, at the least, alter entire world economies. Billions will be spent on preparation. We can also envision riots and looting. If I knew a comet was coming that would end life on Earth, I would not work, nor would anyone else. A worldwide work stoppage like that would create havoc in and of itself. Surgeons not going to work? Police? The ramifications are just too far beyond even our scope."

"That is why we are revealing the comet in stages, to carefully monitor social reaction," said Dr. Cooper. "We can always back out, say the comet's not coming. That's why we've put our comet in opposition, so we can reevaluate our position thirty-two days from now."

"And no amateur astronomer can be looking for it if it's in opposition," said Tennyson. "Within these thirty-two days if we abort the project we will simply say our sungrazer was pulled into the sun."

"The point *is*," said Stofford, "we've agreed that, one, the life struggle to survive is basic and implacable, every species fights to survive, and two, that there are just too many of us competing, that we don't *need* to compete but we compete subtly, aggressively and territorially anyway, and three, we'll continue to fight and struggle against some ideal, or for some boundary, or against some real or imagined enemies until we reach some kind of homeostasis, probably after a global-scale conflict such as a war or viral adaptation, and four, we are attempting to solve the problems we've identified sooner, which we believe is better than later."

"Believe is some immeasurable distance from know," Dr. Stofford," said Cominelli.

So the Sigmas made a statement the comet was coming closer and there was a chance, albeit small, that it could impact with Earth, and the reaction around the world was mixed: some people were frightened; some viewed it as God's final judgement; and some saw it as justification for deeds and misdeeds. Those reactions were correctly predicted by the Sigmas.

But when the Sigmas absorbed world reaction more of the members became less sure of the project. A major block, not surprisingly, were the three Sigmas with families and children, for the spouses called during their week at Mount Palomar, voiced their concern, and they had to be lied to. And the Millennium Project could never be a majority vote, it had to be unanimous—that was agreed on from the beginning. At the end of that week they voted. There were five nays and the whole thing was off. Astronomer Cominelli possibly best voiced the concern of the dissenters:

"We are in an experiment which, like Dr. Stofford stated,

counts on all of human nature to respond with an instinct for survival. A choice that is morally good. But if we believe in the basic good, and trust the instinct for survival, then we must trust human nature now, for the instinct to survive is resulting in positive advances in many ways and in many places. There *is* much good going on as we speak. Along with the great destruction and wars of this century we have also made, some of the people in this room, great strides in medicine. No longer do we fear so many diseases. We are getting closer to curing cancer, AIDS, and heart disease. Common sense is prevailing in judicial legislation, and in neighborhoods around the world people are starting to address problems locally. We *do* want the world to be a desirable place for our children, for *my* children. The Cold War ended in this century, the Berlin Wall came down, apartheid has been overturned. China, for one, has stabilized its population growth. On environmental issues, humans rights issues, society has been slow to react but they *do* react and in many ways life is so much better than August 31st of *1899*. Let us direct our vast energies and resources in a direction that could help alleviate the salient problems we have hereby identified."

The comet wasn't coming.

Stofford and Tennyson thought it would be best if Doj was cut off from the Net. Taft agreed. Doj agreed.

But Doj believed the Sigmas would change their minds. Even Stofford voiced a small ray of hope, evidenced by the fact that the astronomers didn't announce the comet was definitely *not* coming, but perturbed into a different orbit. If Stofford and Tennyson were sure the Sigmas would abort the project they would have had the comet go into the sun, quite normal for a comet entering the inner solar system.

When Doj was cut off from the SigNet he also felt cut off from his life, what came to be his life's mission: to contribute his part to make the planet a better place to live; a planet, especially since Yellowstone, he was building an ever-greater love for. He knew that there were many great minds—not just Sigmas, but academicians, scientists, anonymous philanthropists, working to improve the quality of life. Doj wanted to contribute, but now he wasn't sure what role he should assume. He pondered the fact that, so often in the twentieth century, great minds with similar motivation took a turn down a different path. How often were religious leaders defrocked and political leaders disempowered because of fraud, sexual improprieties, lying, stealing, cheating or conspiring? And how could our battle heroes, or sport heroes, be capable of wrongdoing? Drugs? Alcohol abuse? Why are they tempted? Are their lives better once they give into such temptations? He looked to the writer Joseph Campbell for answers. He found answers—he recognized heroes and gods as myths that left people earthbound, feeling inadequate.

The coat of armor he had grown into—a gift from the island sanctuary of Delta University—had been penetrated.

So Doj was frustrated. Instead of visualizing his part in a successful Millennium Project, he went into the mountains at night and gazed into an empty void. There was no one to blame.

He remembered a Rousseau quote he had read the day after the Sigmas said the comet was not coming: "Every man has the right to risk his own life in order to save it."

Doj could no longer risk his or save it.

The games of conquest he could escape into suddenly seemed immature and inconsequential to the gravity of the Millennium Project.

What helped was the correspondence with Lisen. It was apparent in their long, handwritten letters that the intense, initial physical attraction underlied a natural complement in heart, soul, and temperament.

They shared similar views of music and nature, and in hopes and fears. She was more pragmatic. She wrote, "The awareness of the ambiguity of one's achievements—as well as one's failures—is a symptom of maturity. Keep growing, Doj."

Lisen's letters and running long trails through the forest assuaged Doj, but the outside world still obsessed and angered him. He needed someone to direct it to, and in MTV's *Crossfire* he found the catharsis he needed.

Crossfire was competition. It was in his blood and Doj thrived on it. He had to compete and he had to win—and he had the skill, talent and knowledge to win any competitive endeavor he entered.

But after Survival his blood slowed and cooled and he was back in Jackson Hole. Taft told him the number of Millennium Project dissenters was holding at five and Doj and Taft shared remorse with Tennyson and Stofford after they announced to the world, "There is little or no chance the Tennyson will hit the earth."

Doj was tempted to go when Toby invited him to Jamaica, but that seemed like the easy way out, though he wasn't sure what he was trying to escape. Something needed to change and Doj was powerless to affect that change.

He felt no remorse in killing the hunters that attacked them, for the hunters shot one of the few humans, Doj determined, that needed to be on the planet, besides just being his friend. The hunters to Doj were earth scum, evolutionary failures, as well as former criminals. The two oldest had a prior conviction for poaching, killing one of the few grizzlies left in Yellowstone. The youngest, during the previous winter, had been arrested and fined for driving his snowmobile drunk, crashing into another snowmobiler, injuring her, fleeing the scene, then driving his machine into a Yellowstone thermal pool and clogging it.

The only remorse Doj felt was in that he did not actually terminate the organisms himself, but the fact that the wolves ultimately killed them gave the whole thing an ironic touch.

Toby said, "Those men were not carried by the wolves to the bright light."

When Doj thought Toby had died and Doj commandeered the airways, it caused another rumble among the Sigmas, for the head of CNN News was a Sigma, a strong pro-Millennium voice. He approved of the transmission uplink when Taft requested it. At first they thought Doj was going to reveal the Project. It caused a rumble and some of the Sigmas wanted Doj muzzled.

But Stofford and Tennyson saw Doj's "There is no God" speech as tilling the seedbed in the summer of discontent which made it the perfect time to sow. There was talk of the Pro-Millennium Sigmas breaking off, forming what Stofford called the Delta Faction. But the Italian astronomer, Cominelli, the chief Millennium opponent, vowed he would blow the whistle, he felt that strongly.

That is, until he was murdered outside his observatory near Bolzano, Italy by the neighbor who spent his life savings building half of a comet shelter. Cominelli had spoken brilliantly in justifying aborting the project. His was a passionate voice of reason and hope, and he was an optimistic stalwart amongst the Sigmas. But he was murdered and that was the event that turned the tide.

Dr. Shaku might have voiced the appropriate sentiment when he said, "I knew in my heart that the Millennium Project was the right thing to do. But in my mind I absorbed the smallest ray of hope, Cominelli was the beacon and reflector for our individual rays of hope, but the beacon is extinguished and I see no light down the darkest of corridors. This potentially great civilization is walking down a decaying path, and we have a chance to let everyone glimpse the dead end. We've seen the writing on the wall, now we must reveal the writing in the sky. Dr. Cominelli is dead, tomorrow it could be any one of you, my esteemed and valued friends and colleagues. I change my vote."

So did the three others and the Tennyson was coming. Stofford suggested changing the name of the comet to the Millennium, concerned for Dr. Tennyson's safety.

The SigNet embraced Doj's return. He was back in business, and the Millennium Comet was heading for a rendezvous with Mother Earth.

Doj re-anteed for the most important game he had ever played; he became the white bishop, the rook, and the knight all combined into one.

The Sigmas predictions were correct: People of the world *did* work together. Wars were halted, borders dissolved, grudges put aside, hate and prejudice suspended. People worked together to fortify against the common threat.

Yes, there was greed and stockpiling, for that was the way of some people. They were the exceptions, for some things never change, and hoarders were isolated.

Aisha and Lisen showed up just in time for the fireworks. Doj saw Lisen; she filled a void in his heart, and he loved her.

The Haties guessed correctly—it was dynamite that blew up Blacktail Butte—but the lasers from the IAU satellite, even though a little late, blasted the peaks of the Tetons and Doj had his unwavering following.

The world prepared, and waited.

Though technically it was the eve of the 1999th year after the birth of Jesus Christ, everyone called it Millennium Eve. As midnight approached sacrificial cameras dotted hundreds of square miles around the impact zone. Satellites from outer space beamed pictures. As the white dot appeared on the screen hardly anyone breathed. Many took a good stiff drink. The voice of Dr. Tennyson filled living rooms around the world as the white light grew brighter and the emphatic, scientific voice of Dr. Tennyson grew louder.

". . . six . . . five . . . Four . . . THREE . . . TWO . . . ONE!" and a great white light filled the screen.

Book III

The Gospel According to Caesar's Palace

A deep rumble accompanies the great white light. The tone is deep, resonant, chordal. Ninety-nine times the sound reverberates then suddenly a face fills television screens around the world. It is the face of a man. The man is black, a dark black. He has long dreadlocks tipped with beads. The man is smiling through perfectly white teeth. It is Toby Tiler, also known as the Rastjahmon. A camera pans back revealing that the man is making the chordal sound with a guitar. The one-hundredth sound is a d-minor chord, which leads him into Bob Marley's "Natural Mystic".

He finishes the song and smiles and laughs deeply, "Aaahhh! So good to have you splendid people with us today! Irie New Year! Welcome to the show. Aaahhh yes, now we all have had a near-death experience, have we not? Did you see the white light? Aaahhh yes, I thought so. Speaking of white I would like to introduce you to a very close personal friend of mine, Mr. Doj Bolderton."

The camera pans back and Doj walks into the picture, to a second microphone. "Hello. Today we will be coming to you live from Caesar's Palace in marvelous Las Vegas, Nevada. And in case you were wondering, that was not Sammy Davis Junior. Nope, folks, that was the Rastjahmon, here for your listening pleasure. Now we'd like to take this opportunity to introduce everyone in the band, that fabulous back up group, the Sigmas. I first would like to introduce our brass balls section, on first trumpet, singing the high parts, Dr. Langdon Stofford."

The camera pans back to encompass the entire casino lounge. Sitting there, not with drinks in front of them, but glasses of water and notes, are the thirty-five members of the Sigma Society.

Dr. Stofford sits at the center of the cocktail lounge at a table with Dr. Tennyson. He says, "Ladies and gentlemen, citizens of the planet, we are the members of the Sigma Society. The Millennium Comet does not exist. There is no comet. We'll discover more as we go along, but first let's learn a little about the casino here at Caesar's, shall we? Let me introduce George Greystoke, the owner and CEO of Caesar's Palace."

Greystoke stands and gestures broadly. "Welcome to Cleopatra's Barge, the lounge I like to call 'This Is Your Vice.' Pick a vice. Any vice. Drinking and gambling are the legal ones here. Prostitution arrangements and drug deals have also been transacted in this lounge. Most any vice ever known to man has been bought and sold in this lounge. Is this wrong? I'd like to introduce Dr. Edward A. Johnson of Stanford."

"This lounge, and this bottle of bourbon in my hand, represent the drugs of the world, be they tobacco, alcohol, prescription drugs, illicit drugs, caffeine, et cetera. We'll call them drugs in that they allow escape. The use of drugs is a personal decision that supplies pleasure or relief from mental distress. Drug use has a way of bringing back impulsivity, which we experienced as children and adolescents. Until relatively recently in our human development, few people lived much beyond the age of thirty. Impulsivity, earlier in human development, and in a few places and circumstances today, conferred an evolutionary advantage. People who answered insult with insult, who fought back against any assailant without waiting for a distant government to take charge, who rushed headlong into battle against a common enemy, who plunged without hesitation into the forest in pursuit of an animal—these may have been people who at some point in human development served themselves and their offspring well. But modern society rewards self-control more than impulsivity. But modern society is . . . well . . . modern, a recent development that must cope with a human animal that evolved under very different circumstances. So we drink. We take drugs and we return to the state of impulsivity. Is it wrong? There is pleasure in drugs, there is pleasure in abstinence. Addiction brings incontinence and dependence. Drug use reflects a choice of present pleasure over long-term health. Oh, by the way, welcome to the year 2000. Now, would you prefer drug use or drug abuse? Self-control or impulsivity? Are drugs the only way, or the best way, to recapture a youthful spontaneity? Can we, should we, in the next millennium, move toward free choice or more stringent control?"

Doj jumps off the stage. "That was very pretty, Dr. Johnson. Don't you people out there in television land think he speaks well? Let's move onto the next category, shall we? The roulette wheel! For this segment let's turn to Dr. Evelyn Vasquez, botany professor."

Vasquez stands over the roulette wheel and says, "The wheel spins counterclockwise. Bets are placed when people put their money on numbers, or columns, or colors, or clusters of numbers. The house wins when the ball lands in either of two green spaces, zero and double zero. The ball is spun in a clockwise direction and lands in one of the slots and chips are either paid out or collected. Now let's imagine for a moment, if we can, that the roulette *wheel* is the earth spinning around at a consistent rate of speed. The numbers would be thirty-six random plant and animal species. We are betting that the elimination of one of these species will not effect the earth in any large-scale fashion. If we average the best estimates, we believe there are about five million species of plants and animals on earth, nearly two million are known. Our ball roller today will be David Attenborough, the creator of the television series *Life on Earth*. Let the ball go, please, David."

The small white marble rolls counter to the spinning wheel.

"Now," continues Vasquez, "we are presently playing this game one hundred times a day. One hundred species are becoming extinct each and every day. OK, it looks like its . . . landing . . . in . . . twenty-eight. We've got a twenty-eight. Book twenty-eight, Dr. Vandren?"

Taft Vandren holds a large antique book in his left palm, closes his eyes, flips open to a page near the middle, and Attenborough closes his eyes and puts his forefinger on the page. Vasquez leans over Vandren and peers down.

"Puffins!" says Taft.

"Hey, I *liked* puffins!" says Doj.

"May I set the book down, Dr. Vasquez? It's still pretty heavy."

"We can make it lighter," says Vasquez, who grabs one corner of the open page and rips it out. "That page is all crossed out. But, Dr. Vandren, if I may quote the late Dr. Carl Sagan,

> we have to remember extinction is the norm. Survival is the triumphant exception. The Permian period ended some 245 million years ago. What suddenly wiped out ninety-five percent of all the species then living on earth at that time? Now say, and this is speculation, that we eliminate enough species, or the right species, or the wrong species—whichever way you look at it—or a virus adapts and it triggers mass extinction. Should we be concerned? In ten million years, more or less, the variety and abundance of life on Earth will recover. Then, of course, there will be different organisms around, some better adapted to the new environment, some not. Evolutionary change is full of fits and starts, some blind alleys and some sweeping change. For example it has been only very recently, in the last two percent or three percent of the history of life on earth, that whales have appeared along with horses, pigs, elephants, wolves, bears, tigers, monkeys, apes, and men and women.
>
> She continues, "Is there a God? A hands-on executive that is in control of all this? It does not seem so. If God does exist it seems he is fond of getting the universe going, establishing the laws of Nature, then retiring from the scene. Power has been delegated. Evolution suggests that God will not intervene, whether besieged or not, to save us from

ourselves. Evolution suggests we're on our own, that if there is a God, that God must be very far away. So the nature of God is only a shallow mystery. The deep mystery is the nature of man.

Evelyn starts the white marble again and says, "so the game of roulette will continue, we are simply in the midst of a cycle. The wheel has been spinning since before we humans were here. It's just that we have been playing the game at a much faster rate these last hundred years. But, the wheel will continue to spin around after we're gone. We have a simple decision. How fast do we wish to play the game while we're the ones holding all the marbles?"

The marble trips over the 13, bounces high on the wheel before spinning down and landing in the green slot marked 00. "Ms. Vasquez!" exclaims Doj, patting her on the back. "Nice shot, you scored one for the green team! Now let's all head toward the outdoor stadium, shall we? Ms. Vasquez, I didn't think you were a gambler. How's your chess game?"

Greystoke ushers the entourage past the empty sports betting lounge. As the Sigmas walk into the huge arena lights come up over the boxing ring. As they stop five rows from ringside a three-dimensional, holographically-produced scene materializes in stop motion. It is the reenactment of third Muhammad Ali-Joe Frazier fight that occurred in Manila on October first, 1975. The Thrilla in Manila. Greystoke says, "In this arena some of the world's greatest fighters have met in some of the most violent *legal* combat, outside of declared war, in this century. Ali fought Holmes here. Sugar Ray Leonard and Thomas Hearns fought here twice. Roll the Holodeo, Dr. Shaku."

The bell sounds and round one commences. Crowd noise materializes as Ali dances and shuffles and Frazier stalks. It's as if the fighters were physically there, at their peak.

"Was Ali the greatest fighter of this century? Was this the greatest fight of the century? That's your opinion. Was it physically beautiful, was it an intense thing to watch, and was it violent? Yes it was. Depending on where you are, today or tomorrow marks a new century, a new millennium. Will we want violence and combat in the next thousand years? Will someone be complaining about violence on New Year's Day, 3000? We *are* born with it. Adapting and domination are how humans came to rule the planet. Congratulations. Happy New Year. Again, Dr. Edward A. Johnson."

He leans on the seat, the fight continues in the background. "Combat and violence derived from the need for males to hunt, defend, and attack. Much of civilization can be thought of as an effort to adapt these male dispositions into appropriate channels, such as hunting rituals, rites of passage, athletic contests. In this twentieth century, wars have been the outlet for much male aggression. In modern society climbing the economic ladder, succeeding in the business world has also been a way to channel modern aggression. But modern society, with its rapid technological change, intense division of labor, and ambiguous allocation of social roles, frequently leaves some men out, with their aggressive predispositions either uncontrolled or undirected. Gangs are one result, for example."

Doj jumps up, mimicking a left-right combination by Ali. "I get it-I get it-I get it!" he says. "You're saying that we can channel aggression into real-life war with real bullets and bombs or we can compete in athletic contests or economic quests, or we can channel our aggressive instincts even vicariously, by watching as spectators."

"No. I'm asking, Doj. Is violence and combat here to stay? Will we always be territorial and seek to dominate? If so, should we control aggression and punish for it, or should we accept it and insure outlets for it? Why did people pay three hundred dollars to sit in this seat to watch two men fight, then why do we temper the event by demanding each men wear padding over their weapons?"

"No padding today!" smiles Doj. "There's no one in here. No one on the streets. No one cranking down the one-armed bandits, and no one on the tennis courts. Listen, George, I hear you play a little tennis. And since you own Caesar's Palace you must be a gambling man. Play a match for, say, a stack of those lavender chips?"

The bell rings, ending round one, and Stofford steps up.

"Perhaps we should move on to the basement where Dr. Singer is waiting."

The entourage moves down the escalator to the 'Kid's Level.' They walk past the children's arcade to a rotunda with eight doors spaced uniformly around. Dr. Condesca Singer is at the center of the rotunda. She spreads her arms wide and says, "Welcome to the world of virtual reality! Not active, but interactive. Choose one or choose all. Through this door is the Devil's Mine Ride. Dash and crash through the labyrinth. This one is snow skiing. Stand and experience every mogul and every powder shot just as if you were there. Cold, wind and powder snow, all are experienced. Behind this door is what we call a motion machine. Your child can fly to any country, take in the countryside, the architecture, the culture without ever leaving the safety of their harness. Behind door three is our most popular feature, a raft ride down the Colorado River. Your kid's hair will get soaking wet before it dries by an ultraviolet campfire. This feature comes with wood smoke smell and Class IV rapids. Kids can spend hours in virtual reality while their parents gamble in a climate-controlled, oxygen-rich environment. Isn't it great? The kids come out dry and clean with absolutely no trepidation of foreign countries or outdoor adventure."

"It's party time!" shouts Doj. The procession moves to the show lounge and uncork chilled bottles of Louis Roederer Cristal Champagne. They put on party hats and blow whistles. Lisen and Aisha are already on stage along with Rastjahmon on guitar and various Sigmas on bass, tenor sax, trumpet and congas. Doj picks up a guitar and after a two count they launch into 'Respect', an Aretha Franklin song, Aisha singing lead.

Against a background of new millennium revelry the rest of the Sigmas are introduced to the television audience. One by one they are introduced to the world.

Then all the Sigmas hold up glasses of the expensive libation. Stofford says to the camera, "Our toast is for you, fellow humans. Before you return to your regularly scheduled programming, we ask that you look around. You're getting along today. There are no wars, there is no violence, no crime, and you're alive. It's time to celebrate! Come out of your houses, come to Caesar's Palace.

Mr. Greystoke invites one and all! Today, the chips are on the house!"

And the earth continued to spin around on its axis, and continued to orbit the sun and for some time things were good. Slowly the Ring filled back up with people and the work force of the world started anew and football games were scheduled and all the details of the Millennium Project were discussed and things were good. Life started over with the Millennium. The Sigmas were placed under house arrest at Caesar's while the Department of Justice decided what to do. What could or should they be charged with? The white flash that filled television screens was an atom bomb detonated by the military when they surmised the Hubble was the approaching comet.

Although Toby Tiler was not indicted, he stayed with Doj and the Sigmas. A guardian for Doj was the idea of Stofford, Tennyson, and Stevelin Gordy, the Sigma who owned the record company and recruited Toby Tiler. Only those three knew of Toby's role. Toby was recruited to watch over Doj and test his resolve.

Public reaction was overwhelming, exuberant and positive; the Sigmas were hailed as heroes, almost benevolent saints. Because, for some time, as the earth rotated on its axis and revolved around the sun, things were good.

Book IV

The New Testament

The Gospel According to Jamaica

Jamaica, June 6th, 2000.

There is no artificial thing ever made by humans which can match the color, the texture, the sight, sound and feel of the Caribbean sea on a calm day. Call it turquoise if you'd like, if you need to try to describe it, attach an adjective to it. The sea has been calm for seven days, the water visibility is seventy feet. It is morning, just minutes before the earth rotates toward the sun and longitude 76 degrees, 13 minutes west is exposed. Clouds lying low on the horizon are still and purple-blue, a few fingers of orange appear over latitude 17 degrees, 23 minutes north, the eastern tip of Jamaica.

Seventy feet off shore, above a coral reef, two mammals slowly break the surface of the water and spout before they disappear again, then four fins break the surface and flutter once before they smoothly disappear and concentric ripples glide out from a center. Thirty seconds later and twenty feet offshore the two mammals rise up and out of the water and lift snorkels and masks over their heads. As the Rastjahmon stands on one foot to take off a flipper Doj Bolderton tackles him from the side.

"You crazy mon!" says Toby, laughing, wrestling Doj back. "You still got that violence in you. You better join the Rastjah in a little morning safety meeting rastjah cultural lesson."

"I'll race ya to class," says Doj. They fling their snorkels, masks and fins ahead of them and sprint up the beach to the cabana.

It is a special day for four reasons:

One, it had been a month to the day since they'd arrived in Jamaica. Between Mensa 'Juries' and government hearings and subsequent 'debriefings', as the Feds were calling it, Doj and Toby hit every talk show and profile show they could. They made enough money to purchase a large beach-side villa that the five of them shared, as well as Uncle Jenolee's bar that stands near the road beyond the palm trees. They formed a house band. They started a Jamaican version of Rent-a-Friend that offered "Spice, Herb and Snorkel" tours of the island on a sliding scale.

Two, Spencer Tennyson and Langdon Stofford called the night before. The Royal Swedish Academy of Sciences had extended the deadline and Spencer Tennyson and Langdon Stofford were nominated for the Nobel Peace Prize. Taft Vandren was nominated for the Nobel Prize in Medicine for his work in controlling the HIV virus through biogenetics.

Three, it is Doj's thirty-fourth birthday.

Four, Langdon—Doj and Lisen's son—is exactly two weeks old, and it is his first day at the beach.

The smell of Aisha's lobster omelets fills the air as Lisen tosses Doj and Toby fresh towels. Doj walks to Lisen. She lifts Langley out of his crib, then holds him out to his father.

"Lisen, you mean to tell me this uncoordinated, dribbling ten pound midget will beat *me* in tennis someday?"

"Only if you teach him how to hit the ball one stroke more than you do."

"And not into the net," says Aisha. "Omelets are ready. Does everyone like their orange juice fresh-squeezed? Aaah. Thought so. Bimini bread is on the table, here's a ladle for the gazpacho."

After breakfast they walk to the edge of the water. The two couples silently disrobe, their bodies bathe in the rich orange light of the sun, its nuclear explosions silent here, some ninety-three million miles away. Doj looks at the sun's reflection on the water, like an orange path leading to the horizon. He leads them into the water, to thigh level, then looks at the others. "I was thinking about what the Himbies were saying. I think they were on the right path. It was Heart in Mind — Body in Every Spirit." He pauses and turns Langley toward the sun. "That's it then. They were right."

"Aaahhh, Bolderdoj, your aura is very orange this morning. You see the orange path."

Lisen says, "Yes, Doj, we possess those things."

"Yes," says Doj, "we all have a heart, a mind, a body, and we all have a spirit."

Aisha says, "And it's not necessarily equal from person to person. Some of us have more of one than the other."

"Aaahhh yes," says Rastjahmon, "and we all have it in different blends at different times, in different ratios. Some have diminished body and mind for heart and spirit."

"And some have diminished their heart and spirit for body and mind," says Doj. "Langley, I don't know if there's a God. I can't tell you that. I know there is a spirit. I hope you will see that."

"I think he sees it now, Bolderdoj."

Doj Bolderton nods and lowers his son into and out of the sea. The infant laughs. Doj holds his son over the water and the child starts a paddling motion. Rastjahmon walks farther into the sea and the others follow his path, toward the bright light on the horizon.